High Strung

~

High Strung

~

A Novel

Quinn Dalton

ATRIA BOOKS

New York   London   Toronto   Sydney   Singapore

ATRIA BOOKS

1230 Avenue of the Americas
New York, NY 10020

ISBN: 0-7434-7018-4

First Atria Books hardcover printing July 2003

10 9 8 7 6 5 4 3 2 1

ATRIA BOOKS is a trademark of Simon & Schuster, Inc.

For information regarding special discounts for bulk purchases,
please contact Simon & Schuster Special Sales at 1-800-456-6798
or business@simonandschuster.com

Printed in the U.S.A.

FOR MY FAMILY.

ACKNOWLEDGMENTS

I thank my husband, David Mengert, who read the manuscript, believed it would become a book, and sang "Itsy Bitsy Spider" over and over to our daughter, Avery, while I worked.

Thanks to my father, Jim Dalton, and to my scholarly mother, Nancy Dalton, whose research improved the story. She put me in touch with Dr. Kenneth R. Turner, Director of the No Man's Land Historical Museum, on the campus of Oklahoma Panhandle State University. Dr. Turner put me in touch with Johnnie Davis. Both men gave me valuable information about the histories of the towns of Goodwell and Guymon. Sam Baker of Atlantic Aero in Greensboro, and Robert Cannon, a pilot and University of North Carolina Greensboro professor, patiently explained to me all the things that can go wrong with a small plane. And I can only assume that I am now on file with the Greensboro Police Department after getting information from the helpful Sergeant V. S. Hilton about pipe bombs.

Special thanks to Julianna Baggott, who has been a most encouraging friend and editor for ten years. I am also grateful to my friends Elizabeth Blanchard Hills, Katy Dooley, Julie

Funderburk, Larry Queen, and Matt Wagner, who were honest and careful readers. Thanks to my teachers at the UNCG MFA Writing Program: Fred Chappell, Michael Parker, and Lee Zacharias.

Thanks to David McLean and the excellent artists of King's English, who designed my Web site.

Thanks to Tom Lorenz, editor of *Cottonwood,* the literary journal of the University of Kansas, for publishing my short story "How to Clean Your Apartment," which prompted an inquiry from my agent Nat Sobel.

Thanks especially to Nat, and to the readers at Sobel Weber, who asked the tough questions that readied the manuscript to hope for covers and bookshelves.

Many thanks to my editors Kim Meisner and Greer Hendricks, true professionals who graced me with their thoughtful advice and enthusiasm.

And sweet Avery. You remind me daily why this life is so good.

1

MY LIFE IS A story of flights.

I wasn't technically present for two of them, and they weren't even of the airborne variety, but I count them anyway.

Two were with my mother.

Two others were over the ocean.

All were short on planning and quite nerve-racking.

One made me think about death, and that was when I started to calm down.

The next to the last one: I was running, really, back to Ohio from a shitty London flat over a woodcutting shop where machines shrilled like the trussed characters in a typical X Publishing adult novel, of which I had copyedited hundreds. I was just in time for my birthday and another campus vigil. I was beat up, underfed, sexually exhausted, pornographically overwhelmed. I had been gone ten years. I had a perverted ex-boyfriend and a smoking habit to show for my time, and a friendship with Fiona, a feng shui consultant and breathing instructor who kept me centered and in cheap Silk Cut cigarettes. I was coming home to a grandmother I hadn't spoken to since I'd left, a father I didn't really know, and a brother who had fallen in love with a doll. The beginning of a new century (or the end of the old one?) was a hook trailing three perfect zeros—and we were still round with loss; we all led double lives.

I hugged Fiona good-bye when it was still dark, the windows facing the Gatwick observation deck dark mirrors showing more than I needed. The sky folded open with light as the plane took off and I thought of the photograph, the one that had followed me through childhood until I finally took flight number five to get away from it: my mother and I outside the Morris P. Alston education building moments after the bomb blast, me two years old that day and screaming in my mother's thin arms, her hair tangled in my fist, the dark smudges of police uniforms in the background. She looks angry, or maybe just determined, and her free hand reaches into the air, as if trying to catch something outside the frame.

My father would never talk about the photograph, and my mother can't now, having died drunk in a car accident the night she allowed me to start wearing mascara. I was thirteen. I'm thirty-two now, the age she was when she died, and every time I take a drink I still think about it, how I could get in a car and drive into my next life.

Fiona had instructions to take whatever of mine she wanted before the landlord padlocked my cramped, loud flat. I had also asked her to tell Terence that I'd had to leave on short notice— family issues, I asked her to explain—and that I didn't expect to be back anytime soon. I told her to tell him I'd be in touch.

I pulled on my orange-and-brown-striped clown socks the attendant handed out, and thought of Terence and seven years—one year for each name letter, each stripe on each foot. I couldn't have warned him that I was leaving. He was too persuasive, too good with the guilt trips; he would have talked me out of it. Even so, I worried for him as I watched an extra-long sunrise turn the Atlantic a sequiny brass, which reminded me of Terence's favorite mirrored hip-huggers, and which got me wondering where he would go, at which point I had to remind myself that his father was a diplomat, and he had several houses to choose from. *He should have been worrying about where you would go all this time, Merle,* I told myself, scalding my tongue on the black water Virgin Airways calls coffee. I realized I was pinching the inside of my arm, a habit when I was worried. This kind of compulsiveness started with games every kid played, like skipping sidewalk cracks or breath-holding near graveyards, but somehow I'd never grown out of them. In fact, I had honed and perfected them so that they made a scary kind of sense to me. They were how I tried to correct a life filled with bad decisions. Most of my rituals focused on trying to avoid mishaps while using various forms of transportation; for example, I had to cross my fingers during flight takeoffs and landings. To keep myself from falling onto the tracks while boarding the Underground in London, I had to mouth "Mind the gap" along with the fatherly, firm voice on the speakers.

I could blame this on my family's bad luck with transportation—my mother's fatal car accident, my grandfather's heart-attack death on a tractor while harvesting the family corn crop when my father was eight. But really, it was because I had always been tense, even as a child, walking around with my shoulders crammed into my neck, second-guessing every smile—*Are they laughing at me?* I'd always wonder, no matter who it was. I had to admit that, at the age of thirty-two, after sampling a range of therapies—art therapy, aromatherapy, breathing exercises, crystals, meditation, good old-fashioned eighty-five-quid-per-hour therapy—the fact is, uptight was just who I was.

Terence would be fine, I told myself as I flipped through the in-flight magazine, in which a blind and deaf fifteen-year-old was interviewed after climbing Mount Everest and a supermodel insisted you could travel to the Bahamas with a swimsuit, wrap skirt, and scarf and come up with twenty different wardrobe combinations. Terence would slink like a cat through life, always composed, always true to himself alone. I would have to learn to shed my dog ways, my compulsive habits, my obsessive loyalties for people who didn't extend the same concern for me. *You're going home to grow old alone,* I told myself as the plane lowered into a cloud bank over New York.

2

MY BROTHER, OLIN, would have offered to meet me in Cleveland and let me stay with him, but I couldn't stand the thought of having him do either. I'd left housing issues to my father, who had found me an apartment recently vacated after the death of its occupant, a connection through his job at the Florence Department of Social Services. During most of the flight from New York, I closed my eyes and considered my pride, which allowed me to take free emergency housing rather than accept the hospitality of my only sibling. What it came down to, of course, was jealousy. Olin, now twenty-seven, had already made something of himself right out of college doing marketing, first and foremost for the guy who patented the naked Marilyn Monroe digital barbeque thermometer that sang "Happy Birthday, Mr. President" in a breathy voice when poked into beef, chicken, or pork at the correct temperature, bringing together elements men love: meat, fire, sex, gadgets. My brother sent me one after the product launch, a glitzy affair in Cleveland at the Rock and Roll Hall of Fame. The digital readout ran up Marilyn's belly from just above the crotch to between the breasts like a brand. It was disconcerting, but popular, and my brother had found himself suddenly rich.

He spent it all on the basics—women, a big car—but that wasn't the point. He'd been a success early in life, and hadn't cared either way. When we were kids, he'd been the slightly overweight goof in school and I had been the one with promise, despite being prone to tantrums, but somehow things had changed, flipped in fact. It was right around the time I had switched my major for the fourth and final time, from psychology to English literature, and Olin had gotten a scholarship to Miami University in Oxford, Ohio, to major in sociology and long jumping, from which he still had an angular athlete's build. He dropped out one semester short of graduation though, because he said he missed our hometown. He said it in a way that made it impossible for me to know if he was joking, his even-toothed smile glowing like our mother's. He didn't seem to think he'd given anything up. After all, he still had the car.

Olin stuck around, went to clubs, dated. I left and got tied up a lot, staring at my thick white thighs, wondering how I was going to pay the rent while Terence talked dirty to me.

As we landed, I pulled out a lavender sachet from my carry-on, pressed it to my nose, crossed my fingers, and began the Walrus Belly breathing exercise Fiona had prescribed for calm during family gatherings: a slow, six-count inhale, four-count hold, and release in six short exhales. The woman in the seat next to me glanced over and drew her book closer to her chest. To each her own, I thought; she had laid out pictures of her twin Pekinese on both knees before takeoff. I closed my eyes and drew a red circle around my ambivalence toward my brother's success. I slowly squeezed the circle with each breath, as Fiona had taught me, but I couldn't make it disappear. I tried again and again, while I waited for my bags, and while I alternately dozed and woke up panicking about right-hand side driving during the two-hour bus ride down to Florence.

It was dusk as we came into town from the north, passing the elementary school, the high school, then a left turn, crossing the bridge over the Cuyahoga River, really just a stream where we are, then through town and a stop at the newly built Florence College student union, a concrete box with slit windows like a fortress. I managed to talk a woman into driving me to Baden Lake Apartments, mysteriously named because there was no lake, where my father had found temporary housing after my hysterical phone call only two days before.

My father hadn't asked me why I was coming, and it didn't occur to either of us that I might stay at his house. We had talked maybe half a dozen times in the last ten years. I had no idea if things would improve between us, but I was tired of being alone in the world. I didn't know what else to do except come home.

I dragged my two duffel bags along the grass-seamed sidewalk just as it was getting dark. A streetlight popped on at the corner. Back when my childhood friend Tanya had lived with her divorced mother in the Baden Lake Apartments, they were a neat rectangle of red brick Monopoly houses with bright, white-trimmed windows. Now the brick looked bruised and crumpled, and the dark windows sagged in their sashes. I found the key in a white envelope in the rusted iron mailbox by the door, but when I pushed it in the lock, the door simply swung in, revealing a dark, empty room. I guess I had expected dark and empty, or maybe I hadn't thought about what to expect, but the square, green shag-carpeted bareness shocked me. I found a wall switch, and the emptiness was starker still under the sharp light of one bulb that flickered on uncertainly in what would have been a living room if a couch or coffee table had given it any direction in life. I pulled my bags to the middle of the room, maybe to hold the floor in place, unrolled my sleeping bag in between them, and immediately fell asleep.

The next morning I woke to a knock on the door. I sat up, heart pounding, and caught my foot in my sleeping bag as I tried to stand, tumbling onto my knees. I dragged myself to my feet, grabbed the metal safety railing next to the door— clearly the deceased former resident had been an elderly person, a woman, I thought, judging from the nose-itching smell of scented talcum powder. I threw open the door without considering the fact that I was only wearing a wife-beater undershirt and fuchsia peekaboo boxers, both of which I'd pulled out of my bags in the dark, and that no one besides my father and brother was supposed to know I was here.

Squinting into the light, I saw an old man, a shambles of a human—scruffy several-day beard, wrinkled trousers, and shoulders like a coat hanger under the untucked shirt, face obscuring the late morning sun, white hair a thorny halo.

"Yeah?" I said, trying to sound tougher than I felt.

"Harold Balch," he said, extending a hand, head cocking like a worm-hunting bird to check out my shorts. "Your neighbor, at your service."

I didn't take the bony, knot-knuckled hand. "Look, Mr. Balch?" I paused, momentarily distracted by a swell of dizziness.

"Harold, please," he rasped.

I pressed the side of my head to the metal edge of the door. I was exhausted, my bags slung like bodies in the empty living room, the only evidence of my existence. "Harold," I continued. "This is not a good time, right now."

His hand dropped against his skinny thigh and I felt mean, sociopathic. "Perhaps later?" I said.

"I only came over to say hello," Harold said, shoving his hands easily into pockets that gaped under his cinched belt.

"I'm sorry, I'm—"

"And to see if you wanted to buy a gun."

I looked back up at him—blue eyes like faded denim under bushy eyebrows, a red bulb nose. Thin, sincere, definitely-not-joking lips—the guy never had been a looker. "Jesus," I said.

"He won't help you, missy, 'til you're dead. Before then I think a pretty single thing like yourself oughtta look into something simple, like a Special."

I stared at him. "I'll get a dog, thanks," I said, pushing the door closed.

"Hey, I'll be your watchdog," he said through the crack. "Come by for a beer later?"

I shut the door, locked it, and leaned against it. I thought about the ride to the airport with Fiona, how at any point I could have turned back, could have done anything. Now I was stuck here, completely broke, lost, with gun-toting neighbors, after living for ten years in a country where people didn't even have to worry about their dogs getting rabies. I could feel panic swelling in my rib cage; I started trying Walrus Belly again but then gave up. "Shit shit shit," I said. "What am I doing here? What am I doing?" I sat down on the rectangle of linoleum marking the foyer area where probably the last tenant had put some nice little welcome mat with daisies. I rocked on my haunches, crying, the floor cold through my shorts, which were actually Terence's; why I saved a thing of his I didn't know, but impractical underwear was probably the most appropriate, considering. For years I had believed being with him had somehow made me more carefree, when in fact it had left me completely disoriented, like an actor playing the same role for too long, trying to remember how the real her ordered coffee, styled her hair, got home at night. I slumped against the wall, choking on each breath, sucking in air and snorting. Through my tears the walls seemed to melt onto the floor, the floor wavered, and I thought about the instability of everything and cried harder.

Finally my stomach was sore from heaving. I hauled myself to my feet, dug out a roll of toilet paper I had stolen from the woodcutting shop before I left, and stumbled to the bathroom. I blew my nose and came back to lie down in the middle of the bare living room, bags at my back, something poking me, perhaps a dildo. I'd meant to throw away all gifts from Terence; I imagined one of them leaping into my bag, a stowaway, a determined survivor, and my unwittingly marching it through every security checkpoint in London, New York, and Cleveland.

The thought made me feel strangely calm, and I let it wash over me as my breathing steadied. It was not such a great start to a homecoming. "God help me," I sighed, even though I don't believe in God, exactly; mostly I picture a drunk air-traffic controller who keeps letting planes smack together in the sky—*Oops! Oops!* he says. I thought of my father, of what he would say if he could see me at this moment. He would call me high strung. Theatrical, melodramatic. He began whipping out these terms like stun guns to neutralize me after my mother died. When I got upset because he wouldn't let me go on dates, or kept my curfews earlier than prime-time TV, or grounded me for foul language, he got quiet and called me high strung. And because my mother was apparently high strung enough to drive at nearly a hundred miles an hour into a tree, I believed him.

Maybe my father decided I was high strung because I cried when I lost my hairbrush and he never cried, not even at age eight when his father had that fatal heart attack behind the steering column of a tractor with my father riding along. Not prone to panic even then, my father had the presence of mind to crawl between his father's thighs and stand on the brake, guiding the rig to a stop before it ran into the irrigation ditch.

"Life isn't perfect," he would say, calm as a priest, while I held my breath or threw myself at walls. "You just have to stay the course."

I dragged myself into the shower, dressed, smoked one of my last cigarettes, pulled my hair into a rubber-band ponytail, stuffed a pile of coins in my pocket—a mixture of quarters and quid, halfway worthless anywhere, totally appropriate currency for me—and started out the door. I didn't bother to lock it.

Rubbing my eyes and cutting across the quad, I would have tripped over it if I hadn't looked just in time: a hand-lettered sign stapled to a garden stake stabbed at an angle in the dew-damp ground. Thick, forward-leaning letters proclaiming:

ONCE THE TOOTHPASTE IS OUT OF THE
TUBE, IT'S HARD TO GET IT BACK IN!
HAROLD M. BALCH,
URBAN PHILOSOPHER

I considered this. I wondered if I were being watched, not necessarily at that moment, but in a more universal sense, perhaps by ghosts—my mother, the talcum-scented former tenant of my apartment, old boyfriends—and Harold was their channeler. It seemed possible to me then, jet-lagged and displaced as I was, looking for explanations and willing to believe anything.

3

EVERY FAMILY COLLECTS STORIES, like a string of watches flashed from a thief's coat. So mine has the "only two dates before marriage" story, the "murderous grandfather" story, the "farm heart attack" story. And these are the ones we actually like to tell. Ones we don't include, among others, are the "car accident" and "the bomb."

In my first few weeks back in Florence, I quickly added to this dubious collection: "the in-flight proposal," "the boy and his doll," "the smell of sliced clouds," and "the father who lived a double life." It was my father I was thinking about as I walked down River Street, looking for a phone booth. The one in front of Jinx's, where all the old men used to line up to place bets to their bookies during football season, was gone. Jinx's had closed and now housed a tattoo parlor—where did all the old men hang out now? A house some friends of mine once lived in had become a bed-and-breakfast. Florence now had a day spa. River Street, which used to be grungy before grunge was in style, had gotten cute. Flowers grew in iron-circled plots around young trees lining the sidewalk. I was surprised to see that all the storefronts had matching awnings—that they even had awnings at all.

I found a phone down the street and dialed Olin, wondering if I should bother hooking up a phone for myself since I didn't know anyone here anymore and bitching under my breath at the cost of a phone call here these days, thirty-five cents, what crap. The phone was ringing and I was nervous, thinking about all the reasons I had made up over the years not to come home—twisted ankles, muggings—though somehow the lies seemed to have come true.

"Hello?" I heard the familiar, slightly bewildered upswing on the *o* and was immediately annoyed.

"Olin, damn it," I said. "It's me."

"Merle?"

"Yeah," I said. "I'm in Florence."

"Hey, that's great! Dad told me you were coming. Maybe we could do dinner tonight? Wait, wait, hang on a minute." I heard his voice catch as he shifted position, and then I heard a woman's voice, not talking, but crying, screamy crying, the kind that doesn't stop for a phone call. He cupped the phone and there was muffled conversation, calming on his end, choppy on her end, which I tried to understand but couldn't.

"This a bad time?" I asked. I assumed he was having relationship problems, and I was relieved that at least I wasn't the only one.

"No. Hey—you're really here?" A door slammed and the woman's voice was fainter, but still going strong.

I sighed. An old man wearing a rumpled suit stared at me as he passed by on a sputtering moped. I stared back. "Yes."

"Can I call you back?"

I ignored this. "Listen, you got a car?"

"Oh, let's see . . . yep!" he said, sarcastic.

"Meet me at the Iron."

I hung up and walked down the street toward the Iron, which was open, according to a flickering green neon sign that stuttered BEER. The downtown was almost completely deserted. I was lurching every few steps, dizzy and jumpy. In spite of the eighteen hours of travel from the day before, I felt as if I had just appeared here, and the last ten years hadn't happened. I felt stunned, out of sorts, and I was grateful for the basement-dark of the Iron, even with its sad, abandoned, Sunday-afternoon stillness. There was the wet, bitter smell of spilled beer and ashtrays, the echoey, oddly churchlike silence. The Iron had been my favorite bar in college, a firetrap with carving-scarred booths, a unisex bathroom known as the trough, and a front entrance that curved forward like the profile of an iron handle; hence the name. It was a dank, smelly place but it brought back good memories, of the days when I was on the dean's list at Florence College, which meant I was smart; when I looked good in tight jeans and could stay awake past midnight, which meant I was fun; when I could buy a pitcher or two of beer, which meant I was rich.

It took Olin a couple of hours to show up, by which time I'd had three beers. It's only the first beer that makes me feel guilty. Put simply, I feel I shouldn't drink at all because my mother drank too much—as if my abstinence might lead to a kind of cosmic averaging that would bring her back, so that she could be sitting across from me right now, each of us enjoying a glass of wine perhaps. Except she hated bars, and as far as I could remember she wouldn't even order a drink in a restaurant. She preferred to do her drinking at home, where she could keep going. In fact, drinking was how I told time. It started when my father came home from Social Services, where he got a job coordinating emergency housing after the college laid him off because he was married to an alleged campus agitator (more on this later). My mother would fix him a scotch and soda, and of course she'd have one, too. One drink each the entire evening, just a little more ice, then a little more scotch, with less and less soda. There was no binging, no screaming, no falling down, just a slow slide to nightfall, when, in my earliest memories, my father would help get me ready for bed because, as he would explain, my mother was so tired. She almost always fell asleep before I did.

But I have to admit: when I was little and my father tucked me into bed, I loved the sour sweet alcohol on his breath. It was part of him, and my mother too, like her White Shoulders perfume or the dye that turned her hair a bright chestnut once a month. I suppose with time she would have gotten worse—she would've gotten lost in town, left the fridge open, started fires. And I wondered if by drinking alone on a Sunday afternoon I was tempting the same fate— but of course that was such an American viewpoint. I mean, try drinking and driving in very tiny cars on skinny, busy highways with not very well enforced speed limits. It's enough to make you love America for its safety, its sobriety, its railings, and wet-floor signs.

The door cracked and I looked up, expecting Olin. There was no one else in the bar except Angel, the bartender, who hadn't recognized me, which didn't really surprise me, and in fact was a comfort, considering the numbers of glassware and social taboos I had broken there. But instead of Olin I saw Watson Puckett and Ivy Penrod, my first lover and high school nemesis, respectively. They walked in with arms linked, not an easy job in the code-flouting narrow doorway of the Iron. They looked absolutely, tormentingly the same, both tall and willowy, Watson a little hairier than I remembered, Ivy a little bustier, both of them looking just in from sailing, walking Nautica adverts in white shorts and yellow and blue golf shirts. They ordered beers from Angel and took a booth across the bar. I positioned myself behind some obviously rotting support posts and tried not to attract attention.

I was scared that they would recognize me and scared too that they wouldn't. I couldn't figure what they were doing in a shabby bar like this on a Sunday afternoon; they seemed too bright, too crisp for the place. They radiated the social exclusivity that I imagine is common to all small towns, the way it's just high school magnified: the rich kids go to college and become doctors and professors and the poor kids finish vo-ed and become hairdressers and mechanics, and the two groups don't mix, except when the professor needs a haircut or the mechanic needs to go to the doctor. I didn't fit in either group in school. I was overly competitive and needy with boys, and without a mother to advise me on things like hair and makeup, I went for big: glitter hair gel, heavy black eyeliner and lipstick, a sort of cross between Diana Ross and Joan Jett. I realize now I was trying to cover up my face entirely; the makeup was a ploy to distract people, a disguise. For the most part it worked—usually people looked at me and then quickly away, as if passing a wreck in their cars. It got me through the days.

But things changed when I started going out with Watson Puckett, my first and only boyfriend in high school and also the first boy I ever slept with—which is really not accurate because we never actually slept together. Our sex was sneaky by necessity—scraps of time in cars and parks and occasionally at one of our houses when no one else was home—it was quick and, looking back after eight years in the porn publishing industry, quite tame.

We met during the school drama teacher Mrs. Perelli's ambitious production of *The Seagull*. He played the depressed, petulant playwright Konstantin and I was Nina, the shallow and tragic actress whose spirit is broken in the end. I loved that role, as if it could offer an explanation for the lack of focus or resolve that I already suspected was derailing me. Because Watson was six-four he got all the leading male roles, even though his blond hair stuck straight up no matter how much gel was applied to it, and he was so thin his clothes hung from his shoulders and hips like drapes. He was too shy to ask me out, but we managed to hook up after the cast party, our faces and clothes smeared with Max Factor cake makeup, and we went out for two years after that. I can still remember the soft pale skin of his chest against mine, the way his gray eyes narrowed in concentration as he struggled to put on a condom for the first time. And I remember how he looked the day we broke up while he was home from college for fall break, tears caught in his long pale eyelashes as he told me he was so sorry. He felt guilty for hurting me, I knew even then. I was a senior in high school and already trying to figure out a way to escape. But I would end up going to Florence College with a scholarship, and it would be five more years before I left.

I watched Ivy and Watson from the corner of my eye as they leaned into each other, smiling and whispering. Ivy had never liked me, probably because I beat her out for roles in school plays. She was taller, slimmer, and better looking, with her ski-jump nose and flawless skin, but was bad on stage— flat, shaky voice and tense gestures, arms seemingly glued to her ribs. It wasn't pretty.

While I would have liked to talk with Watson, the last thing I wanted was to have to get through a pretend conversation with Ivy—you know, the ones where the women nod and smile a lot and then make comments about each other afterward, as in, "She carries the extra weight well," and "I always thought she was going to get her nose done." I finished my beer and was about to make a break for it when the door opened and Olin walked in, white shirt like a spotlight, silk trousers swishing as he approached, looking past me in the gloom. I stood up and hugged him, placing him between me and Watson and Ivy, who had looked up when he came in.

"Hey, Merle—" Olin started to say, but I held a finger to my lips and he stopped.

"We gotta get out of here," I whispered. I took his arm and tugged him toward the door and into the too-bright day.

"So you really are in the FBI," Olin said. I ignored him. I was heading for the river park, where I had once spent many an evening, trying to score a nickel bag with Watson.

Olin followed until he saw me going for the muddy, steep trail zigzagged in the grass by years of drunks short-cutting to the tracks. "Hey, I'm not dressed for this. I just came from church!"

I spun to look at him at the mouth of the trail, nearly slipping. "You what?"

He smiled, shook his head at me. He was standing a few feet uphill from me, sun in his light brown hair. He was thicker at the shoulders and hips, but still lean, the breeze rippling his pants against muscled thighs. I remembered the woman crying in the background during our phone call and wanted to ask about it but decided against it.

"Fuck you," I said, smiling. "Since when do you wear silk?"

"Since I found out it feels good." He rolled his eyes and turned. "You hungry?"

I followed him into Fortuna's, which didn't feel safe, as it was practically next door to the Iron with a plate-glass storefront, near where Watson and Ivy still very likely lurked, but Olin insisted. When I was in high school Fortuna's was a shabby, underground kind of place where shaved and leathered punks hunched over their sandwiches and smoked cigarettes while eating, a talent I never mastered. The sandwiches were prepared by young, similarly punky women who flinched whenever the owner, Mr. Fortuna, was around, as if he might box their ears for putting a sweet pickle with a Reuben when it was clear a Reuben called for a sour crunchy pickle. Mr. Fortuna was serious about sandwiches, and Fortuna's was a serious place. Now there were airbrushed posters of Elvis, James Dean, and Marilyn Monroe in a neat row behind the long prep counter, the tables and chairs sported matching cherry red covers, and the menu was short, with no complicated combinations likely to stump the unsophisticated sandwich customer. Fortuna's had gotten cute. I shook my head.

Olin saluted the Marilyn Monroe poster and ordered two meatball sandwiches and lemonades.

"Since when do you go ordering for people without asking what they want?" I muttered as the order was rung up by a skinny blond girl with a nose ring. The girl radiated a heroin calm, and there was no Mr. Fortuna hovering near the meat chunks.

I led the way to a table partially hidden by a large fern, plant life also being a new idea at Fortuna's as far as I could recall. "Ah, the Fortuna meatball special. How did you know I was craving this?" I said. But secretly I was glad he had ordered for me. It made me feel taken care of and, after the last few weeks I'd had, I needed it.

"It's time you ate a good meal," Olin said in a stern voice that I knew was meant to emulate Dad. Then, "Have you seen Ernest yet?"

I couldn't remember when we'd gotten in the habit of calling our father by his first name. It made me think of him as a kid with a high shiny forehead and a squinty careful smile in old photographs. "Nope, but he got me a place to stay," I said. "Things happened kind of fast."

Olin bit into his sandwich and nodded. "So what brings

you back to the center of the revolution?" he asked, a reference to the Morris P. Alston building bombing, with which my mother and I had been associated ever since that unlucky photograph when I was two.

I snorted on a gulp of lemonade, took my time swallowing. I had asked my father to let Olin know I was coming, but neither of them knew about Terence and the swinging ferry incident, which had been a contributing factor to my last-minute flight; only Fiona knew that. "I'm not at liberty to say," I said, affecting my best West London accent.

"Aw, come on."

"Nope, you don't have clearance. So how's work?" I asked, changing the subject.

"Oh . . . well, I'm kind of in between jobs right now," he said. But then he brightened. "I'm thinking I'll go into comedy."

"Ofay," I said, chewing.

"No, I mean it. I'm serious," Olin said. "Former adman trades tag lines for gag lines; gets funny."

I wanted to ask him how he was living without any income, where he was living, if Ernest knew. Then I had to smile at how I'd fallen right back into playing big sister when I was in exactly the same position as Olin—worse, because it terrified me and didn't seem to bother him in the least.

"You think that's funny?" Olin said, thinking I was laughing at the adman line. "Maybe I could use that. The advertising thing could be my shtick. What do you think?" He pulled a pen from his pocket and scribbled a few words on a napkin.

I was about to say he couldn't really be serious, but his eyes were wide, sincere. "I think you'll be great," I said.

Just then Watson and Ivy strolled by, holding hands. I leaned back to hide behind the fern and Olin turned and craned his neck to look. "Jesus Christ," I said. "Could you be more obvious?"

"Who are they?"

"That's Watson Puckett. Remember?"

"Your old squeeze?"

I nodded. "And Ivy Penrod." They passed, laughing, all white teeth and highlights.

"Man, I remember I wanted to take sailing lessons to be like Watson when you guys were a thing," Olin said. He had a good memory; Watson and his father were into sailing. In fact, he had tried to imitate every guy I went on a date with before I left Florence, sometimes with disastrous results. For example, there was George, who made sculptures out of old musical instruments and a blowtorch. Olin was a freshman in the high school band then, and he had experimented on his saxophone—a low point in his relationship with Dad. I was glad he had gotten over the copycat phase by the time Terence came along. Of course, he had never met Terence, and it was just as well.

We dumped our trash, stacked the red plastic sandwich baskets and headed out in the opposite direction of Watson and Ivy. "I gotta call Dad," I said, stopping at the pay phone.

"Here, use my cell," Olin said, slipping a slim piece of black plastic from his pocket and handing it to me.

"Oh, my. Do they want you that bad?"

He laughed as I tried to figure out how to dial the number and then finally gave up and let him do it. My father picked up on the first ring.

"Well, I made it. Wanna meet up tonight?" I said.

There was a pause, the whisper of him releasing a breath. "Oh, Merle. Right. I got us a table at the Depot. Seven-thirty."

Neither of us said anything for a moment. A breeze blew in the receiver and I heard an ocean, wind over a field. "I'll see you there," I said.

"Lettie's coming, too, by the way."

"What? Wait a minute."

"Don't you want to see your own grandmother? I think you owe it to her," my father said.

"I don't need you to tell me—"

The line squeaked, the connection ended. And then, a feeling I thought I had long since packed away: a tightening in the chest that had been an early signal of adolescent anger at my father, how he kept scores, made demands. His operating procedure had always been to fling quiet accusations of selfishness and melodrama at me like nets over a duped criminal, followed by white-knuckled trips to Lettie's house, where he left me when he had given up entirely, Olin in the backseat trying to act as if we were just on a rather high-speed Sunday drive. This was the extent of my father's anger, taking corners too fast in his eagerness to get away from me for a while. *Do something with her,* he used to say to Lettie.

Meaning, *Make her more like me.*

I'd planned to see Lettie when I was ready, but I didn't feel close to ready yet. I could refuse to go to dinner, of course. But then, why would I have come all this way just to stay away? My father had me, and he knew it. I snapped the phone closed, handed it back to Olin. "Lettie's coming," I said. I wanted to cry, and Olin could see it in my face. He put his arm around me; I leaned my head against his shoulder. I had forgotten how tall he was. Even though he had been the only one to visit me in London—twice, once when he graduated from high school and then once again after he finished college—somehow he had shrunk in my mind over the years, back to the boy he had been long before I left. I inhaled the bleachy smell of his shirt.

"How is she these days, anyway?" I asked.

"A little looped. But mean as ever."

I laughed, blinking back tears. I was worn out, boozy and stuffed from the beer and subs, nervous about the evening to come. Olin led me to his black Bronco, one of those hulking sport utility vehicles that were all over the place, Americans having apparently decided to drive around in their houses to avoid the curb-to-door commute. The Bronco was five or six years old and looked saggy and tired now, a holdover from his thermometer days. We took off, heading north. I watched the rows of narrow-windowed houses pass, the sunlight blinking through the trees. I didn't ask where we were going.

I had missed Lettie more than anyone, even Olin. She was my father's mother, the one who had told me that my father had never cried, not since the day he brought the tractor to a stop by standing on the brake between his dead father's legs, that and many other stories, even the ones that hurt to hear. My memories of her were physical—the frayed hem of the blue jeans she always wore, the rough edges of the straw hats she hung in the hall, the soft, raised green-blue veins on the backs of her hands. She had taken care of me when my mother died and I had a nervous breakdown, mascara all over my face like a bottle of ink. She had told me all the family stories except one. And so she was the one I had blamed the most— even more than my father—for letting me believe she had shared everything she knew about my mother, Joanie, the night-shift motel worker turned hippie turned alcoholic. My father was tight-lipped by nature, but I had trusted Lettie to give me the full picture, to layer in the details I wouldn't be able to make sense of otherwise, a human Shakespearian aside.

It's true that I fell in love with the love of my parents, even though it was failed and tragic. In fact, maybe the failure made the falling even easier. I knew every story Lettie told about them by heart. I had added my own details over time. I hadn't talked to her for ten years.

4

IN 1966, Ernest Winslow was twenty-three years old. Having spent his life on a farm, he became attracted to the idea of making buildings because he wanted to create something that would stand for more than a season; something that could be added to, improved upon. Corn and wheat demanded a constant starting over, constant prayers for survival; he suspected praying and farming would never be enough. He began to dream of amphitheaters, cathedrals, and arcades—not just the buildings themselves but the structures within, what held them together and lifted them to the sky: flying buttresses, pre-cast, post-tension concrete systems— the stuff of skyscrapers. He began sending out applications like seeds he hoped would take root. He chose Panhandle A&M in Goodwell, Oklahoma, because he felt he needed a change of landscape to open his mind. When he told his mother of his plans, worried that she'd be angry with him for leaving her alone on the farm—he'd always been a little afraid of her, the way she cursed at the hired hands and smoked like a man—she surprised him by buying him a two-hundred-dollar car, and he drove halfway across the country to become an engineer.

My mother, Joanie Madison, was barely seventeen and had graduated a year early from high school in Guymon, up the road a razor-straight ten miles from Goodwell. She was driving to Goodwell twice a week to take two art courses at Panhandle A&M and was working the graveyard shift in the Star-Lite Motel owned by her parents near the Pioneer Rodeo Arena on Twelfth and Sunset. She had grown up around cheating businessmen, crying whores, drunk cowboys demanding a room with not enough cash in their smashed hands. She was unimpressed by the posturing or threats of men. But she was not prepared for Ernest Winslow, who with his Buddy Holly glasses and ill-fitting clothing and purposeful plans for the future of America's cities, awakened in her a sense of possibility, of great change.

Ernest knocked on the glass front door of the Star-Lite at four in the morning, looking for a cup of coffee. He had driven to Guymon from Goodwell, where everything was closed, because he didn't want to go home to the hunched bungalow he was renting with its tiny windows and bare rooms. He had been up for two nights in the studio, gluing tiny pieces of white board together for a model due that day. Some of the glue had gotten into his hair, clumping it into horns at his temples. He reeked of cigarette smoke, as it was part of his student persona to smoke heavily while pulling all-nighters. He'd left the studio when his friend Hall McLendon, who had also been up for two days, tripped and fell on his own project, which had been drying on the floor near the open windows. Hall had picked up his crushed model and smiled like a small child or perhaps more like a mental patient upon realizing that he had destroyed twenty hours of work. He tucked it under one arm and ran to the far end of the studio. "Go long!" he screamed at Ernest.

Ernest ran toward the door, caught the spinning model,

sailed it back to Hall, and ran out of the door before Hall could pass it back, leaving him shrieking "What a catch! What a catch!"

Ernest was nervous and he couldn't quite get his eyes to focus. He was no longer sure what he was doing there at all; he was already in danger of flunking all of his courses, tacking with his portfolio to get home every day through a heavy, dry wind, staring at a garage-sale television set that didn't clear no matter how many beer cans he balanced on it, while tumbleweeds and other debris slapped at his door. The plains beyond his square patchy yard yawned into the white horizon. He needed sleep but he decided to find some coffee instead.

Then he saw Joanie sitting at the front desk and forgot about the coffee. My mother was not just beautiful. She was striking, in the sense that people were struck still by her, men and women alike, but she didn't seem to know it. She was as direct and economical in her actions as a harassed editor perpetually on deadline.

So, when Ernest knocked on the glass front door, it being locked after midnight, she slapped her book on a table, kicked her feet down from the shelf behind the counter where she always propped them, stood up as if she had ten customers in line, all of them cussing at her, and walked in an almost-run to the front door. For the few seconds it took her to cross the lobby, Ernest had the opportunity to observe how her reddish brown hair shone against her shoulders and her dark eyes glistened like lakes at night, and how she was biting her bottom lip as if concentrating on some problem. She wore a lime green A-line dress that she had made for herself that day and sandals tied with matching ribbons around her slim ankles.

Ernest felt a biting pain in his chest that was the beginning of the heart problems to come, caused most likely from smoking and drinking too much and never crying. The pain came whenever he got excited, and he would try to breathe shallowly, as if to keep his lungs from pressing too hard against his heart, to protect it from the pressure that had killed his father.

Joanie cupped her hands around her eyes to see him through the glass. "Yes?" she said.

Ernest leaned in, so she could get a better look at him. They squinted at each other. "Are you open?"

"You a guest here?" Joanie asked in a twang as flat as the plains around them, her voice muffled through the glass.

He tried to think. His brain felt dry, dusty. "No, I was just looking around," he said. He looked at his shoes and shook his head. "Are you, uh, getting off anytime soon?"

"Maybe," Joanie said. She bit her bottom lip again, concentrating on some important question, Ernest thought. He remembered wanting coffee. He stuffed his hands into his pockets and asked if she would go with him.

"I'll have to ask my father when he wakes up," she said. "In the meantime, you should go comb your hair or something. I get off at six."

Ernest wandered the wide streets of Guymon, his stomach growling and pinching, smoking cigarettes until it was time to come back to the Star-Lite. He watched the sun rise, throwing pink light on the low pole fences of the rodeo grounds, and it reminded him of the eyelid-purple morning he'd arrived in Santa Fe after driving through a desert night with the bright moon stuck in his windshield. He'd been sent by his technical drawing professor, Clink Johnson, after failing a test, so he could see how "God don't come out of a damn mechanical pencil." He had walked from the Palace of the Governors across the empty square, following the Old Santa Fe Trail that ran past the thick-walled San Miguel Mission Church and rose into the mountains, and he remembered the still air inside the Loretto Chapel whispering like the early morning street where he stood now, the voices floating from the Mexican bakery like hymns. He could close his eyes and see the *milagro* staircase, the silken pulse of its cool wood spiraling two complete turns to the loft. Clink Johnson, or Professor Clink, as he was called, had told the class about it: how engineers and architects from around the world had studied it, and no formula could explain how it stood. "It's simple," he'd said. "You've got the Sisters of Loretto who can't make it up the ladder into the choir loft anymore to sing their devotions. They hold a *novena,* nine days of prayer, to ask for help. Next morning, a man knocks on the door, builds the staircase with no nails or visible support, and exits into the desert." Professor Clink had scowled, eyebrows crowding his nose. He was trying to explain why anything was built; he was talking about need. "You've got form and you've got function. And then you have the Spirit."

There were nuns and miracles and then there were beautiful young women watching over sleeping cowboys in rundown motels. Either way, Ernest knew he wasn't at home and he was glad of it. It felt like something. It was true that people had shot each other over land rights and less out here, and the windstorms could knock a man down. He had to admit it was an altogether difficult place, nothing like the black-soiled, gently rolling farmland of northeastern Ohio that he had left, where birds were small and rain was regular, and trees divided the landscape to human dimensions. And the people—Florence's German farmers were an industrious, friendly lot, hearty but not overbearing, religious but not zealous. The people of Goodwell seemed unused to focusing at close distances, their farsighted gaze trained on whatever weather might be billowing on the horizon. Most were polite enough but short-spoken, a few harmlessly crazy, and one or two aggressively menacing. He would learn that Joanie's father fell into the last camp.

Ernest bent to inspect himself in the side mirror of a broken-down car, working at the clumps of glue in his hair. He had bushy eyebrows, gray eyes like his parents, and light brown hair that went blond in the summer. He tried smiling at himself in the mirror, which helped, because his teeth, although crooked (one broken in front from an unfortunate baseball pitch in his youth), were friendly teeth, and his smile made his squinty eyes seem less skeptical. He polished his teeth with the hem of his T-shirt and started back down the road to the Star-Lite.

The wedge-shaped sign mounted on the roof of the lobby was spangled with various colors of glittering stars; the *i* in Star-Lite was dotted with a star. The pale turquoise doors to the fifteen rooms made my father a little queasy that morning as he stood across the street, trying to see my mother through the glass door. Instead he saw a man he correctly assumed was her father, lanky with a bony face and black hair, staring back at him. Ernest shuffled across the broad, flat street, pushed open the door, and walked inside.

"Help you?" my grandfather said.

"I'm looking for—" Only then did Ernest realize he didn't know her name. He looked at the clock. It was 6:05.

"Well?" my grandfather said, impatient. He loomed over the counter and my father saw that behind him was a shotgun propped against the paneled wall, a cleaning rag tossed over the end of the barrel like a gray wig. It unnerved him, even though he had grown up with shotguns. But they had always been carefully stored in his father's dark wood cabinet, which had a brass lock and key.

"I think I'm in the wrong place," he said. He turned to go,

sneaking a glance down a short hallway to his left, hoping to see my mother.

"Maybe you are," my grandfather said.

My father didn't look back as he walked out onto the street. It was one of the two times he would see my grandfather before he and my mother ran away together.

5

BEFORE MEETING OUR FATHER for dinner, Olin took me to Cleveland. We came in on I-77, and I could see the whole skyline—the Terminal Tower, the Society and BP buildings—and bits of the lake winking behind it. I stared through the brown-tinted glass of Olin's Bronco, the sky and road and grassy banks on either side warm-toned like a Kodachrome slide. It was late afternoon, the sun angling through the buildings, sharper than in England, where the light is pale and muted. Cleveland has among the fewest days of sunshine in the country, and maybe Lake Erie is what makes them seem too bright, the colors snapping against each other like a child's drawing.

"OK, now for the tour," Olin said, pointing. "There's Jacob's Field and Gund Arena." At a nearby sidewalk café a group of sturdy-looking men drank beers in various shades of red and gold. College-aged kids wearing black handed out flyers in front of a string of small theaters. A young woman in a blue dress on a bicycle veered around us as we slowed for a light. There were signs pointing to the Rock and Roll Hall of

Fame every couple of blocks. When I'd last been here, twenty or so years old and going out with friends to old munitions warehouses to see aging punk bands, or to piano bars where people sang along to endless Billy Joel and Bruce Springsteen cover bands, Cleveland was still a joke to the rest of the country, known for the Cuyahoga River and the mayor's hair catching fire in the same year.

In the Flats, the old warehouses now bristled with brightly painted steel and neon towers, not yet lit for the evening and looking anemic in the afternoon sun, like an actress without her makeup. We parked on the street and I followed Olin into a short alley, where we entered a building through a dented metal door and rode a service elevator to a tall-ceilinged fourth-floor apartment with exposed brick walls, black marble kitchen countertops, leather furniture, and a view of the lake. I thought of my flat over the woodcutting shop in West London, with its hallway afterthought of a kitchen and curtained bathroom, and of the similarly dreary flats before that, two of which Olin had seen, and, most recently of course, the apartment our father had just gotten me, emergency housing with the powdery scent of the woman who'd lived there before.

And then I saw this: a life-sized Marilyn posed next to the window, wearing the white dress from *The Seven Year Itch* and smiling like a hostess.

I squinted at her against the light off the lake until spots danced on my eyeballs.

"What do you think?" he asked me.

"Nice place. Where'd you find the doll?" I asked.

"What? Oh, she's not a doll. Dolls are small," Olin said, laughing and shaking his head as if I should have known the difference. He pulled a bottle of beer from the stainless steel refrigerator, poured it into a chilled glass from the freezer, and offered it to me, but I shook my head.

"OK. What is it then?" I realized I was pinching myself on the soft skin of my upper arm—the whole thing made me nervous, the doll, the spotless apartment; it wasn't Olin. I couldn't figure out what was going on.

"Well," Olin set his glass of beer on the coffee table on his way over to her. "She was a gift, originally. But now she's sort of become company." He straightened the dress at the shoulders, pulled a thread from the skirt hem.

"Company?" I sat on the slippery leather couch.

"Yeah, she's the perfect date, really—looks good, keeps quiet," Olin said, grinning. I knew he was trying to see if I'd get irritated—I'd been heavy into Gloria Steinem in the late seventies with my best friend, Tanya, and he'd never let me forget it, how I'd quoted constantly from the article "If Men Menstruated" and later tried to collect signatures for the ERA. My mother had been accidentally labeled as a revolutionary, but I had tried earnestly to earn the title before just trying to pay the bills became my biggest priority in life. When exactly had that happened? I wondered. Meanwhile, Olin was talking about someone named Sandy who was no longer speaking to him.

"That's her?" I asked, pointing to a picture on the coffee table of a tanned blond woman smiling magnificently at the camera, wisps of hair blown attractively around her face.

"Yep. She's a lawyer. Great girl. Neighbors hate her, though," he said, pantomiming a screaming orgasm. He grinned at me with a foamy beer mustache, expecting me to be shocked, I guess, but after you edit books about S&M for a living, you start thinking that anything short of group sex seems quaint. I gave him a thin smile as he plopped onto the couch across from me.

"So you're living together?" I figured she'd been the one crying in the background when I'd called.

"Well, actually, I'm living with her. This is her place."

"Oh?" Now it made sense to me, how this place didn't jive with the string of shabby but cozy apartments Olin had lived in, which I knew from the snapshots he'd sent me over the years, usually at holidays. He'd had a sagging beige couch, a toughened fern, and a beer bottle collection. I wondered where he'd put his stuff—surely Sandy wouldn't let him keep it in this museum. "You're a kept man?"

"Not bad work if you can get it," he said, propping his feet on the gleaming coffee table next to the picture. "You know, you got me thinking, maybe I do need a new career—not just the comedy," he said. "It's all marketing, right?"

"Sure," I said. "Me, too." I thought of the dingy X Publishing offices, your typical hastily built British post–World War II office building, cramped and badly heated, Terence in there working away on his latest bondage novel. I had told Olin and my father that I worked in publishing, but they didn't know what kind. I had no idea what I would do next, and it scared me. I'd always thought that, like my father, I'd feel called by a profession, even if it didn't work out. But that hadn't happened. I tried to think positive; I could hear my voice yelling like a game-show host, *You're going to do something really great, really exciting!* But so far, nothing came to mind.

Olin jumped to his feet. "Hey, got something for you," he said. He drained his beer, and for a moment he looked like those sun-kissed kids on Mellow Yellow commercials from the seventies, lovingly throwing back their sodas in preparation for rope-swinging across a creek. He disappeared down the short hallway—I heard a closet door opening and closing with a heavy metallic click—and came back with two tickets and a Marilyn thermometer, which he tossed on the couch next to me.

"What's this for?" I said, picking up the tickets first.

Running down one side were the words "Cleveland Improv" in a jittery font.

"For you and Dad," Olin said. "I got my first gig. Well, OK, a friend got me in. Amateur night. It's a few weeks off yet."

"So you're really going to do it!" I said, trying to sound enthusiastic when in truth the idea made me nervous. I wondered what he'd find funny if not a life-sized Marilyn in an apartment that wasn't his.

I picked up the Marilyn thermometer, studied the poof of white-blond hair, the red mouth, the absurdly round breasts and tiny waist. The plastic eyes glittered. "You already gave me one of these." He'd brought it with him on one of his trips, and I'd lost it on one of my moves, maybe on purpose.

Olin frowned, disappointed. "Hmm. Well, hey, she can keep the other one company."

"I don't cook much meat these days," I said, tossing it on the table. "So when Sandy screams, how do you tell whether she's getting pissed or getting off?"

Olin waved the question away. "So I wonder what my joke list should be for the Improv?" he asked himself, stroking the line of his mouth as if there were a mustache.

"Well," I said, deepening my voice to sound serious, responsible. The Ernest voice. "If the Lake Effect jokes don't work, you can always get a day job."

"There she is, the sister I remember. Someone's got to be the good child around here, the responsible one. Where the hell have you been, anyway? I'm the fuckup, remember?" he said, and then he grinned a grin I knew as well as my own face. That grin had stared up at me through our childhood, every time he outran me even though his legs were shorter, every time he had gotten out of doing the dishes. I had changed his diapers, helped him with his homework, held him when he cried for our mother, nights when he had crawled into bed with me because our father was so deeply asleep with the pills he took for a while; but even in his grief Olin had been somehow freer than the rest of us, more able to move on without going anywhere at all.

He stood up, flicked his keys in the air, held open the door for me. I picked up the tickets and followed him.

6

THE DEPOT, a yuppie restaurant that used to be the Florence general store, overlooks a shallow stretch of the Cuyahoga River, which flows calmly through town after some dramatic rapids and waterfalls north of here. Our father was waiting for us at a table near the tall windows. I had gotten fired from this restaurant one summer in high school by the troll of a manager, Mr. Lick, who didn't appreciate my nontraditional style of serving—meals at separate times, condiments as it occurred to me, sneaking sips of too-full drinks as I carried them to the table—that sort of thing. I'd had good intentions, but I didn't really have a good grasp of details, which hadn't helped my editing career either, not that readers of the X Publishing novels were deeply concerned with apostrophes being in the right place or the correct use of semicolons. However, those things had mattered greatly to my boss, Chet Peterson, a devoted publisher who was also the only three-time winner of the Diva Award at the Vauxhall Tavern, where began the glittering careers of such drag-queen talents as Julian Clary, the Divine David, and Lilly Savage. He was patient with my mistakes but meticulous in correcting them. Terence had idolized him; we both had, but for different reasons. While Terence was enthralled by the creativity of Chet's costuming, down to the diamond chips pressed into his glossy nails, I was most impressed with his gentleness, his way of looking at you as if you mattered more than anyone in the world to him at that moment. Maybe it was his large, beautifully painted eyes or his fine, translucent skin, but he made me feel supremely loved, and I craved it; it was the main reason I stayed so long at X Publishing. That and the fact that he paid me in cash and took me out for curries with his drag-queen friends, where I felt like the most well-adjusted woman in the world.

My father's hair was the first thing I noticed when Olin and I spotted him. It was a silvery gray now and thinning, cut very short so that it stood in a fuzz at his crown and over the ears. His face looked reddish, puffy. Sitting at the table with a menu cradled in his hands like a prayer book, his shoulders seemed narrower, curving into his chest. He sat alone, no Lettie. My first reaction was relief. I didn't want to deal with her outbursts; her hand-waving drama, her habit of pinching waitstaff on the ass, male or female. But somehow I could sense her presence, a residue of cigarettes and harsh laughter in the air.

My father stood up and smiled as Olin and I approached. He turned to me and the smile tightened, but remained. We hugged. He seemed thicker and shorter and I was surprised by his smell, something like damp wool. I didn't remember him having a smell other than cologne, or alcohol, of course. As he patted my back before sitting, his hands seemed stiff, tentative, and my earlier frustration with him drained, feeling that slight tremble.

Olin and I took seats on either side of my father. "So where's Lettie?" I asked.

My father gestured toward the rest rooms, and just then the door swung open, slapping the wall and turning heads at nearby tables. Lettie bustled past, muttering to herself, pocketbook clutched in both hands in front of her like a shield. She wore blue jeans, a faded work shirt, untucked, and field boots. She was skinnier than I remembered, her elbows poking tiny tents in her shirtsleeves, her hips sharp points. Her gray hair had gone white and was pulled into a pompom on the top of her head. "Goddamnit," she said loudly as she reached our table. "Why they can't keep enough toilet paper in these places is beyond me."

"Well, you know, maybe if you didn't steal it," my father said calmly, sipping a glass of water.

Lettie looked at him. Olin and I watched; I was conscious of how still we were both sitting, like startled rabbits, I thought. As Lettie turned toward me I willed myself to meet her eyes and not flinch. "Well, well," she said, hand on her hip. "Miss Merle is back in Florence—call the press!"

I stood up. "It's good to see you," I said, feeling immediately idiotic.

Lettie laughed and shook her head, as if I were too absurd to answer. "What does it take to get a martini around here, anyway? Hey!" She called to a sullen, forty-something-looking woman with mascara smudges under her eyes, bright red lipstick, and a name tag with SHOOPIE engraved under the "Hello! I'm . . ." heading. I was skeptical; I wondered if they still made fake name tags here so angry customers would fill out complaint cards about bad service from someone who didn't exist. The woman came slowly over to our table, eyeing Lettie warily. "Three martinis," Lettie said, leaning into her as if she might have a hearing problem. "And speed it up, toots; I'm an old woman." She didn't order one for my father because he rarely drank after Joanie's death, his own cosmic averaging, probably.

My father was watching Lettie with the slightest hint of amusement gathered in the crinkled corners of his eyes. At this point, everyone at the surrounding tables was also watching us, but not with the same kind of appreciation. Olin stepped around the table to her, cupped her elbow. "Come have a seat, hmm, Lettie?"

"Don't coddle me, boy," she said, shaking him off.

Shoopie came with the martinis. Lettie plucked hers off the tray, nearly knocking the whole thing off balance. Shoopie glared at her; Lettie glared back. "Back off, bags," she growled.

I had to admit, Olin was smooth. He took the other two martinis from Shoopie, thanking her profusely, pretending he hadn't heard Lettie. Shoopie sidled away as he handed a glass to me and raised his. "A toast!" he declared.

Lettie rolled her eyes but lifted her glass. My father raised his water. I had to prop my elbow on my free hand to keep from shaking the gin out of my glass. "To homecomings!" Olin said. "And to our family, together again," he finished, grinning brightly at me.

I took a big gulp of gin and then noticed that Lettie had drained hers. I gave Olin a look that asked, is this normal? Olin just shrugged, a lip-and-eyebrow shrug really, no shoulders; that would have been too obvious. Lettie set her glass on the table, patted my father on the head. "Well, I'm off."

"You're not staying for dinner?" my father asked.

Lettie flashed an indulgent smile. "That's what I mean when I say 'I'm off,' darling." She waved her fingers at us and marched toward the door.

We looked in that direction for several seconds after she'd gone, as if we expected she might reappear, changing her mind. It seemed as if twenty people had left the room, not just one rather small old woman. That was my grandmother. I sat down, took another big gulp of gin.

"So, tell us about the trip," Olin said to me then, settling next to me. I could see he was trying to help me recover, but I didn't want to talk about it at all.

"My trip?" I said, buying time. I felt flattened by Lettie's appearance. Even my father seemed dazed by it. The trip had been terrible, from slipping out of bed at four in the morning, leaving Terence asleep and unknowing, to the bumpy ride to Gatwick with Fiona, who had never mastered certain driving basics such as stopping consistently for red lights. I had spent most of the flight teary and nauseous, chiding myself for coming home at such a bad time, but of course I had come home precisely because things were so bad. I caught myself worrying about whether Terence was managing alone and I had to pinch myself hard on the thigh. I winced. "The trip was fine. But thanks for fixing me up with a place," I said to my father. "I promise I won't need it for long. I'm just getting . . . I don't even know how long I'll stay, or if—" My father was looking at me with a benign expression, waiting politely for me to finish. I cleared my throat. "So, you wouldn't happen to have any of my old furniture, would you?"

"Sold it," my father said, coughing dryly. "Needed a home office, you know?"

I looked at him, trying to smile and say I understood. But the words wouldn't come. Tears burned at the corners of my eyes—why, I couldn't be sure. Had I really expected him to keep my room intact the way he'd done for a while with the master bedroom after Joanie died? I thought, Do you have to die to demand any permanence?

"Speaking of the home office, I saw a couple of great infomercials last night," Olin offered.

This was why he'd been so good at marketing, I realized.

He could make anything relate to anything else. Hair dye and cat food? Sure thing. Meat thermometers and sex? No problem. It was a natural gift. Meanwhile, I felt as if I had suddenly been cut free, like an astronaut who'd pulled the wrong cord. "Oh, really?" I said.

"One was about the Mask. It's this plastic thing that gives women an instant face-lift! You just 'put in on and plug it in,'" he said, pantomiming. "And it vibrates or something like that, removes wrinkles and warts, you know—"

"Olin?"

He ignored me. "The other one was, like, a total program on seventies music, selling a CD. The Smooth Seventies! There was this married couple talking about each song, and the man kept reminiscing about how he used to be on *General Hospital* when it was really big—but who knows if that was true, because I totally didn't recognize him—anyway, they had their hair feathered and—"

"Is this going in the act?" I asked.

"What act?" my father said, looking back and forth between us. I realized he didn't know yet about Olin's comedic aspirations.

Olin seemed to be fumbling for an answer; it was clear he didn't want to talk about it, which was odd, since the Improv tickets he'd given me were supposed to be for me and Dad.

"Oh, you know, at work," I said, and Olin knocked my knee with his in thanks. It was no problem, I wanted to say, but Olin knew more than anyone how true that was. I was an everyday, addicted liar growing up. I lied about everything. I wish I could blame this habit on covering for my mother's drinking, but I can't. I lied even before I became aware of her drinking as something not quite normal, before I had to make excuses to my friends about how it was not a good time to come over, ever. By the time I was out of college and newly arrived in the UK, I had a habit. If someone asked me where I was from, I told them Bugtussle, Oklahoma, or Kitchen Table, Montana. If they complimented me on my earrings, I told about how they had been given to me by my rich, dying aunt before her third boy-husband left with all her money. When we were kids, I got Olin to walk down to the Cinema Six with me and pretend we had been dropped off by our parents from another state until my sixth-grade teacher Ms. Montaigne spotted our Styrofoam cup and sign, which said, HELP, WE'RE ORPHANS FROM MAINE, as she stepped out of the Dairy Queen. She was less than pleased, and that was perhaps the first time I remember that tired, what-do-I-have-to-do-to-get-some-sanity-around-here expression on my father's face as he came out to the parking lot in front of the Social Services building to collect us.

We ordered. I finished my martini. "So tell me what's been going on with you these days, Dad," I said, exhaling gin fumes through my nose, my eyes watering.

"Nothing much, just working," he said. "There's this Habitat project for low-income housing on the southwest side of town, and it's been nothing but battles all the way. The zoning, the permits, the neighbors don't want it. Nothing ever changes," he said, shaking his head. "In fact, I hate to rush, but I'll have to take off as soon as we eat—I have to get something ready for tomorrow."

Our meals came, and we ate in silence. The dinner, I realized, was just what a family did for a reunion—not getting together upon my return would have been odd, so here we were, trying not to be odd. Lettie had told me once that when my father brought Joanie home he was so happy his forehead shone, as if his blood might burst through his skin, both of them smiling like prison escapees. They had been wildly happy once, redeemed in each other. But somehow it had

worn off. I had always wanted to know why, and now I understood why I wanted to know: I thought it might be the key to
my own unsuccessful love life. I had stuck with Terence for so
long because I mistook his flamboyance as a sign that he was
someone totally different from my father, someone I could
really communicate with, but that wasn't the case at all. In
truth he was just as remote, and someday he would undoubt-
edly relinquish his platform boots and neon mesh shirts for a
flannel suit and a nice bank job. If he'd fooled me it was
because I'd wanted to be fooled. When it came down to it, I
knew more about bondage equipment than relationships.

My father wiped his mouth with the oversized linen napkin, folded it, and sat it neatly beside his plate. I knew that,
once we were all finished, he would insist on stacking our
plates with the silverware collected on the top plate to make it
easier for the waitress. He would pay for the meal with a credit
card but leave her cash so none of it would be taken by the
manager or have to be reported on taxes. That was the way he
was: unfailingly concerned for the poor, the underrepresented,
the lonely, but somehow tuned out from the people closest to
him.

Olin was talking about his former client who wanted to
launch a line of celebrity cleaning implements: a Jimi Hendrix
sponge, a Cher mop with a spangled handle. My father was
talking about a developer who wanted to build a mall on
known wetlands, and people were protesting, carrying posters
of bullfrog photos with a crosshairs painted over their big-
eyed, wet faces.

"Well, you two, I've got to go," he said when Shoopie
brought back his credit card. "Early day tomorrow." He was
eyeing the door, as if measuring for a leap. "Give me a call," he
said, apparently forgetting the detail of my not having a phone.
"Oh, and you'll call—?"

He didn't have to say Lettie; I knew what he meant. "I will. Definitely," I said. My heart squeezed tighter for a beat. Angry as she had made me, I loved her—her stories, her independence, the way I had once thought of her as my friend as much as my grandmother. But she was also unpredictable, laughing one moment, mean-spirited the next. As Olin and I followed our father to the door and watched him walk away, I had to ask myself who I was kidding, thinking I could know any of them again. It had been too long. I felt as if I had been asleep all this time, a neurotic Rip Van Winkle. My father and brother were perhaps just being polite, letting me believe I belonged to them until I found somewhere else to go.

7

THE OPPORTUNITY FOR ERNEST to revise his model project came from the grouchy but sympathetic Professor Clink a couple of afternoons after Ernest met Joanie, when Ernest came to Professor Clink's small and cluttered office for a midsemester conference. Professor Clink informed Ernest of his age, sixty-eight, and birth year, 1898, during which people still called the Panhandle Beaver County or No Man's Land, the narrow strip of land left over after Texas lopped off the top end of its panhandle at the Missouri Compromise line to avoid being counted as a free state. Ernest wasn't sure where Professor Clink was going with this information, but he was willing to listen.

"God's Land, that's what they called it here," Professor Clink said, twirling a string of his bolo tie around one finger. "But hard living, I'll tell you. I was born before the railroad came. Yep, that was 1901, and I remember it. Those Rock Island boys came in here laying steel and named the place Goodwell after they drilled down and found all that cold fresh water—they wanted steam, you understand? They had wagons and tent cities and they worked all night. Back then you could still hear the grass waving under the wind, just calling. Like a woman sighing sometimes, or shushing a baby." Professor Clink leaned back in his cracked leather chair and closed his eyes, as if hearing it again.

"I think I might be in the wrong profession," Ernest said. He looked at Professor Clink across a massive deck piled with blueprints and papers and books.

"You aren't in a profession, son! You're a student." Professor Clink's eyes flew open again, bulged as he raised his voice, his pale irises awash in twin seas of milky ivory.

"I guess I mean I'm in the wrong course of study then."

Professor Clink stared back him. "Well, I don't know about that," he said slowly. "Things happen that you can't plan for. Them Russians, for example, coming out here with thistle on their coats, in the wheat seed they brought. Now we got tumbleweeds. Damn things can knock down a barbed-wire fence. Nobody planned for that but there it is."

Ernest stood up, picked up his model and Professor Clink's spidery handwritten crit, and headed for the studio.

That night he tried to respond to Clink's suggestions, to simplify, to avoid extras that would never be supported in a public project. But there was no detail he could part with.

Over the next couple of weeks he skipped his theory class because the assignment, which was the single assignment for the whole semester, was to prove a mathematical theorem, which, it was rumored, had taken a building full of government supercomputers to solve. He hadn't started on it. He could no longer follow the discussions in class, as students, working in teams, pelted Professor Luckado, a thin-faced Polish Jew from New Jersey, with questions, hoping to determine if they were on the right track. Professor Luckado beamed at the questions, and flipped his stringy ponytail in frustration when students were, as he put it, "going the wrong way on a one way street." Ernest had never seen a man with a ponytail in person. Hall called him an East Coast radical. "The FBI will be in here soon to haul his ass away, I expect," he whispered one day in class.

"The math knows only one direction," Professor Luckado would say in his nasal, gangster accent. "If the government can do it, surely you can." Professor Luckado hated the government uniformly, as if it were one thing, like a make of car, or a flavor of ice cream. He would be crushed under a burning car rolled on top of him accidentally by rioting students in Berkeley five years later, 1970, the year of the Kent State shootings and the Morris P. Alston building bombing, the year things changed violently between my parents, and were never repaired.

Ernest and Hall were on the same math team, which was how they had met. During the two weeks when he'd given up on Luckado's theory class, Ernest worked listlessly on models for Clink Johnson and thought about Joanie. He didn't know her name yet, so he tried various ones: Melissa, Katherine, Patricia (the name of a girl he'd dated in high school who had let him take off her bra; he remembered how the skin of her breasts glowed bluish white against her tan lines in the dark of his mother's car, the nipples upturned like little faces, which, he remembered, unnerved him as he bent to take them in his mouth). None of the names fit. As each day passed without a visit to Joanie, Ernest wondered what Hall would have done in his situation. Ernest figured rangy, confident Hall would have talked his way right past Joanie's father that first morning. Hall was six-feet, seven-inches tall and had grown up on a ranch outside of Texhoma. He had four older brothers and his mother wanted one son to go to college. He wore jeans he'd shrunk to a snug fit by soaking in a horse trough, and cowboy boots made from the leather of a bull he'd had to kill the summer before. "Went heat crazy," Hall had explained to my father the first time they'd gone out for a beer, lifting his booted foot in the air like a peeing dog to show my father how he'd tooled the leather. Ernest figured if Hall could kill a bull, he could work up the courage to get a date. The whole thought of it hurt Ernest's stomach, and he felt weak and useless, slumped over his drafting table in the empty studio, night after night.

Hall pounded on Ernest's door one afternoon after Professor Luckado's class let out. He slowly came to from a fog induced by jalapeño-spiced beef burritos and Lone Star beer. Ernest had seen Hall's rebuilt model the night before, and he'd had to admit it was the work of a budding genius— economical, crisp, and realistic. Ernest pulled himself to his feet from where he had been sleeping on the floor and wove toward the door. He was beginning to believe his talents resided elsewhere; where, he wasn't sure.

When Ernest opened the door, Hall took a step back. "You look like hell," Hall said.

Ernest leaned against the door and let Hall come in. Hall waved at the air. "You smell like hell, too." He peered at Ernest's drawn face. "You sick?"

"Maybe." Ernest sat down on the bench he had built with two boards and some cinder blocks. He stared at matching shelves that lined the facing wall.

Hall nodded solemnly. "Son, I know I am not exactly ready for Jesus, but you are fucking up something fierce."

"I know," Ernest said.

"What are you gonna do?" Hall said. His head nearly reached the ceiling.

"Not sure yet," Ernest said. He tried to run his fingers through his hair, but there was still glue in it. He winced, untangling his fingers. "I think I've got food poisoning."

"Hell. Nothing some three-alarm chili can't kill."

"I don't know."

"You're feeling sorry for yourself. Some alcohol will clear your head."

Hall and Ernest drove to Guymon, since there were no bars in Goodwell. Guymon had beer halls and a couple of clubs where you brought in your own liquor and paid an entry fee and a setup charge to the bartender. They had a few beers at the Y-not, but Hall wanted liquor. "Let's get out of here," Hall said, throwing a couple of limp bills at the bartender, a rat-faced man named McCreedy who seemed happy to see them go. "I know where we can get some liquor."

"I don't want any grain alcohol," Ernest said, following him outside. "Stuff can blind you."

Hall laughed, "Boy, what do you think we do out here? This fellow's got good liquor, bonded. Tequila, whiskey, anything you want. They say the only traffic light they need in this town is in front of his house."

They drove down to a trailer near the railroad tracks that Professor Clink had watched being laid down a lifetime ago. Ernest waited in the car while Hall managed the transaction with the fellow, whom Ernest couldn't see because he didn't seem to feel the need to open his thin metal door very wide. Hall came back with a bottle in a paper bag. "Crack her open," he said, climbing in.

They drank half the bottle by the time they made it back to Goodwell. They sat unsteadily on stools at the Aggie Inn and ordered steaks. By the time their meals came, Ernest felt solidly drunk, the meat doing nothing to soak up the alcohol as Hall had promised. Hall seemed unfazed by the sips he was sneaking from the bottle whenever the waitress wasn't looking, one after the other.

"Let's walk," Ernest said, lurching out of his seat after they finished eating.

They ended up by a small park near the campus, where my mother sat in Bermuda grass, sketching the Chinese elms, which had been planted by the Goodwell Garden Club and which threw long shadows in the early evening light. The park was the only place around Goodwell that had trees in any number, other than the cottonwoods that grew along the draws and ravines outside of town. Ernest imagined that someone had imported them fully formed to this place, along with white bread and refrigeration.

He and Hall sat on a stone bench, backs against a picnic table, and smoked, watching the light shift and fade. The sky was now deep golden with streaks of pink and purple. It changed its character at night, softening and flattening, lowering from the day's endless upside-down bowl of blue, so that Ernest felt it looked almost familiar.

"Well, I'm in love," Hall said, staring straight ahead, his long, pointy-kneed legs stretched out like fence posts. He was drunk and slack-faced; Ernest could tell even though he too was dizzy with alcohol.

"With who?" Ernest asked, thinking of Joanie, whose name had been Alice last time he'd thought of her. He considered mentioning her to Hall, to ask for suggestions on how to approach her, when Hall lifted his arm and pointed straight at her.

Ernest could not see that it was Joanie; he saw only a tall, long-haired woman in silhouette, over to the right where shadows streamed under the elms, bending to gather her belongings and place them in her bag. Then she began walking toward them, and Hall elbowed Ernest hard in the ribs.

"All right, here goes," Hall said, leaning forward, trying to stand. His head dropped to his chest and snapped back up.

"Here, I'll help you up," Ernest said, standing. He reached for Hall's elbows, turning to glance at the woman. But by then she was close enough to recognize, and Ernest stood up quickly, as if kicked. Hall flopped back against the table edge.

Joanie stopped a few feet away, recognizing Ernest. "Well," she said. She glanced at Hall and then back at Earnest. A wind lifted her hair and bent the grass against her ankles. She squinted, looked them both up and down, unimpressed.

"Ernest Winslow," my father said. He took a step forward and held out his hand, but she didn't take it.

Hall pushed himself to his feet, swaying, a full head taller than my father. He stared at my mother as if she were an apparition, a miracle. "Hall McLendon. Pleased to make your acquaintance," he slurred, bowing unsteadily. Ernest cringed.

"Joanie Madison. You both are stinking," Joanie said. Her dark eyes were steady on them, not angry, but not amused.

"I'm sorry," Ernest said. He was trying to think of a way to save the situation, but his ribs seemed to be knitting together, tightening around his lungs and heart, and he couldn't find his voice.

"I guess so," she said. She cocked her head looking back and forth between them, tapped her foot. "If one of you is going to ask me out, you'd better get on with it."

This pronouncement, combined with their drunkenness and Joanie's beauty, left both Ernest and Hall shaken. But Ernest recovered more quickly. "OK," he said. "How about coffee? Tomorrow?" he asked. "Or a movie. Whatever you like."

She considered his question. "I'll meet you here at four, and then we'll decide," she said. She looked in her bag, as if checking for something, and turned to go. "Nice to meet you, Hall," she said as she walked away.

They watched her. "Well, damn it," Hall said under his breath. "You are a rat, Ern."

Ernest laughed, throwing his head back. Above the elms

the first stars were coming out. They were pale and flat, but soon they would grow fat and glittery, and bigger than any stars he had seen in Ohio, and although he knew they were the same stars, they seemed entirely different. The air was rolling in cool from the plains, and he felt it all around him, like an ocean.

Hall stalked off toward the bar they had come from. "I mean it," he called over his shoulder. "You mess up once with her, I am right behind you!"

Ernest strode across the grass after Hall, feeling triumphant, generous, as if he owned the park and everything around him, and Hall was his friend to protect and indulge. He felt for a moment as if he had entered the body of his father, with his long stride, his powerful hands. Ernest had been a baby when his father reached the same age he was at that moment, his heart perhaps just beginning to worry over a weakness in its fabric that would tear and kill him seven years later. At age eight, when Ernest had steered the tractor to a stop just short of the irrigation ditch, he had thought his father must have been an old man, that he must have been ready to die. He had believed it like the predictions in the *Farmer's Almanac* and decided it was time to be a man, to replace the one taken.

Stumbling home to his small, square house so drunk he'd forgotten he'd driven, he fried some Spam and stood on the patio, eating directly from the pan. Afterward, he smoked and thought of Joanie. He said her name and enjoyed the light touch of his tongue on the roof of his mouth, the puff of air across his teeth required to voice it. At twenty-three, he knew his father had not been ready to die, any more than he was. He wanted to live, to be in love, to build great buildings, to build something, at least. He finished his last cigarette and watched the smoke spread and thin against the star-poked sky. He was ready to begin.

8

THAT NIGHT AFTER DINNER with our father, Olin drove me around Florence. We passed the river and park to our right, historically correct iron lampposts winking amber light. Over the trees the moon was rising, just a sliver, with the shadow of the rest of the curve barely visible. "Why didn't you want to tell Dad about the comedy gig?" I asked Olin.

He shrugged. "Oh, with Lettie there and him worried about you coming home all of a sudden—"

"He's worried about me?"

"Of course he is. I am too. One day you're talking about how great the publishing business is and then the next day you're leaving the country. You kill someone or something?"

I ignored this. "You know, I feel like walking," I said. "Let's head back downtown." We crossed the bridge toward Baden Lake, and I watched passing rows of tall, narrow houses perched close together with small, square windows and screened porches in front, painted gray and maroon and brown. Shallow, scrabbly yards with bushes leaning hopefully against bony fences, the occasional flower bed. The streets, stretched and crunched by winter ice and summer heat, pot-holed and patched like a gray quilt, crumbling to gravel at the edges. And yet it looked cleaner, crisper than I remembered, during those years when I was plotting to get out.

Olin looped around the lake and, on the way downtown, pointed out the Department of Social Services, that square, beige building. "And of course, Ernest's workplace, built in the bunker tradition of the 1950s," he said in a tour-guide voice. "So, really. What made you leave?"

"Oh, because I couldn't take it anymore. My career was going nowhere. My relationship was a mess. I felt I had to do something drastic."

"Like when you left in the first place?" He said it like a question, but he wasn't really asking, so I didn't answer. He parked on River Street and cut the engine.

I dug around in my purse for my cigarettes, popped one in my mouth, and searched for some matches.

"That's a lovely habit," Olin said.

"Off my case about it," I said. I sat on the steps of the gazebo where there were concerts in the summer and watched the college students filing into the row of bars lining River Street. I felt drowsy and unfocused; I needed sleep but I didn't want to go back to my bare apartment and be left alone.

Olin bought a gyro from a cart on the corner and sat down beside me. "Want a bite?"

I was so tired I couldn't even answer; I just waved it away. I was disoriented, everything around me familiar yet changed. I figured there were things that I didn't really recognize at all, but my mind had decided to recognize them because it felt it should. I was considering this, glancing back and forth between Olin munching on his gyro and the college students who looked like children, like they needed baby-sitters, really, and I was thinking of saying yes to the bite of gyro when a

huge, mint green Cadillac convertible with fins and a lot of
chrome rounded the corner. Next to the small, mostly rusted
student cars, the Cadillac looked like royalty among cars, a car
celebrity. It seemed to float down the narrow street, jostled
only slightly by the uneven paving. The radio was blaring an
easy-listening station; Christopher Cross singing about sailing.
The car paused to allow some students to pass. "Nice car!"
someone yelled. A woman was driving, her big blond hair
tinted pink by the red neon beer signs in the windows. The
middle-aged man next to her had narrow shoulders, a silvery
buzz cut, and thick glasses. He sat with his arm propped on the
door, his fingers tapping lightly to the music. He turned to the
woman and said something. The woman threw back her head
and laughed out loud. "Ernest! You kill me!" she crowed.

The whole picture came together for me then, like a
reverse explosion. That was my father sitting in the Cadillac,
making comments to a heavily made-up blond woman wearing big rings on every finger. I elbowed Olin. "Look!"

They were right in front of us. "Wow," he breathed, voice
muffled by a mouthful of gyro.

I sat as still as possible, shrinking behind a gazebo post,
hoping they wouldn't see us. My father had changed from the
gray sweater and corduroy coat he'd worn at dinner to a dark
leather jacket with shiny silver snaps. As they passed, I saw the
back of his head, the pale skin of his scalp gleaming through
the thin hair at his crown. I saw the familiar slope of his shoulders. Even though he passed not fifteen feet away, I kept trying
to decide that I'd actually seen someone else.

The Cadillac paused for some more crossing students,
revved the engines, and disappeared around another corner.

Olin grabbed my arm. "Let's go," he said, tugging me to
my feet.

"Oh, sure," I said. "That's a great idea."

"You want to wait here?" He started jogging.

"Fine, I'm coming." I caught up with him. We turned where they had and saw them stopped two blocks away. I was completely out of breath, panting after running less than a hundred feet. It was embarrassing, but Olin didn't seem to notice. We watched as the car coasted over the hill toward the movie theaters, the shiny Cadillac seeming to hover over the pavement until it disappeared. We stood watching for a moment, even though we couldn't see it anymore.

"Can you believe it?" Olin said, hands in his hair. "That's the first time I've seen him out with a woman, ever!"

"Well, I'm happy for him."

"Me too, me too. But did you *see* her? I mean, whoa!" He slapped his knees and laughed. It made me feel better to see that he was slightly out of breath, too.

"Don't be a mook," I said. I still felt a kinship with women who didn't know where to stop with the hair spray and makeup. Since high school I'd learned—I'd cut off my hair and had culled my makeup usage to lipstick only. After the glam-rock look I had maintained for Terence, it was a sort of cleansing, but I didn't feel better yet.

"Ernest and Zsa Zsa!" Olin said, laughing harder.

I looked at him, his dark hair perfectly ruffled by the cool night air, his smile even over orderly white teeth. He had gotten our mother's teeth, while I had cavity-prone teeth that were happily at home in England. "Yeah, let's see how long your lawyer babe keeps you now that the money's stopped coming in, huh?"

Olin looked hurt, but then flashed a broad grin. He was trying to cover up, but I could see I'd gotten to him. And what did that mean? I asked myself. So what?

"Hey, it's temporary. Anyway, she'll love me even if I'm poor," he said, mock pouting.

"I'm sorry. I'm an idiot."

"No, honey, you just don't understand how women react to me. They love me."

"Please."

"I mean, it's a blessing and a curse, you know?"

"Save it for the stage."

"OK." Olin patted my head as if I were an upset child, and while ordinarily that would have irritated me, in that moment it brought back a memory of us standing on that street corner years ago in bright sunlight, waiting to cross with our mother. She was standing just in front of us, leaning forward slightly to see if traffic was coming over the hill. I held Olin's hand—he was about eight years old—since it was my job to keep him from running out into the street. He had a habit of running away, bursting out of reach like a cat, and I squeezed harder than I needed to, to punish him for this, making him whine. My mother looked down to say something to me—she wore a light blue dress, white sandals, and her hair piled on her head—one hand pinching the back of Olin's shirt, and just then a truck pulled alongside us. There were two men in the seat, and the one on the passenger side opened his door and leaned out. His hair hung in a thin, greasy curtain to his neck. "Get in," he said to my mother. Grinning open-mouthed, rasping. "Come on."

My mother backed away, pulling us to her, and the man laughed, a wheezing exhalation, and slammed the door shut, and they took off. I remembered looking up at her, frightened, thinking that she was, too. But she seemed calm, one hand pressed against Olin's chest to hold him against her, the other hand on my head, watching the battered truck disappear over the hill. Instead of frightened, she seemed disappointed, as if she had actually expected someone to stop for her. I was thirteen years old, and I registered that disappointment, how she might have wanted to get into a truck—not specifically that one, and not with those men—but with someone else.

I followed Olin back to the Bronco and let him drive me home, and I thought of her face that day, only weeks before she died, how she seemed so lonely, ready to leave. She'd spent her life running to the next thing that would help her figure out who she was, not just because she wanted to, but because leaving was part of her character, and she would show us that again and again.

9

ON THEIR SECOND MEETING, Ernest saw Joanie again in the park. This time she wore a red sundress with a small gold locket, the chain like a thread around her throat. She told him about the two art classes she was taking, one of which she was skipping to meet him. In one class she was painting emotions—all very sixties—and in the other she was etching metal sheets with acid, to create reversed images. She had started a sketchbook, a wishful visual history of her life. She had painted her birth in pinks and purples, her mother's face peaceful, her father smiling, reaching for her. She had created an etching of the Star-Lite Motel, except there were mountains in the background and a lake.

They went to the No Man's Land Historical Museum on Sewell Avenue on campus and walked through rooms set up to reproduce the frontier life—rifles, tin pans, chipped washbasins. In another room there were Indian artifacts and dinosaur prints cut out of the sod. Joanie interviewed Ernest, extracting his age, his town of origin, his reason for coming to Goodwell. He explained his theory of landscape, and his deci-

sion to find a new one, and the chapel in Santa Fe that my
mother had heard about but never seen, and his belief that
buildings could change not just the landscape of a town, but
also the behavior of people.

"I may flunk out of school," Ernest said.

"Oh, come on," Joanie said.

"I'm worried about it," he said.

"I dreamed I was in class and spilled the etching acid on my
face the other night," Joanie said to Ernest as they stopped at a
stand in a small courtyard near the museum to buy grape Sno-
Cones. Ernest winced.

"Everyone decided I had become someone else," she said.
Her lips were purple with the grape flavoring. "I had to have a
new family, new everything. I looked at myself in the mirror,
and I didn't mind." She smiled at him, teeth purple too, and
Ernest saw how she was just a girl, several years younger than
he, and he felt as if he could see her as a small child, too, even
a baby, and he tried to imagine what she would look like when
her hair went gray—would her cheeks grow hollow or plump?
What pattern would the wrinkles form around her eyes? He
wanted to know.

And what they didn't tell: Ernest did not talk about his
father's death, the tractor brakes squealing at the edge of the
ditch, all the plans squeezed to nothing in his father's heart,
and how now his own plans weren't working out; he couldn't
follow the math, couldn't make the concepts concrete.

Joanie did not talk about how her father sometimes disappeared for days or weeks, leaving her to run the motel and care
for her mother, who wandered the house in her nightgown and
had seizures whenever the windstorms came in or when she
felt insulted, which was often. She did not talk about the Star-
Lite Motel, how her father had won it in a card game from a
rancher. And she didn't talk about the secrets she knew about

every one of the fifteen rooms, all of them marked by a leak there, a stain there, how she knew them all, the smell of bleach in the sheets, how they snapped over the bed, how good it felt to look in on a row of rooms, straightened and ready for guests, clean and open with possibility. Or how she tried never to be alone with her father when he was drunk, because he had no judgment then, and how he hated weakness, and he thought women were weak, corrupt, perverse. Nor did she talk about the screaming, the nights when she took to one of the empty motel rooms rather than stay in the five-room house her father had built in back of the motel, listening to her parents' voices rising like frightened horses, like bobcats.

They stood in the courtyard, holding their ices away from their bodies so they would drip on the brick instead of their clothes, slurping the last slush from the soggy paper cones, the words swirling around their heads like smoke, dispersing in the breeze. Ernest took Joanie's paper cone and threw it away. She shaded her eyes with one hand and watched him. He turned back to her, and now she was a woman, her face amused and knowing, and Ernest wanted to kiss her but the thought made his stomach pinch. He wanted a cigarette, wanted to feel the warm smoke against his cold purple tongue. "Do you want to go back in?" he asked her, his voice tight in his throat.

"I have to go," Joanie said.

"Already?" Ernest looked at his bare wrist. He realized that his watch had been missing for days.

"I have to be home at six for dinner, and then I have to do chores and start work at nine," Joanie said. She was matter-of-fact, not resentful.

"When do you sleep?"

"From about six-thirty to two-thirty. My father takes over at six," Joanie said.

"I know," Ernest said. "I came back that morning and it was just a couple minutes after six and you were gone."

They walked through the gates of the courtyard onto the street, and stood on the sidewalk, watching cars passing. Ernest felt as he once had one summer when he had missed the Erie Ferry he took to work on Kelleys Island by only seconds, and he had stood on the pier watching the white boat slowly pull away, thinking about how one's life could be changed forever by such an event—what if that boat sank? Or the next one?

"Are you going to stay here?" he asked her.

"No," Joanie said, as simply as if he'd asked her if she wanted a cup of coffee. She pulled her hair off her neck, squinted into the sun. "I've got to go now."

"Can I come see you tomorrow?" Ernest asked her.

"No, no thank you," Joanie said, her tone firm and formal.

He searched her face for a reason. He could see nothing but amiable distance in her eyes, which were nearly level with his own. They were dark hazel in the sunlight, like deep water. He leaned forward and kissed her, and she kissed him back, and they stayed that way, arms at their sides, for several seconds as if afraid to part and face each other, until a passing car honked, and they both pulled back at the same instant.

"Let me walk with you then," he said. She turned and started walking and he followed her. He followed her the way he had wanted to follow the ferry that day, leaping into the air across the green water, landing heroically. He felt as if he were perched at the edge of something, his legs trembling in anticipation of the effort.

They came to the corner of the street where Joanie's father's car was parked. She pulled the keys from her purse. Ernest knew how her days fit together now—she would drive back to Guymon, fix dinner, and go to work at the Star-Lite all night, maybe working on her art projects while everyone slept. Where would he fit in with all of this? Ernest grabbed Joanie's hand, stopped her. "When can I see you next?"

She shrugged, looked at the ground and back up at him, and he kissed her then, so urgently they knocked teeth, and then he hugged her. His heart felt bruised, pushing against his chest. He felt her arms light around his waist, and it balanced him. "Joanie, what if I asked you to marry me, would you say yes?" He took her hands and looked down at them so that he wouldn't have to see her face.

"Are you asking me?"

"I'm asking."

Joanie was aware of the pressure of his hands around hers, the sound of orders called in Spanish floating through the open doors of the Mexican bakery, carried on the warm, yeast-sweetened air. She felt as if she could see the entire town in which she had lived—the broad streets carving a grid in the plains, the churches in the center, the rows of sun-bleached ranch-style houses and the scattered low-roofed huts on the edges where the poor lived in shadows and heat, the brick walls of the schools. She thought of her father and mother, on good days falling asleep together in front of the black-and-white television in the living room of the house her father built—and how would she live in all of this? Who else would she find in this town of ranchers and cowboys, laborers and pilots on leave, puffing their glittering chests and then flying away, the occasional winking storeowner or banker with soft white hands? She wanted not just another town, but another existence, someone who could know her and help her know herself. She took a long breath. "Well, then, yes."

They decided Ernest would come for her in three mornings from then, after they'd gotten their blood tests and finished the waiting period. They could've driven to Clayton, New Mexico, only a hundred miles away, where there was no waiting period, but Joanie wanted to marry on land she knew, and Ernest was happy to do what she wanted. For the next few nights he drove to Guymon to see her in the early hours, when he was sure her father was asleep. He parked his car at the rodeo grounds and walked to the Star-Lite, standing in the shadows beyond the glass front door, which Joanie propped open so they could talk. They planned that he would come for her on the third morning, again before my grandfather got up, and she would leave a note promising to be in touch soon, and they would go to Ohio to live with Lettie, his mother, until they found a place of their own.

Two evenings before they left, Ernest packed his hard-sided brown suitcase that had belonged to his father, dismantled his wood shelves and bench, cut the planks into pieces that would fit in his trunk.

Then he went to see Professor Clink at his house to tell him he was giving up his studies. Professor Clink answered the door in his robe, bourbon in hand. "Ah, yes," he said, as if he'd been expecting him. He waved him inside and Ernest followed him into a dark living room piled with newspapers and books and scrolled blueprints and animal skins slung over the leather couch and chairs. He sighed as he lowered himself into one recliner. "All right then, let's have it."

Ernest felt Professor Clink already knew this speech; surely he'd seen dozens of young men come to his door, heads lowered, confessing they couldn't do it, the math, the hours in the studio. Maybe, like him, they had come from small farms or sprawling ranches, hoping something would reveal itself from within the slick-covered textbooks, the classrooms shiny with linoleum and fluorescence. Still, he struggled with adding himself to the list of quitters. He had always been a deliberate person; the decision to leave home had been huge, and he wouldn't have done it if Lettie hadn't encouraged him. After all, she ran the farm far better on her own after his father died and she didn't really need his help. She had a mind for numbers and futures and returns, while these things numbed him. He'd gotten his father's head, his dogged desire for simplicity—big ideas, the details scattered and forgotten.

But he heard himself doing it anyway, giving up. And then telling him about Joanie, and how he'd fallen in love. "I was wondering if you could help us find someone to marry us and be our witness," he finished, the words rushing from his mouth.

Clink Johnson leaned forward, grunting with the effort. "And what else can I do for you, boy?" he asked Ernest in a near growl. It wasn't really a question; he waved it away like an insect. "I promised myself I'd never say this, because it would mean I was finally old, but the youth of today confounds me. What on this earth can you bear down on? You have one or two setbacks and you sit on your haunches, head in hands?" The bourbon sloshed in his glass, and he slammed it on a ringed tabletop. "By God, the people of this windy country would have died, starved to death! If they'd been as—" he stopped himself then and took a slow breath. Ernest stared at the floor, heart pounding with shame. But Professor Clink wasn't finished. "This young woman is not a project, she's not a class you can drop. Marriage is a fine and noble act, but you can't go back on a vow before God," Clink said, gesturing at the ceiling, as if expecting God to weigh in on this point. He touched the silver frame of a photo of a young woman then that sat on a side table. Ernest presumed she was a granddaughter, and he watched Clink for a long while, waiting for the old professor to speak again. Finally, he cleared his throat and got to his feet with some effort. "Of course, I'll get you a preacher, of course," he'd said, leading Ernest to the door.

They made arrangements to meet in the park at dawn, two days later. Clink patted Ernest on the shoulder and smiled, a blessing Ernest hoped would at least see them home.

The next night, he found Hall in the studio and asked him to be his best man. Hall was building another model for Professor Clink, a courthouse this time. He had glue all over his fingers and red eyes from the fumes. He seemed not to have heard.

"Look, could you hand me that T-square?" Hall said, reaching for the instrument across his littered drafting board. He was irritable, tired, distracted, displaying all the signs of what engineering students referred to as the Swoon, the sleep-deprived state when great ideas surfaced.

Ernest handed over the T-square and worked the combination on his locker. He piled his drafting tools on Hall's table. "I'm not going to need these," he said.

Hall didn't look up. "You're not gonna die just because you're hitched, though God knows it might seem that way," he said.

"No, I'm dropping out. Joanie and I are going to Ohio."

Hall turned to him then, hands on his skinny thighs. He dropped his head, as if considering what could be done next. "How long have you known this woman? Six, eight hours?"

Ernest looked at Hall, hands in his pockets, tapping his thighs.

"Well, shit," Hall said, shaking his head. He slapped his knees, squeezed his eyes shut, and wagged his head as if shaking off a fall. "I guess you can explain it to Clink in the morning," he said.

"I've already talked to him," Ernest said. He took the instruments—his compass and mat cutter and white board and broccoli trees—and placed them carefully in Hall's locker. Hall stood, clapped Ernest on the shoulder, and walked with him outside.

Professor Clink was waiting beside the largest elm tree in the park at a few minutes before six the next morning. He had trimmed his white beard and put on his best bolo tie, a silver and tiger's eye clasp. With him was a preacher by the name of Sam Tracy. The two men had grown up eight miles apart and were each other's closest neighbors and boyhood playmates. Clink called in dues to get Preacher Tracy out of bed so early; Tracy had crashed his pickup into Clink's toolshed the previous winter when he took a turn too hard into Clink's driveway and lost traction on a patch of ice. "Wake up, old man," Clink said when Ernest and Joanie arrived in Ernest's car. "You got customers." Preacher Tracy rubbed his eyes and pulled his prayer book from his shirt pocket, standing with his feet apart like a man accustomed to bracing against wind. Clink clapped his shoulder and they smiled at each other, perhaps already imagining the coffee that would warm their hands at the Aggie Inn after the boy and girl left them alone again.

Ernest parked and turned to Hall, who was stretched out in the backseat, still drunk after a night in Guymon bar-hopping to "celebrate," as he had put it to Ernest, but mostly it had consisted of Hall doing shots from another bootlegged bottle and trying to sing with a Mariachi band that was playing out of what appeared to be an old feed barn they'd run across on the edge of town. The purple sky made Ernest's white shirt glow against his skin. His face pale in the gray light, Hall slumped in the backseat, singing softly or maybe moaning, until Ernest opened the back door, eased him into a sitting position and then onto his feet, while Joanie checked her hair in the rearview mirror.

"Oh, God, don't do this to me," Hall moaned.

"It's going to be OK," my father said. He pulled Hall's arm across his own shoulders and guided him out of the car.

Joanie leaned to look in the rearview mirror and applied frosted lipstick that matched her pale pink sheath dress and jacket set, the closest outfit she could find to a wedding dress on such short notice. She opened the trunk to retrieve her birth certificate. She had altered it by one year that night, using ink from her etching class that, mixed with water, looked just like the original ink she had carefully scraped off the paper. She had changed 1948 to 1947, erasing and erasing the curves of the eight into a seven and thereby changing her age from seventeen to eighteen—not a huge fib in the scheme of things, although her father had been on the road then, looking for work during the time her mother would have gotten pregnant with her, which meant she could be the daughter of another man, something she had often wished.

It was a small but crucial lie, because Professor Clink was an honest man, and would not have been a witness if he had known the truth. And my father? I don't know what he would have done, had he known. But he wouldn't notice the careful change to the birth certificate until it was time to bury her. On their first and only date, he had asked my mother when she had graduated from high school, an indirect way of asking her age, and she had told the truth but hadn't mentioned graduating early.

And the fact was, she had fallen in love. No matter what happened later, she had loved him the way she had loved the row of vacuumed, freshly sheeted, scrubbed motel rooms, a line of doors waiting to be opened. He was sensible, smart, even-tempered; she knew she would never have to wonder what would or wouldn't set him off. He would be dependable. Kind. As she had shaved the ink off the yellow fake parchment paper of her birth certificate with a razor, she felt as if she were scraping clean her whole life.

To look at the certificate today, you'd think she could have done a better job, but it was early morning, and both Preacher Tracy and Professor Clink's eyesight had been fading for a number of years. Added to this was a fine mist that further blurred Clink's vision, which happened to him whenever he saw young lovers, because it reminded him of his wife, Marilee, who had died of the Spanish flu in 1918, when they had been married less than a year, leaving him with just the one photograph that Ernest had seen and mistaken for his granddaughter.

Joanie was about to close the trunk and join Professor Clink and Ernest, who were both holding up Hall while Clink introduced Ernest to Preacher Tracy on the lawn a few yards away, but then she noticed that her sketchbook was missing. She opened each suitcase, knowing she had deliberately left it out so she could put it in the car and sketch what she saw during the long trip north. But she had forgotten to put it in the car. It was full of things she didn't want to leave behind. In fact, it was the only thing from her life so far that she didn't want to leave behind.

Across the park she thought she heard a shout, and she looked up, heart pounding, expecting to see her father striding across the grass, but then she saw it was just Hall, throwing up in a flower bed. I'm sure she could not have imagined what would happen the next time she saw Hall, fifteen years later, during the summer of 1981.

She closed the trunk. She decided she'd have to go back and get the book.

She crossed the lawn, her dew-damp sandals slipping on her feet, her birth certificate fluttering in one hand, the air already gathering heat. Ernest watched her approach, smiling, his hair wet against his ears. He held out his hand to her and she took hold of it like a rope to a boat pulling away.

10

I KNEW THAT I HAD to go home the day Terence told me about the swinging ferry. It was 7:00 A.M. and he was leaning against my clinking radiator, which we were still using even though it was mid-April, the windows misted wet, Terence smoking one of his hashish cigarettes, eyes glassy, dark red hair wreathed in yellow smoke. He was wearing his favorite turquoise ultrasuede trousers, silver-tipped Converses, and a gray jersey with a pink flower embroidered on the left breast. He may have been a ridiculous dresser, but he pulled it off—he had a lanky athletic frame, sky blue eyes fringed with dark lashes, a square-jawed face—he was extremely good-looking and he knew it. He drew on the 100-length cigarette, the excellent hashish supply one of the many perks of being the son of a British diplomatic envoy to Denmark. Not that he was provided with hashish, but he had diplomatic immunity and therefore he was almost in no danger of being charged for possession or other misdemeanors, although he had tried hard at it, getting arrested often, once for dancing naked in the pigeon shit-encrusted fountain in Trafalgar Square, another time for public indecency on Shaftsbury Avenue for trying to act out the street name, and another time for driving at 120 miles per hour down the A-1 beltway while blindfolded.

Terence had come up with the ferry weekend to celebrate our seven-year anniversary. The fact of seven years together was shocking enough; it meant I had been editing what was being marketed as erotica novels for eight years, another shock. It meant I had been in England for just under ten years, the first two spent working in a pub on the Thames, where, after watching the mating rituals and broken-bottle fights of the London citizenry, I lost any illusions that the English were more refined than Americans. It meant I had to ask myself how I lost track of the high achiever who'd gotten a 4.0 in high school and in college (B..A., English, with a senior thesis on Victorian women writers, during which time I became so immersed in the syntax of the period that a boyfriend broke up with me for talking like Jane Eyre). Looking back, I can't say that I was good at anything except going for the highest score. So I found the real world, the one I had been so eager to step into like the off-limits room of a house, impossible to navigate. Even going to England had been a cop-out—I chose it because I'd heard it was easy to get under-the-table work, and I spoke the language. I'd told myself I was taking control of my life by starting over in a new country, but of course I had just taken my old life with me, like an outfit that was ill-fitting and too revealing, but stuck to my back.

Terence was the best evidence of this. In believing I was starting a new life, I consciously looked for a man who was different from my tight-lipped father, as well as from a disappointing string of past boyfriends—the business major who quoted constantly from leadership books and taped motivational sticky notes to the ceiling over his bed, the sports aficionado who always wore shorts and pumped his muscles so big, I suspect, to make up for his robin's egg-sized penis; the pothead who listened to Pink Floyd's *Dark Side of the Moon* constantly and considered getting his chin done so he'd look more like Roger Waters. And before him was Watson Puckett, who actually was quite sweet, even though he broke my heart.

Looking back, the notion itself was pathetic, that a man could help me change my life any more than a new hairstyle. These are, at best, temporary measures. But Terence had started as a temporary measure and turned into policy before I knew it.

His plan for the getaway weekend was to drive to Torquay, where there was a swinging ferry—of course I imagined a houseboat swinging from a tree limb or something—which cruised up and down the Channel, until returning to dock at dawn. It cost two hundred quid per person, and the explanation for this exorbitant cost was apparently that couples were allowed to have sex with each other and whomever else they chose under the watchful eye of retired off-duty Cornwall bobbies who were there to make sure things didn't get "out of hand," as Terence put it. I wondered what would constitute "out of hand" in such a scenario—condom slingshots? Going over the orgasm limit?

"It'll be the bomb," he said.

"I don't think so," I said.

"No really, it'll be fantastic," Terence said. "I've heard it's splendid."

"No," I said.

"What do you mean, exactly, by no?" Terence could get terribly formal with his English when he was frustrated.

"I mean I am not going."

"Oh, please, Merle," he said. "You're always like this. Remember the first time I wanted to tie you up?" His cheeks were getting red under his freckles, and his voice rose slightly. "You just automatically said no, as if it wasn't even worth considering. And now we do it all the time. You enjoy it!" he said, triumphant.

"Terence," I said, feeling unbelievably weary, as if I had been up all night, or actually, a lot of nights. "That's in private—"

"And the dildos. You love those, too."

"Oh, stop," I pleaded.

He was used to getting his way. He was an only child, and his parents lived in separate households, which permitted him to flit back and forth whenever one annoyed him—his father in London and his mother in a fourteenth-century stone cottage that had once belonged to the local cardinal in Norwich, surrounded by roses, which she tended when she was not riding horses. When Terence was a child, she had been an avid reader of Dr. Spock and let him dress himself as he preferred, so he picked out pink plastic platform shoes and polka-dotted jumpsuits. He chose to wear his curly red hair long, and even though he now kept it short, so short that it was like a silky fur against his neck, he was still vain about it. He still had a certain flair for dress and a temper. Even as a child I'm sure he knew how to use his looks to his advantage. He knew how to flatter and pressure at the same time, and he saw no shame in doing it.

We stood in silence in the hallway that was my kitchen—a stove, refrigerator, and sink poking out of the wall like they were lost travelers on the way to somewhere else—the light from the bedroom window souping in gray and shadowless. Terence stubbed out his half-smoked hasher, as he called them, and put it back into the flat silver case he carried in his trouser pocket. When he was flush with cash, he would simply throw out half-smoked hashers, but not today.

"Look, I've already bought the tickets," he said finally. "I was going to surprise you." He looked lonely, dejected, and I wanted to comfort him, which is how he always won our disagreements. I treated him the way I wanted to be treated—I wanted to be coddled, lavished, forgiven—and in the process, I got run over, flattened by his dotty ideas.

"You know," Terence said, inspecting his springy red hair in the mirror. "You only live once. And sex is living to the tenth degree. It's free, the little death, if you haven't forgotten."

"My God," I said, rolling my eyes. I had never been able to say no to him, in all the years we'd been together. Somewhere along the way he had convinced me that if I said no I was close-minded, negative. He was so cheerfully manipulative that I found it impossible to hold my ground in any disagreement.

"You'll go then?" he said, as if he'd just asked me to the prom.

"Of course," I said. "Of course I'll go."

That night I dreamed we were driving up Mantle Street in Florence, the street of my childhood home, except we were driving up the wrong side of the road. I was in the backseat, being chauffeured by Terence, who turned full around to talk with me, ignoring oncoming traffic. I ducked and screamed, waving at him to turn around. And then the bugs appeared. Big, brightly colored jelly bugs like my father's fishing lures, climbing the half-rolled-down windows, crawling in. In his sleep, Terence turned over in my bed and brushed my shoulder, and I lurched sideways, whacking my head against the dresser. I sat up in the bed, shaking, my head throbbing. Terence didn't even wake up. He had the gift of being able to sleep wherever, whenever, and for however long he wanted. I rubbed the small knot forming on my scalp and thought about what I had agreed to do. I knew I couldn't go through with it, no matter what I'd been willing to do in the past. It was true, I had agreed to the bondage, the sex toys, the role-playing. At the time I thought it was evidence of how uninhibited I was. I wasn't high strung; no, I was a free spirit! But over time I had started to suspect that I was really just engaging in one long role-play torn directly from the flimsy plots of a typical X Publishing novel: hardworking editor of smut novels by day, sexy provocateur by night. But I was just Merle Winslow from Florence, Ohio, who missed her mother and wanted her father's approval so much that she had never admitted to him what kind of books she edited. Whenever my father had asked during our brief and rare calls, I always said "how-to."

But there was of course more to it, more that made me leave, than Terence choosing the swinging ferry, although I knew that reason would pass in Ohio. First, there was the issue of the other woman. She snuck up on me, really, and I never knew her name or made one up for her. It wasn't as if she hadn't been in front of me for a long time; she had appeared before my eyes, but it took me a long time to put it—her—together. Let me explain.

First there were the feet. Terence had kind of a foot fetish; he liked to tickle, suck, bind, etc., and I was simply too ticklish to go along with it—for once my body took care of me when I couldn't stand up for myself. So one day I came home and there was a perfect pair of long-toed, red-nailed women's feet, arched for high heels and poised on the bed like two pale cats. He'd scored them from a department store somehow.

Then there were the breasts—rubber, with armholes so you could slip them across your chest, wear them as a party gag. But Terence took them rather seriously. They were huge and sloppy, with orangish nipples that looked like the yolks of two fried eggs, sunny side up. Terence tried wearing them once, citing our need to try different sexual roles (it was always experimentation for the greater good with him—he couldn't just admit he wanted to try something different; it had to be in the name of science or personal growth). But role-playing either made me laugh or made my mind wander. I was happy to play along but I got confused, lost the thread of the game, started making shopping lists for the chemist.

Then there was a wig, and then an entire torso—anatomically correct, if I make myself clear enough. Finally, there was the gaspy, red-lipped mouth, mounted on a plastic stand, with a long, open throat and a hand grip on the stand. That put it all together for me. It was only a couple of weeks before Terence came home with tickets to the swinging ferry, and I had just gotten home from work—Terence was "in the field" with our drag-queen editor, Chet, interviewing a hermaphrodite for research for an upcoming book—and I saw the mouth on the dresser, a little trophy. The wig was draped over a lumpy armchair stuffed in the corner. It partially concealed the breasts. The torso peeked out from under the bed, as if hiding; the feet stood as if ready to tap dance in the dusty corner.

I could see her then. I could see her striding into the room, a long evening gown to conceal her lack of legs, spiky sandals strapped to her ankle stumps. She would smile her open-mouthed, "I'm gargling" smile; she would say nothing and rape us both.

But that's not all. It wasn't just Terence. I have to confess something, too. The truth was, Terence and I hadn't had sex, real sex, in months. We played games, there were sometimes toys involved, and sometimes I was even into it. Oddly enough, it helped me to close my eyes and pretend I was getting paid for it, that he was a stranger, that anything could happen, not the new standard ending with Terence quietly getting off in the bathroom instead of with me. We'd had sex in every imaginable way in the past, and I'm not sure what changed with him. We didn't talk about it. I for one wanted to pretend it wasn't happening, that it would go away on its own—maybe I had finally been totally assimilated into British culture. Or maybe it was the natural next step for someone as self-involved as Terence, making love to himself only.

I told myself the woman's lie, that it was really my fault, that I had just lost interest in sex after being introduced to so many forms of it through Terence and X Publishing, but I knew there was something more. And the day he came home with the swinging ferry plan, I understood what it was, why I was playing along in this relationship that wasn't real: I had seen real intimacy in my parents. After everything that had happened between them and everything else I learned later, I know they loved each other. Maybe they had loved each other from the moment my father stumbled to the lobby door of the Star-Lite and saw my mother. Maybe their love was impulsive and uninformed, so the relationship was doomed from the start. But I knew this: If my parents were an example of intimacy, then it was dangerous. It could get you killed.

I quietly began looking through my drawers and closet for my passport. I found it lodged in a pair of bunny-eared slippers my mother had bought me, long since frayed from overuse, the plastic bottoms melted in a grill pattern from wearing them while propping my feet on scalding college dorm radiators. They were one of the few things I had left that came directly from her, along with some photographs, a couple of her dresses that I couldn't fit into, and the half-filled sketchbook she had taken with her when she eloped with my father. That night, I flipped through those delicately drawn pictures and wondered what had stopped her from drawing more. After the escape to Ohio, she'd never added to it.

While Terence slept, I slid these things in a duffel bag and began to plan for my own escape.

11

THE NEXT MORNING after the dinner with my father and Olin and Lettie's brief but dramatic entrance, I woke at 6:00 A.M., smelling talcum powder in the still air and thinking of the old woman who'd lived there before me. I wondered what had happened to her—how she ended up alone—as I massaged my temples and tried to breathe deeply to ward off a rising panic, exhausted but unable to go back to sleep.

Olin had dropped me off at midnight, and I had rolled into my sleeping bag expecting to sleep for ten hours or more. But apparently my body was confused this morning; it still thought I was in England, where it was eleven on a Monday morning, almost time for a quick run to the snappily named Hot Drinks to Take Away stand on the corner, one of the few places you could go in London for freshly made coffee that didn't strip the outer layers of your tongue. Somewhere in my biorhythms, I felt I should be in the middle of final edits of one of the books slated for our fall list, a special series on bondage and consensual slavery. And of course I also thought of Terence, who had woken up Saturday morning expecting to meet the swinging ferry with me, only to find himself alone in our bed. I thought of Fiona, looking dashing as always at 4:30 in the morning with her shiny black hair swept into a hasty bun, her amply curved figure draped in a plum-colored knit wrap dress, reminding me to breathe, and helping me load my few possessions into the back of her Mini before we left for the airport.

I got up, pulled on my jeans, drank some less than clear-looking water from the tap, shook my last cigarette from the pack on the sliver of kitchen counter, and sat outside on the concrete stoop, my bare feet on the sidewalk. Across the quad stared the three other weary buildings, their dented doors and cracked windowpanes the shape of defeat.

Harold's apartment door opened, and since it was too late to go inside without appearing rude, I smiled weakly in his direction. He didn't look at me. He was carrying a hammer and a sign mounted on a scrap of wood that looked rather like the floor molding from the apartments. He walked quickly past me, head down, frowning, and hammered the sign into the grass a few feet away from the sidewalk. The marker-written sign read, IF THIS IS THE FIRST DAY OF THE REST OF YOUR LIFE, THEN WHAT THE HELL WAS YESTERDAY? He bent slowly to pick up another sign, which had fallen facedown, and marched back inside, slamming his door.

I contemplated this. I couldn't imagine even the black-bereted Marxists scurrying from pub to pub in Camden doing this sort of thing. Sure there were the occasional political slogans or the usual graffiti on alley walls or the Underground cars, but the slapping of signs everywhere was a particularly American fascination. I wondered what Harold had done for a living before retiring to a life of sign-making and gun advice. I wondered what I was going to do for a living, how I would tweak my résumé enough to gloss over eight years of X Publishing.

While I had fallen into the smut-writing business the way our paperback heroines fell into trapdoors or dope rings, Terence had sought it out. He had been called the way his father had been called to international diplomacy and his grandfather had been called to the one true Church of England, as he called it. He was a true believer in pornography, while I was simply a subscriber to its economics. After my first year there I was not only bored by the books but by the idea of sex itself. I tried to view this as enlightenment, but really it was just sad.

A woman emerged from the apartment directly across the quad from mine. She was short with a boxy haircut and wore a brown pantsuit. She marched across the quad to Harold's sign and slapped it down. She stomped on the wooden stake, grabbed the planting end, and broke it off. Then she wiped her feet on the sign like a bull pawing the ground and started back to her apartment. "Good morning," she said to me before she turned back.

"Morning," I said reflexively. I watched until she shut her apartment door behind her with an echoing slam.

I decided I'd seen enough. I grabbed my boots and started walking toward my father's office. On the way, I stopped at Fortuna's for a bagel and some coffee. The old man was there alone that morning, salami bouquets under each arm, which he gently rolled into the display case, as if they might bruise. In ten years he had changed barely at all—his eyes may have receded further underneath his wiry eyebrows, the flesh slightly looser under his jaw, the left side of his face hanging slack with nerve damage from, it was rumored, a childhood sickness. He had at one time propped the drooping cheek with a pipe, but now the weight of his thick jowl pulled down his lower eyelid, making his stare seem even more baleful on that side. His wide left eye stayed trained on me suspiciously until

I ordered. He rang up my purchase, lips pursed, thick fingers stabbing the register buttons, then poured barely two-thirds of a cup of coffee and handed it across the counter to me.

"Top that up, please," I said, eyeing him steadily. As a college student, the stare would have cowed me, but ten years later I was tougher. And on my last few dollars, tougher still.

Fortuna glared at me, the coffee still held over the counter, as if daring me not to take it. I folded my arms and waited, but my heart was pounding, even at this slight confrontation. *Coward,* I thought to myself. I remembered he'd never liked young people, which had made life difficult for him in a college town. I wondered if he had been teased as a child because of the way his face was alive on one side and asleep on the other, the milky white eye an accusation.

Slowly Fortuna withdrew the cup, filled it until the coffee ran down the sides of the cup as he handed it back to me. It burned my fingers but I tried not to show it. "Thanks," I said. "And the bagel?"

Fortuna shuffled to the bread case and picked out a hard, shiny bagel. He opened the cream cheese bin.

"Heated, please," I said.

Fortuna didn't act as if he had heard me, but he did put the bagel in the toaster oven, then leaned against the counter, regarding me coolly. "I know you," he said, his thick Old Country accent gurgling in his throat.

I assumed he had somehow remembered me from the occasional newspaper retrospectives of the Morris P. Alston building bombing. It was my turn to pretend not to have heard anything. I looked out the window, tapped my foot.

"Yes, yes. I've seen pictures of you."

"You done with that bagel yet?" I snapped.

"No. You like things just right, I make them just right." Fortuna chuckled to himself. "People think I don't know what goes on in this town, but I know. I know. The boom!" he said, arcing both hands in the air, his pronunciation making me think of the Pink Panther, which would have been funny if it weren't clear that he had indeed started in on the Morris P. Alston bombing. "You know how?"

"OK," I said. "How?" I remembered Fortuna's had been one of the businesses vandalized during the protests leading up to the bombing, so I couldn't imagine him having forgotten that episode in the town's history.

"I see people's faces," he said. He stepped around the register and came toward me, hands outstretched, cupped as if trying to catch a fly ball. My coffee sloshed as I backed away.

"What are you doing?" I demanded. I backed to the wall, the counter to my left, Fortuna blocking my escape toward the door on my right. I froze as he reached toward my face; his callused fingers tapped my nose, then my cheeks and chin gently.

"I see the child in everyone's face. Heh, yes. You, you were the one always at the edges. Am I right?" He laughed at this, his breath spicy and meaty, and I thought, absurdly, of Yoda in *The Empire Strikes Back,* how his bulbous nose and slow-blinking eye were a dead ringer. He wagged a pepperoni-like finger at me. "But, I see you have good reasons for returning. Yes, you have things to do." He grinned, one side of his face unaware of the expression, pinched my nose lightly, and dropped his hands. The toaster oven dinged. He shuffled back behind the counter, pulled out the bagel, and slathered it with cream cheese. I watched from where I still leaned against the wall, trying to calm down. When the bagel was ready, Fortuna summoned me with a wave of his fingers and handed the heavy bagel across the counter to me with a nodding smile.

I balanced it in one hand while digging in my jeans for money, but Fortuna shook his head. "Keep your money," he said, waving my change away. "You need any help, come see me."

I walked the rest of the way to the Department of Social Services, dazed and nervous. The old man had never so much as looked at me when I was growing up in Florence, not even when I was in college and stopping there at least once a week. He had never said a word to me except to bark "No!" when I tried to angle for extra cream cheese or meatballs. As a child, I had always veered back and forth between wanting to be invisible and wanting someone to point at me and say: "You're chosen, make a wish!" And so what if it had happened in a sandwich shop? Maybe it counted. I decided to take it as a sign. I decided it was time to go see Lettie.

12

I FOUND MY FATHER in his office across from the bathrooms on the third floor of the DSS. The tiny beige room offered barely enough space for the desk, chair, and floor-to-ceiling bookcase. Sunlight winked through the beige metal blinds as they rattled in the spring breeze. He was on the phone, nodding but not saying anything, as if he didn't realize nodding didn't work in phone conversations, looking intently through one of the taller piles of paper on his desk. The receiver tipped his glasses so that they sat off-kilter on his nose. He noticed me and nodded again. "Let me call you back," he said, but then continued listening for a while. I glanced around, wondering if he'd actually have a photograph of the mystery Cadillac woman, maybe in a neat little frame, but there weren't any photos at all. "I'll call right back," he said then, and hung up.

"Hi, Dad," I said.

My father stood up, straightened his glasses, and peered across the desk at me, smoothing his hair across the small balding part of his scalp. I had to hand it to him; he hadn't fallen prey to the hair flap combed to one side that so many balding men have succumbed to—and believe me, this is an international problem. I tried to reconcile the tired-looking, frumpy man in front of me—rumpled off-white shirt with a too-wide collar matched with a brown tie, also too wide—with the leather-jacketed man in a Cadillac laughing with his bombshell date as if he were the most clever guy in the world. After the run-in with Fortuna I wasn't even sure I had really seen it.

"Merle, come in. I, uh, don't have anywhere for you to sit."

"That's OK," I said. I took a step inside the doorway and leaned against the bookcase.

"Be careful, that's a little wobbly."

"Oh, OK." I stood up straight. "Listen, I wondered if I could borrow the car keys," I said.

"Oh, yes, well." He pulled the keys from his pocket and handed them to me. I waited for him to ask me why I needed them, but he just stood there, looking uncomfortable. I thought of how I'd said good-bye to him, ten years ago; I'd said it with a question, really, and then I'd driven off, determined to get away from him and everything he'd hidden from me.

"I thought I'd go see Lettie," I said.

"Oh, good, that's good," he said. He sat back down, riffled through some papers; I had the feeling that he wanted me to leave, but then he looked up again. "I was trying to find the job post. I have a printout, but it's also online. Do you know how to use the Internet?"

Americans always think that Europeans are completely without technology. I decided to save for another day the revelation that I'd helped build the X Publishing Web site, so that our customers could buy e-novels. In any case, it made me feel good that he was looking out for me. "Sure," I said. "Is there a computer here I can use?"

"Just use mine." My father backed out from his desk in order to let me stand beside him. I scanned the screen while he made another phone call. Most of the jobs were temporary clerical, catering, or "light industrial," which sounded like a list category at X Publishing to me. There was one for an "office assistant" in client intake downstairs. I thought about that, working in the same building as my father. I thought of this secret life he had, this woman he clearly had no intention of discussing with me, and I thought of how Fortuna had said I had things to do—wasn't that always the way? You wanted a bagel and you got a bunch of advice or predictions or maybe just a come-on on top of it all? Maybe, I thought, this was a chance to get to know the man, and this was one of the things I needed to do.

"There's one for a clerical job here," I said, when he got off the phone.

"Probably doesn't pay much."

"Well, would you be my reference?" *My valentine?* I thought, too, ridiculously, remembering how as a child I had banged on the door when he came up the drive, home from work, waiting for him to open it and pick me up, my mother in the kitchen, maybe mixing the first drinks even then, ice clinking like teeth in the glasses, me drawing little hearts on the cocktail napkins.

My father rubbed his eyes with his thumb and forefinger. He sighed and smiled. "Certainly."

"Thanks," I said. He bent to pick up his battered leather satchel, the same one he'd carried to and from work every day, and handed me an overnight package from Fiona.

"This came this morning," he said about the package.

"Thanks," I said. If I planned to ask him about the woman in the Cadillac, I had to do it now. My father waited with a patient expression, eyebrows slightly raised. As soon as I opened my mouth, I realized I couldn't do it. I was afraid—of what? Of angering him? Of knowing the answer? "Well, I'll see you." I stepped past him.

"Merle," he said. I stopped in the doorway. He bit his lip, adjusted his glasses, gestured as if trying to coax out whatever words he was contemplating. "I'm glad you're back," he said. It was a lot, coming from him.

His phone was ringing again. "Thanks," I mouthed to him as he picked up.

I headed downstairs. Before I went to the HR office, I decided to open the package from Fiona. There was a carton of Silk Cuts, cheap cigarettes that I had gotten hooked on within weeks of starting work at X Publishing. I walked outside and cracked open a pack, lit up. And read the letter, written in sparkly purple ink:

Merle, love,

Terence is wrecked, let me tell you. I'm not trying to make you feel guilty, I'm just telling you, he has gone down to the White Dragon to get pissed, and I don't know when he'll ever be over the shock of it all. I feel a traitor for spiriting you out of the country, or at least to the airport, and yet at the same time I can't blame you for wanting to go back to your family and work things out, can I? Someone has to make the first move. Take me for an example. My parents still don't understand the public service I have shouldered with the feng shui consulting. I try to explain that there are plenty of people with so much money that they've forgotten how to live! They are positively choked by their wealth! But once they understand how to focus their energy in simple ways, their lives are immeasurably enriched. It all comes down to what you surround yourself with, I know you know what I mean. Just the other day a woman I've been working with near Downing Street took her child's stuffed fish—I

High Strung ~ 89

believe it was called Finny the Fin—and placed it in the wealth
area of her solarium. Not that she needs any further wealth,
now, mind you, but this was just a test, you see. And do you
know what happened? She got an unexpected check (for 300
quid!) from the cosmetics company that custom-mixes her eye
shadow! She had overpaid for their last shipment. Almost every
day I hear a story like that one that lets me know in a deep and
fundamental way that I am doing the right thing.

I hope you are practicing your breathing right now as you
read this. You have such terrible breathing habits—you're so
hard on yourself! Remember, baby breaths. Big deep belly
breaths. If you did an hour of baby breathing every day I feel
confident you could quit smoking these horrid cheap things. But
I send them anyway because I think what you need most right
now is continuity. You've put yourself through an awful lot,
Merle, and I hope all turns out for the best.

Write soon if you can manage it, love. Cheers to your father
and that cute brother of yours. Give him a kiss for me, why
don't you? And remember, right now you're a fragile flower.
Just think, fragile flower, baby breaths.

Love,
Fiona

Reading the letter, I could hear Fiona's flute-like voice,
could see how she'd roll her eyes at the phrase "horrid cheap
things" and purse her lips during the "fragile flower" bit. I
missed her so much right then that my stomach ached. I
missed her more than Terence, that was for sure. I wanted her
to sit down next to me on a scratchy concrete bench, waving at
my cigarette smoke and saying "good riddance" when I
stubbed the butt in the sand-filled tray. I wanted her to hear
the rest of the story, which had begun right here.

To my right, I could see the north side of campus, where

the Morris P. Alston building sat at the top of a hill. The Morris P. Alston historical museum, which chronicled the 1970 bombing, was the first place I had thought of to go when I learned that my mother had not been alone in the dark blue Buick we called the spy car on the night of her death. I could have found out back when it happened; I could have read the papers or watched the evening news. But like most thirteen-year-olds, I didn't read the paper. And my father gave our television set, a tank of a Zenith, to Goodwill the day after the accident. He told us he didn't want us having to see the accident on the news. In fact, he railed against journalists and their appetite for human misery.

Joanie died in June 1981, and Olin and I spent the rest of that summer with Lettie. When we came back to school, people did us the favor of not talking about it to our faces. It was at once too mundane and too messy, my mother dying drunk late at night with her lover in the car. That, of course, was the other part of the story, the one Lettie and my father had decided not to tell, the fact of that other man in the car. Everyone else must have either followed suit or assumed we knew.

I went through high school knowing there was more to the story of my mother's death other than the obituary that Lettie had given to me to save. I had always had the sense that something was missing, like people whose twin didn't survive the womb, and of course they can't remember them specifically, but they have a general sense of the loss—an ache in the ribs or the small of the back where a knot of tissue remains. I had been conditioned from the day of my mother's funeral not to ask questions. Instead I asked Lettie to tell the stories of my parents' meeting and brief courtship—which I assumed my mother had told her—and what she had observed herself when they arrived in Ohio, my father bruised and my mother nervous, but the two of them clinging to each other, survivors. I knew something had been left out of my parents' story, but I also knew I couldn't address it directly, the way some people manage never to talk about a bachelor uncle who has a "room-mate," or a cousin who once did time.

In the spring of my senior year of high school, I was plan-ning to go to Ohio State a couple of hours away just to get some distance. I was saving money, working in a camera shop where the FPD brought their mug shots to be developed; I could look at those drunk, swollen faces every day, and so I believed I was ready. I asked the cop who dropped off the film how I could look at the police reports on my mother's acci-dent. To my surprise, he told me I could go to the station downtown and just ask for the file. It was shockingly simple.

The only record I had until then was the newspaper clip Lettie had saved with my mother's brief obit and the Fredemeier and Thigtree Funeral and Cremation Services announcement—it was in the middle column in between ads from the three other funeral homes in the area, which seems like a lot for such a small town, but people here are particular about funerals, eschewing cremations or curtains drawn in front of dark wood caskets for the latest in metallic finishes, propped open of course, with human-sized flower arrange-ments all around and a pink light hidden discreetly between two ceiling beams shining on the deceased's face.

Joanie's read JOAN MADISON WINSLOW, 2 P.M. VISITING HOURS FOLLOWED BY GRAVESIDE SERVICE, ROSEWOOD MEMOR-IAL PARK. That was all. She was listed with two other people, Mr. Cecil Conyers and Mrs. Lucille Palladino, who were clas-sified under the heading INCOMPLETE, which is probably not a thing you need to think about for too long.

But in her police file, labeled "Joan Maddison Winslow"—the two *D*s in her maiden name a misspelling—there was much more to the story. First I found the traffic accident filing and the coroner's report. I read both while standing at a tall, narrow counter in the station. When my legs started shaking, I hooked my elbow over the inside edge of the scratched veneer counter and read the file again. I read the officer's impersonal listing of my mother and the man's physical characteristics— their race and sex, approximate age. I read about the make of car, its crushed frame against the tree, the positioning of two bodies, found tangled and bloodied. I read the officer's quick assessment, "driver loss of control, possible alcohol, other subs. involved." The efficient abbreviation, the unintelligible signature.

And then the coroner's autopsy report on my mother. More basic descriptions of my mother, the adult female, Caucasian. The assessment of blood alcohol level. The determination of accidental death.

There were also three photographs, black-and-white, their filmy surfaces scarred and oily from handling. One of the car from the side, the driver's door pried open, and I searched the shadows of the interior for some sign of them, but of course they were gone. The front of the car pressed against the broad skin of the tree as if in embrace, the hood jaggedly ribbed. Then one from the front left of the car, to show the impact, I guessed. And another from the back of the car, at some distance, to show its final path, the pavement pale and moonlike in the flash's contrast.

I went back to the coroner's report and noticed a mistake: her age. A surge of hope—I realize now that I was thinking that if I could find one wrong detail I could void the whole file, demand she be returned to me. The form said thirty-two, but I knew she was thirty-three when she died, six months before her thirty-fourth birthday. At first I thought it was a typo, a simple slip of the finger from the three to the two, perhaps the myopic clerk sitting at the desk across the counter from me had done it, the one with the dark glossy hair pulled into a bun, hair that looked too luxurious for her thin cheeks and pointed chin, and I wondered if maybe she lived a secret life, just like my mother. She didn't look up at me as she moved files from inbox to outbox. I was ready to ask her about the mistake, confront her, and then I found the photocopy of my mother's birth certificate, the smudge on her birth date, 1947. The shaky slant of the seven looked ghostly and too careful. It was circled. A note beside it said, "Tampering. 1948." I stared at it for what felt like a long time, and right then I felt as if the papers in my hands could float into the air, catch on fire, disappear—they could have told me anything and I would have believed it.

At the library that same day, I found my mother and the man's names together in a four-paragraph article describing the accident in the *Daily Record* on June 18. There was his obituary in the *Cleveland Plain Dealer,* and two more stories, one reporting the accident and another a couple of weeks later mentioning it in an article about rising drunk-driving statistics.

The man's name was Hall McLendon.

I read the stories at the library on microfiche, printed them, and drove to the Morris P. Alston building. I sat on a bench in front of the photograph of my mother and me, our mouths open in exactly the same shape, her face young, her hair tangled in my hand.

I folded the photocopies I had of my mother's file and the articles and slipped them into an envelope. As I sat there, the envelope lightly balanced on my lap, I thought about when and how I would tell my father that I knew everything.

13

LETTIE'S HOUSE, the house where my father grew up and where I spent summers until I started college, was on the corner of two former farm roads, now paved and yellow-lined. Lettie had sold the surrounding land years ago to an equestrian school. I pulled into the driveway next to the broad, tree-bordered lawn and looked up the hill, where glossy-backed horses stood in small groups, bobbing their heads like cliquey teenagers. Beyond it, the two-lane state route became four lanes lined with superstores, hulking gas stations, comic-book-colored fast-food restaurants. As a child I had stretched on my stomach on that hill when it was still farmland. I'd arch my back, chin up, arms straight, pretending to shoot into the sky like a rocket.

I was looking up, thinking of this, when I noticed a small plane coming in from the north. The plane was flying low, engine buzzing irregularly like one of Terence's multisetting vibrators, the "big guns" he'd called them, which even he'd had to admit were more for show than anything else. I fought the urge to duck as the plane passed too low over the house, then watched it barely clear the trees and disappear behind them. I listened for a crumpling of metal, an explosion, but there was nothing beyond the farty sound of horse snorts carried on the soft air.

I took a deep breath to steady myself for the visit to come, climbed the steps to the front porch, felt the give of warped wood. Knocking on the screen door, I cupped my hand over my eyes to peer inside. Lettie was twenty-seven, an old maid, and Randall was seventeen, when they married in 1939 and bought this land and house from a retired judge. She was a teacher, educated at the Reserve Normal school with plans to move east, but then she met Randall in her high school math class and fell in love as she tutored him on long division. She got fired for sneaking sips of whiskey behind the school. She told me she had done it so she wouldn't have to quit; it was her idea of a graceful exit.

Lettie had a small frame and a big, commanding voice that had served her well in the classroom and on the farm. People said she was a man in disguise because she wore her hair short and refused makeup; they laughed at the sight of her pregnant and shook their heads in disbelief when my father was born healthy in 1943 when she was thirty-one. When her husband died before his thirtieth birthday, people said God had cursed him for marrying her.

"Who's there?" I heard her demand from the back of the house.

"It's me," I called. "Merle." I stepped inside, let the screen door tap closed behind me. The tall windows of the front room were open, and a breeze nudged the corners of the open newspaper on the footrest.

Nothing had changed. Not the color of the walls, not a piece of furniture. I took my time walking down the hallway, glancing at photographs of myself at various ages, some with

Lettie and my father and mother, some with Olin as an infant, a toddler, a skinny-legged boy with a smile like our mother's. Then there were no more photographs of Joanie; by the time I was a furtive-looking teenager with bad skin and my brother had started wearing his hair in an eighties version of a pompadour, my father stood between and slightly behind us in photographs, as if trying to fill two spaces. At the far end of the hallway there were no more photographs of me; just Olin's high school and college graduation pictures and one apparently recent shot of my father and Olin, unshaven and smiling, in a restaurant with Christmas lights in the background.

One new thing in the den as I passed on the way to the kitchen: a sleek black TV looking as out of place as a spaceship on its antique table perch, a faded moon-and-stars rug on the floor before it like a worn-out galaxy. The last time I had come here, it had been to demand explanations. I was waiting for a plane ticket that, in the age before e-mail, was being sent overnight. My bags were packed, and I stood in the foyer, not really even sure I wanted to leave—maybe I wanted to be begged to stay, but Lettie wasn't the begging type—and if I thought I could make her apologize for the decision she'd made to follow my father's wishes and keep my mother's affair a secret, I was wrong.

"It's me," I said again. Lettie stood in the kitchen, hips against the counter's edge, cigarette pinched between her lips as she stirred something in a large bowl. She was wearing the same work shirt and jeans from the night before at the restaurant, her feet bare and her white hair pulled into a cloudlike poof at the top of her head. I waited in the doorway, wondering if she'd heard me, then deciding she had. I walked to the refrigerator and looked at the magnets, one for emergency cat services, one for Golden discounts, one for the fire department.

"Grab the mayonnaise," she barked, ashing into the sink. "I need to get this goddamned tuna salad done."

I opened the refrigerator and found a nearly empty jar and put it on the counter next to her. She waved me closer. "Go ahead, dump it in the bowl. How old are you now?"

I decided to roll with this. "Thirty-two," I said, grabbing a spoon and scraping the sides of the mayonnaise jar over the pile of canned tuna chunks and chopped celery. "I don't think you have enough," I said.

She looked into the bowl. "Well, crap." She tossed her spoon onto the counter, reached for her pack of Parliaments on the windowsill, and shook one out. She tapped it on the counter and lit it off the old one, which she dropped, still smoking, into the sink. "You've gained weight."

"Thanks," I said. My nervousness at seeing her again was quickly eroding to irritation. I watched her exhale, smoke mushrooming against the windowpanes. She turned to me then. "Why don't you go on and have a baby, anyway? I mean, even I didn't wait this long."

I ignored this. "What's with the chain-smoking?" I asked, even though I wanted a cigarette myself. But I realized I didn't want to smoke in front of her, a startling idea when I considered the things I had done in front of other people, namely Terence. I shivered.

Lettie leaned to check her teeth in the reflection of her stainless-steel toaster, one of those fat, rounded tanks from the fifties. "Don't try to distract me," she said. "Come on, sit down."

We sat at the kitchen table, which looked over the vegetable garden she had always kept, now vine-snarled and weedy. She noticed me looking at it and shrugged. "I've had enough of digging in the dirt. I have my groceries delivered these days." She took another drag. "OK, let's get to it."

"What?"

"Why are you here?"

"I wanted to see you?" I asked, as if trying for the right answer on a quiz.

"Oh, give me a break." She shook her head and laughed, a dry cough. "Let's go in the other room. These chairs hurt my butt."

I followed her into the den. There was one faded easy chair opposite the TV, a tin ashtray like the kind they give out in diners balanced on the chair arm. "Pull up a seat," Lettie said, sinking into the easy chair with a grateful sigh. Finding the remote control, she pointed it at the TV, sighting from her shoulder like aiming a gun. I had to go back to the kitchen for a chair, and when I came back and sat down she was clicking rapidly through stations.

"I love the clicker," she said. "Nothing I hate worse than a slow clicker, though." She leaned toward me, voice lowered conspiratorially. "I got a theory. Men click faster than women because women gotta know what's going on before clicking to the next channel, while men—" she paused for another drag, "Men make a split-second decision based on the image. You get it?"

I just looked at her. I wondered which men's clicker habits she'd been studying.

"Men are interested in looks and women are interested in stories! But not me, see. That's the crux of the issue, right there. I ought to be on talk shows."

"Yeah, you'd be great," I said.

Lettie didn't miss the sarcasm in my voice. She regarded me coolly, as if trying to decide something. She stabbed out her cigarette in the ashtray and sat forward, looking up at me. "You've got nerve, showing up here after all these years, you know that?"

"What?" I said, unable to think of anything better. It was possible, in spite of her harsh tone, that she was complimenting me, but I couldn't tell and I didn't think knowing the answer would've helped me. I wanted to leave but I felt almost too exhausted to move, my legs heavy. I clutched the seat of the chair I was sitting in. My mouth was dry, sticky. I had thought about this moment for years, had practiced over and over the speech I wanted to make about honesty, which is a form of respect that leads to trust, and how she had failed on all three counts—I had pictured myself ticking them off on my fingers, pictured her looking penitent, wearing something dark and tasteful, something that shouted I'm-sorry-I-hurt-you-and-I-take-your-pain-seriously—I had imagined her crying gently, asking my forgiveness, taking my hands and pulling me to her, at which point we would both cry until we laughed, then split a bottle of wine and some takeout on the front porch, candles lit all over the place, the smell of earth and flowers and freshly cut grass rising in the cool evening air. I had pictured this scene many times, and nothing, not one detail of it, jived with what I was seeing at that moment, my grandmother smoking and talking trash in a La-Z-Boy recliner, not a hint of regret in her crinkly gray eyes. I was about to go ahead and cry myself—at least that part of the scene would play out as fantasized—but then I heard the creak of footsteps on the front porch and a soft knock on the door.

"Did you hear that?" I managed.

"What?" Lettie said, standing up as if the extra couple of feet of height would help her hear better.

"Someone knocking?"

"Oh," Lettie said, stepping past me. "You go see. I'm going to finish that stupid salad."

I walked down the hallway, viewing my family's photographic history in reverse. Through the screen door I could see the outline of a man leaning against the doorframe, body half turned away as he gazed toward the lawn.

"Hello?" I said, staying a few feet from the screen.

He turned, surprised. "Hmm," he leaned back as if to check the house number. "You don't look like Lettie," he said.

This irritated me more than it should have; I chalked it up to listening to Lettie's clicker theories when I had hoped for something different—what, I wasn't even sure anymore. "Can I tell her who's here?" He was younger than I had originally thought, maybe late thirties, early forties. Not bad looking, though I detected a little sheepishness in the curve of his shoulders, as if he knew he'd made a mistake at some point; he just wasn't sure when.

Lettie rounded the corner with the bowl of tuna salad in her hands. "Frank!" she said. "Out of gas again?"

"No, just a minor maintenance issue. Can I use your phone?"

"Come on in. You know where it is."

Stepping inside, he held out his hand and we shook—I'd forgotten how American men loved to shake hands, even with women. British guys took your fingertips as if ready to help you into a carriage, a quaint habit that I liked, even if to some degree it had to mean they thought you couldn't withstand the tougher grip of palm to palm. His hand was rough and warm and steady. "Frank Bryson," he said. He seemed amused to find me here, and I wanted to ask him what he thought was so funny, but I also didn't want to give him the satisfaction.

"Merle Winslow. Nice to meet you," I said, which wasn't exactly the case; I mean, I hadn't decided if it was nice to meet him, but it gave me a chance to look him over some more. He had an interesting face. His nose looked like it had been broken a couple of times; the line of the bridge ambled a little east and a little west before culminating in a slightly hooked tip.

His dark hair seemed undecided about what direction it needed to go. His flannel shirt was untucked; the laces of his hiking boots drooped on the dusty floor. He smelled like gasoline-soaked leather.

Lettie and I led him to the kitchen. I still felt shaky, Lettie's accusation turning in my mind. *You've got nerve.* I didn't feel that I had any nerve at all anymore. I stood in the kitchen doorway and watched Frank dialing. Lettie leaned in close to me, crunching a celery chunk next to my ear. "Pilot. Got his own air taxi service," she shout-whispered at me, which Frank could certainly hear, though he pretended not to.

"Yeah, I think it's the gas line," I heard him explaining. "Well, I'm going to need to get someone out here . . . about an hour?" he paused. "Do you think it'll spoil?"

"Air taxi? And he doesn't have a cell phone?" I asked Lettie. "I thought everyone had cell phones."

"He's a funny guy."

I rolled my eyes. Lettie calling someone funny wasn't saying much. He hung up and shrugged his shoulders. "Well, thanks," he said.

"Hungry?" Lettie asked, shoving the bowl of tuna salad at him. "It's fresh made."

Frank took a look and gave a regretful shrug. "I gotta go."

"Why don't you walk him out, Merle," Lettie said, stage-winking at me, mouth open. I looked at her as if she were a stranger bird-dancing on the street.

Frank followed me to the front door. "That you?" he asked, pointing to a particularly horrific school portrait of me—it was the mid-eighties, and no one had ever told me that getting a perm and teasing the bangs up in a vertical crest was a bad idea, or that large bright scarves, bangle bracelets, and frosted eye shadow would never work for me. I winced, glancing at it as we passed. It was my senior portrait; my mother had been dead for four years by then; Watson Puckett had just broken up with me; I didn't know what to do next.

"My sister," I said.

"Oh, really? Older or younger?" he asked.

We were almost to the door, and I stopped, ready to chat, now that I had started lying about life details, a personal specialty. "Oh, younger. She's a, uh, consultant out west."

Frank grinned at me before opening the door. "You don't really have a sister, do you?"

"No, I don't," I admitted. "But I've always wondered what it would be like to have one." I wanted to ask him how he'd known I wasn't telling the truth, or just adding to it, as I preferred to think of it.

"Well, nice to meet you," he said, carefully stepping outside and closing the screen door behind him.

"What are you delivering anyway?" I asked as he went down the steps.

"Horse sperm," he called over his shoulder, walking away.

There was no chance of coming up with an appropriate response to this—good luck? Happy travels? Enjoy? I heard Lettie coming from the kitchen and turned around. I was thinking about where we'd left things when Frank showed up, trying to come up with a way to make my often-imagined Lettie apology scene play out, the one that ended with us staying up all night talking the way we did when I was a kid, but then she breezed past me carrying a pair of tattered tennis shoes and her pocketbook.

"OK, how about you take me downtown. I need something to wear."

"For what?"

"Your father's wedding, that's what."

14

LETTIE TOOK ME to lunch at the Lotus, a vegetarian restaurant around the corner from the Iron. As we stood in front of the chalkboard menu dangling over the register, she loudly made fun of the sweet-potato and cinnamon fries, insulted the server's nose ring, calling her Torro, and launched into a short speech about the dangers of a meat-free diet.

"Then what are we doing here?" I asked.

"Because you didn't want to go to Fortuna's," Lettie said.

"I was in there this morning and he said all this weird stuff to me, said he knew why I was here," I said.

"Oh, he was just making a pass at you, the old goat."

"OK," I said. But I wasn't convinced. He had recognized me; that was for sure. Beyond that, I didn't know what to make of it. I grabbed a handful of recycled-paper napkins and followed Lettie through the crowded restaurant to a table, passing a bulletin board with various announcements—Vegan Roommate Wanted, Lost Dog, Going to California? Take me with you. On the way to the restaurant, I had asked Lettie for details about my father's wedding—when it was, and, more important, who the woman was—but she said she didn't know. I still couldn't believe it: my father, in love. A gray-headed groom. I tried to picture him in a tux, but Lettie was swiping a salt shaker from the table of neighboring patrons without asking, which distracted me. "Anyway, I've had enough with filling in the blanks for you, Merle. Ask him yourself," she'd said. Of course I figured it had to be the heavily made-up woman in the Cadillac, but I wasn't sure of anything anymore.

In her work shirt and faded blue jeans, Lettie looked right at home with the lunch crowd, mostly college students and a few professors sitting around rickety tables on mismatched chairs. This place had been a travel agency when I was a student here; in fact it was where I had bought my ticket to Heathrow. I looked at the doorway, the uneven wooden floor, and imagined myself walking in, having just come from the university, not trusting myself to drive, still shaking from what I had learned about my mother, what I had really, in retrospect, put off learning as long as possible because of course I had always sensed that something was missing—why else was I always asking Lettie to tell me the same story again and again about my parents, as if somehow, over time, I'd put it all together?

Our server, née Torro, a slim, pale-skinned girl wearing long beads and long straight brown hair that dangled in parallel lanks on either side of her face, her nose punctuated by a little silver hoop, brought our drinks—coffee for me, mango juice for Lettie—and glared at Lettie, who shrugged. "I can't help it if you can't figure out any other way to get attention from boys other than mutilating yourself."

The waitress rolled her eyes and walked away. Lettie rummaged in her bag and pulled out a pack of cigarettes.

"You can't smoke in here," I said.

"Oh, right. Just as well," Lettie said, dropping the pack back into her bag and gazing out the window. I was still getting used to being near her again, the crackling sound of her voice, the way she narrowed one eye when making a point, the way loose wisps of her fine white hair lifted in the air.

"Why are you smoking so much, anyway?"

"Oh, it's something to do. You know? It's a little entertainment."

"You ought to cut it out."

"Don't start with me."

I knew I needed to quit, too, but I also understood what Lettie meant—sometimes, it was a necessary distraction. "OK, then. How about this—why don't you tell me why you got so huffy when I showed up?"

"Me, huffy?"

"I thought you'd be happy to see me." This wasn't entirely true, but I was stretching. I was trying to get her to go back, not just to when I'd knocked on her door earlier, but when I slammed it behind me a decade before. I figured if my father could move on, I could, too.

Lettie narrowed her eyes. "What are you after?"

I looked at her. "I want to know why you and Dad never told me about the affair."

Lettie sighed and fell back in her chair, as if deeply bored by the topic. "You know what's funny about this?" she asked, giving me a look that suggested there was nothing funny, in fact.

I waited, ignoring the question.

"How come your brother didn't get all in a twist about it? We never told him, either. Until you blabbed, of course."

I leaned forward. "Olin was only nine years old. He barely understood what happened. I'm not saying he didn't suffer, but all he needed was comfort." Then, as I continued, I looked straight at her. "I needed someone who would be honest with me."

Lettie leaned forward, left eye narrowed and twitching. "Oh, and you're the grown-up with no secrets around here? Ten years in London and nothing to say about it?"

She had me and she knew it. She sat back in her chair again, bony arms crossed, foot tapping a table leg. She was right; I didn't want her or anyone to know how disappointed I was in myself—not really because of the X Publishing work itself but because of the time wasted and nothing to show for it; no way to say, "This is what I wanted in life and I've done it." Which begged the question: What did I want? It frightened me to ask it, even silently, because to ask was to risk the realization that you're not qualified, not chosen after all. Better to pretend you want nothing. But what would be the truth? A great career? I didn't give a shit about any kind of work beyond paying the bills. To be in love? Sure. I could tell myself that I wanted to get married and have children and live the life my mother might have lived if she had been able to allow herself any kind of peace, a choice made every day. The truth was, I didn't know.

Lettie must have seen it in my face, a kind of defeat. "You were a difficult child, Merle. Always. I tried to warn your father and mother both. Know how I knew?" Lettie wagged a finger at me, working up to something now. "It was the bed-wetting—"

"Please stop it," I said. I winced, realizing I was biting the inside of my cheek, hard. "That was only once or twice—"

"Whatever you need to remember. You want to hear an explanation? Fine, I'm talking. I didn't tell you about your mother's affair because I wanted to keep you focused."

"Focused?"

"Yes."

"On what?"

"On her death. I didn't want you all caught up in the affair, thinking it was somehow romantic. But that's what happened anyway. You've let it run your life for ten years! Why not just let it go? The whole thing was ugly and selfish. Your mother loved you but she loved her problems more."

That was the thing about Lettie—I wanted her to talk, but when she did, it pissed me off. I wanted to defend my mother, tell Lettie she was wrong. But I didn't necessarily believe she was wrong, or at least I couldn't come up with any reasons why. I checked my wrist, knowing there was no watch but wanting to do the pantomime anyway. "That's nice, very nice," I said. "Where do you get your dialogue, hmm? Daytime television?"

"I wanted you to be happy, Merle. Or at least alive. Even if you decided to hold a grudge because of some nutty notion of yours that you should always get the truth from love." She threw her hands up, slapped them palms down on the table. "Look. After your grandfather died, I saw something close down in Ernest. He never cried, just walked the fields. But then he came back from Oklahoma with your mother and he had this blush all the time, this blood glow, so that's why I can't figure out—"

Lettie stopped and gazed out the window, remembering. "Once she tried to talk to me about it. The affair. But this was my son here, and I didn't want to hear it. I said, 'Haven't you got enough trouble in this town? I mean, you stop small talk just by walking through a room.'" Lettie shook her head, and I was glad she wasn't looking at me because I wasn't sure I could cover the shock on my face. I thought of my mother confessing to her. What did she want? Comfort? Permission?

Lettie tapped the table with one finger as if she'd decided something. "Men are weak, that's the problem," she said.

"They're guided by things outside of themselves, things they can't control. As a rule, I've preferred men because, really, that weakness makes them easier company—you just stay off disputed territory and there are no surprises. Women, though, you can never tell what they're thinking. They can never be satisfied. A man's happy with a steady job and a hot meal on the table every night, a little sex every few days or so. Women always want something more." She was trying to sound calm, resigned, but then she pressed her fingers into her forehead until the tips whitened, and I realized she had started to cry.

"Lettie," I said, reaching for her. She waved me away.

"Stop it," she said, crumpling her napkin and dabbing at her eyes, and I wasn't sure if she was talking to me or to herself. I watched her and remembered how, when I confronted her with my discovery, waving my mother's birth certificate and the photocopied newspaper stories at her, I had known even then that her decision not to tell me and Olin about the affair was motivated by a desire to protect us. I couldn't say I would've done differently.

Our server came with our garden burgers. "Will there be anything else?" she asked in a tight, shaky voice as she totaled our order in jabbing pen strokes.

"No thanks," Lettie said, dabbing at her eyes. "This should be poison enough."

I couldn't help but smile. It was a relief to move into the next moment, to see that even in her grief and regret, Lettie could still sting when she wanted to.

The waitress slammed the ticket on the table and stomped away, beads clicking.

Lettie looked at me, patted my hand. "Cheer up. You could be waiting tables and telling yourself the nose ring was a good idea."

I tried to smile, but I think I just pressed my lips together in a grim line. I could not get over my mother coming to Lettie, confessing to her, and what that must have been like for her, watching her son's marriage disintegrate and not being able to do anything. I decided I'd try not to think too much about the mistakes I'd worked to convince myself were good ideas in the past, like my so-called editing career, my relationship with Terence, my theory that I could become a different person if I just put enough distance between myself and my family. I realized that what I was missing now was not so much the way things were, but the fact-free beliefs I'd gotten so used to carrying around, like an alcoholic who still needs a drink at a cocktail party, even if only soda, for the familiar weight in the hand. I bit my bottom lip, and what I thought then was that I needed to talk with my father.

15

I THINK MY FATHER knew what would happen once Joanie told him she needed to go back to the Star-Lite to get her sketchbook. They were just married, but there were no hearts drawn in soap on their car windows, no cans clanging their love on the street; they left Clink Johnson and Preacher Tracy holding up a hungover Hall McLendon in the park, and Ernest knew Joanie's father would be there, waiting for them; it was inevitable.

They drove away from the park in silence, the signed marriage certificate sitting on Joanie's lap. When they pulled into the gravel parking lot, Ernest tried to see him through the glass door, but he couldn't. He got out and walked around to open her door, but she had already opened it.

"Please just stay in the car," Joanie said. Her breath was tight in her chest.

Ernest said nothing. He offered his arm, which Joanie did not take. She started for the glass door, and he followed her.

The lobby was empty. The note Joanie had left on the front counter was gone. She stopped and looked around.

"He's looking for us," she whispered. She lifted the dividing counter at the front desk, pulled out the sketchbook from where she'd left it on the deep shelf under the counter, several of its pages used as blotter when she was changing the numbers on her birth certificate, and eased the counter divider back down. It landed with a small thud, which made them both jump.

The toilet in the hallway bathroom flushed and the door opened. There was no time to move, so Joanie stood beside Ernest and faced her father as he entered the hallway, shotgun dangling from one hand—he had taken it to the bathroom with him, as was his habit.

My grandfather did not seem particularly surprised to see them standing there together, my mother's knee-length pale pink dress showing the soft curves of her hips and breasts, her hair in a shining chignon with a few wisps dark against her long neck, my father looking slight in a suit that had been his father's, a chrysanthemum from the park in his lapel, his glasses slightly crooked on his nose. My grandfather surveyed them, his face flat and expressionless, set in a way that Joanie knew meant he had already started drinking for the day. He stood across from them in the lobby and leaned on the shotgun, the heel of his hand on the mouth of the barrel, the sight of which made Ernest's chest burn.

"Well, well. Two thieves," my grandfather said, looking at Joanie and then at Ernest.

"I wanted to tell you—" Joanie began, but her father cut her off with a swipe at the air.

"You even planning to kiss your poor mother good-bye? She's back there asking for you, doesn't even know you're gone. Leaving the office wide open, anyone could rob us blind. Kill us in our beds."

Joanie dropped her head to her chest. A tear ran down her

nose and her shoulders shook. Ernest took her hand, wanting to pull her into his open jacket and wrap it around her.

"Don't you touch her!" my grandfather yelled, his voice filling the room, shaking them.

My father did not let go of my mother's hand. "We're going now," he said. He turned to his right, reached for the door. My grandfather stepped forward, making my mother cower backward, and he swung the gun like a baseball bat, the stock sighing as it arced, cracking against the back of my father's skull.

Ernest lurched forward, heard screaming, and then nothing for what seemed like quite a while. He awoke being dragged across the parking lot by his collar, the edge of the cloth cutting into his skin. He heard his breath very loud in his ears. He could see his heels bouncing on the gravel; they seemed to be someone else's feet. One of his shoes was gone, the gravel cutting into his feet and hands. His glasses were gone. He felt heat on his neck, something wet, and knew it was blood.

My grandfather pulled him to his feet, threw him against the car, stepped back, set the shotgun on his shoulder. "Get in the car."

Ernest slumped against the warm metal door, his head thick, pounding. He wanted to throw up. He thought of his mother, what she might be doing at that moment, what she would do if he were killed.

My grandfather cocked the trigger. "Get in."

"I am waiting for my wife," my father said, the words thick against his dry lips. My grandfather uncocked the trigger, turned the gun, drew back to swing, but my father ducked, ran to the other side of the car. "Come on, Joanie!" he yelled, shuffling dizzily, keeping the car between himself and my grandfather.

Joanie moved forward, even though her legs felt shaky the way they did in dreams when she tried to run but her knees went to rubber beneath her. She had the sketchbook in one hand and Ernest's glasses in another. She thought she could hear her mother screaming. She thought she could hear Ernest's heart beating. She saw how sweat had darkened the back of her father's shirt in the shape of an hourglass and she started running.

Her father was breathing hard, his face was red. He lunged for her and missed as she angled for the passenger side of the car and then jumped in, locking the door and rolling up the window. Her father ran to the door, tried the handle, raised the butt of the gun over the window.

My mother pressed the side of her face against the glass and closed her eyes, thinking of her dream of spilling the etching acid and how her new face would make her a different person. But her father did not bring the gun down. He stepped back, rested the butt gently on the ground, leaned on it. He was exhausted, deflated, his shirt sticking to his ribs, sweat rivering in the creases of his sun-scored skin. He looked at the ground and spat.

My father opened his car door. He sat down, pulled the door closed, put the keys into the ignition. Out of the corner of his eye he watched my grandfather staring at the ground, breathing hard, blank-faced as if he had forgotten why he had come outside.

It was only when my father began to slowly pull away that my grandfather raised the gun to his shoulder again, peered through the sight, seemed to aim, tracking them as they turned onto the street. My father saw this but was in too much pain to worry about being shot. Foggily, he thought of a salute. He turned a corner, and he couldn't see my grandfather anymore, and he thought of his mother and father, who had grown up on farms within three miles of each other, and of how their marriage, unusual as it was for the time, with Lettie ten years older than her husband, had almost happened without their trying, as natural as rain.

Joanie sat forward in her seat, face cradled in her hands, until Goodwell had disappeared and the ranch lands surrounded them. After a while Ernest saw his glasses on the car seat, the lenses smudged, one of the earpieces broken off. He put the glasses on. As bad as his vision was, he hadn't noticed he was driving without them.

They didn't speak until a low-roofed gas station appeared on the horizon, its large rounded pumps gleaming dull red in the now high sun. My father pulled the car to a stop at the pumps, dust rising from the gravel. He cut the engine and Joanie seemed to notice him for the first time since they started driving. She pressed her fist to her mouth, her swollen eyes almost slits. She reached toward his neck. "Your collar's all bloody," she said.

My father craned his neck to look in the rearview mirror and the first pang of a long headache hit him. He winced and Joanie touched his hand. "Come on."

The gas station owner, a round-faced man, sunburned skin shiny, called out from the shadowed doorway. "Fill 'er up?"

"Yes," Ernest called back. His voice felt brittle, cracking in his throat.

Ernest got out of the car, moving slowly. Joanie didn't wait for him to open her side. They walked into the tiny hot cinder-block toilet together. Inside, my mother peeled off my father's shirt, soaking it so that the blood ran pink into the dirty sink bowl, and touched the wet ends to Ernest's neck where more blood had caked. "You're going to need stitches," Joanie said.

Ernest touched Joanie's waist, pulled her to him, pressed

his forehead against her neck. They leaned against each other in the orange-yellow light, the sound of their breathing magnified against the cement walls. They stood there until the gas station owner at the pumps became nervous, until the air inside was almost too hot to breathe. Then they opened the door and stepped outside.

16

IT WAS EARLY EVENING when I dropped Lettie back at her house with a red, sequin-trimmed pantsuit, a wispy flame caught in a crinkly plastic hanging bag knotted at the bottom. Angling for wedding details, I wanted to know if she needed a jacket, or open-toed sandals. Was she buying for a particular season, or time of day? "Honey, I buy whatever I like, as long as it doesn't bind," she'd said, brushing my questions away like lint. "I'm too old to care."

Driving back into town, I thought of calling my father at the office to see if he might still be there. I imagined him wandering through the parking lot outside the DSS, lost for a moment upon realizing he didn't have his keys, maybe even thinking of that hot morning years ago in the parking lot outside the Star-Lite Motel, disoriented from the shotgun butt blow, my mother crying, clutching his broken glasses, my grandfather dragging him toward his car, his body throbbing as he jerked free, searching his pockets for the car keys, then, perhaps, coming back to the present moment, remembering he had loaned me the car, the muscles in his chest loosening.

That was a story in our family, "The Day Your Grandfather Tried to Kill Me," and when my father told it, in the nonchalant, distracted tone you'd use going over a grocery list, Olin and I had always laughed. We'd laughed because my father meant for the story to be funny, and my mother played along, shaking her head at the part when my father recounted how he drove for several miles before realizing he wasn't wearing his glasses. That's what passed for humor in our family.

I pulled into the parking lot of the Department of Social Services and drove around the side of the building to where I could see the window of his office, which was dark, evening sunlight filtering through the trees so the building looked draped in a kind of shadowy lace. I remembered how, looking up at that window as a child, I thought it impossible that a small square could contain him, everything that he was to me. I drove down River Street toward our house, my father's house—I could hardly think of it as mine anymore—passing the southern edge of Florence College, the old, ivy-bearded brick buildings gone purple in the waning light, cars in front of me looking wet and sunset-smeared. I passed Fortuna's, turned at the Iron, passed the Lotus, then the bridge over the river where a man stepped slowly along the rock-dotted banks, picking up cans. After that it was uphill into my old neighborhood, the tall, narrow houses seeming to lean inward to the street, the huddling trees secretive, hoarding shadows.

I pulled into the driveway, cut the engine, got out and lit a cigarette, regarding the house. My father had lived here alone for nearly ten years now, ever since I left the country and then Olin left soon after for college. I wondered what it felt like to live in rooms full of memories of his dead wife, his children before they left. Did they keep him company or make him feel lonely? I thought of how I got a little nostalgic when it was time to buy a new toothbrush and wondered how he had decided to marry again in such a businesslike way, it seemed, planning a wedding without even mentioning it to his kids. But then, he had proposed to Joanie after only two dates. Maybe it was because he, and Olin after him, really could move through life without getting tangled in it, without regret—while, whenever I tried to ape those traits, it was nothing more than pained pretending.

I heard the crunch of gravel, and saw him walking up the driveway. I wondered which way he had taken home since I hadn't passed him on my way. I leaned against the door, tapping my foot, feeling a little absurd, like a silent-movie gangster. As he got closer, he looked up and smiled, a kind of squinty smile that was almost a wince.

I folded my arms. "Can I ask you something?" I asked.

My father blinked and smiled the squinty smile again. He was steeling himself; I could almost hear him thinking: *Here she goes.* He raised his eyebrows, as if to ask what I meant.

"You know, I got like six greeting cards from you the whole time I was gone," I said. "Do you think we cracked double digits on the phone calls maybe?"

My father sighed, slid his hands into his pockets. "Is this about the wedding?" he asked.

"I—yes," I said, surprised at his directness.

"I figured Lettie would have told you. She's excited, you know? Always the mother." He clicked his tongue against his teeth and winked at me, smiling still, a bit apologetically now, and right then I could see him as a little boy, her only son, the one who never cried, who wanted to grow up fast so he could take care of her. And that made me think of Terence as a little boy, and all of a sudden I felt sympathy for them both in their tender years until I remembered that I should be pissed that my own father wasn't including me in his wedding plans. I bit the inside of my cheek to jumpstart my resolve. My eyes watered and my nose started running.

"So is there anything else?" I said, sniffing. "I mean, who is she? How did you meet?" I paused, then held up a hand to stop him. "No, wait. I'm going to go first, OK? I'm going to bring you up to date," I took a deep breath. I thought of Lettie asking me what I'd been up to for ten years, not really asking but pointing it out, this gap I wouldn't discuss. "OK, first thing, I worked in the porn industry for eight years."

As soon as I said it, I realized what my father thought I meant, that I had been in movies—but the worst part of the moment was the flicker of disbelief in his eyes; somehow, realizing he thought I would make up a story about being a porn actress was harder than having to admit that my dazzling editing career was actually one of rewriting hack novels in a badly heated converted warehouse in Clerkenwell.

"As an editor," I clarified. "Beyond that, I haven't paid taxes since 1990. My last boyfriend was a hash fiend and a crossdresser and a shitty writer of sex scenes. He made my job hell and he disappointed me on top of that. So, I need my family right now. I need to see a dentist. I want to know why you didn't let me know about the wedding. I mean, could you make me feel at least somewhat a part of this family? At least tell me the major plot points?" I was crying by then, my father standing a few feet away, stiff and uncomfortable in the driveway. I wanted him to be the father of my childhood, to comfort me. But he had never been good at it in the first place, and now it had been so long, he was out of practice.

I wiped my eyes and tried to steady my breathing. "OK, now you go. Your turn."

"Her name is Doreen, and I meant to tell you, I did," my father said, blushing, a smile spreading from his cheeks to the crinkly skin around his eyes to the ruddy skin of his forehead.

"But then you were coming home anyway, so I thought I'd wait until you got here."

"Why?" I demanded. He didn't say anything. "What if I had changed my plans? Would you have even bothered to tell me?" I sounded childish, I knew, but I didn't care.

"I didn't want you to worry."

"You didn't want me to worry," I repeated slowly, as if I didn't understand. But in fact I thought I did. He'd wanted to protect me, avoid upsetting me. I was his dangerously emotional daughter, teetering close to unstable, perhaps. Maybe he'd been right about me. But I knew his own balance was delicate, always masking control with protection. "When is it?" I asked.

"Two weeks," he said, shrug-smiling in a way that asked for a forgiveness I wasn't sure I could give.

17

I TOLD OLIN about the wedding, and of course he took it right in stride. He suggested we throw Ernest and Doreen a party. A few days later, we were wandering the aisles of the ACME Sparkle Store, and all we had picked out so far were potato chips, bean dip, and beer. "Well, I'm just about ready for Friday," Olin said. "My act, you know? Dad's bringing Doreen." He was so pleased with himself I could barely stand it. I gave him a defeated look, and he rolled his eyes. "OK, what?"

"What the hell am I doing here?" I said. I stopped in the middle of the snack aisle and leaned on the rusty cart.

"We're shopping for the party," Olin said, speaking slowly, as if to an amnesiac. "Stay focused, will you?"

"You know what I mean," I said. I knew I was being whiny, but I wanted sympathy.

Olin shook his head. "Can't you just take things day by day? Play the good recovering addict. It'll come to you."

"That's what people think in their twenties. But when you hit your thirties and there's still no big news breaks, you start to get concerned."

"OK, so what do we know about this Doreen chick?" Olin asked, clearly looking to change the subject. "Isn't it weird that Ernest is playing things so close to the chest?" He tossed some streamers into the cart.

"Those are tacky," I said.

Olin gave me a look that said consider the source, and I let it go. "Yeah, it is weird. Should we go spy on him or something?" I tossed in some paper napkins and plates.

Olin contemplated this. "Not a bad idea. Should we ask ourselves what things have come to when we're spying on our own father?"

"If you say so," I said, watching as he ran over to a half hidden stack of Christmas lights in the clearance section, stragglers the store hadn't shipped back. He grabbed several boxes.

"Look, only a dollar!" His eyes were bright with excitement.

I watched him stack the dusty boxes carefully into the cart. "So, how's the routine coming?"

"Oh. Actually," Olin said, pausing to bite a hangnail, "I decided to take more of a performance art kind of approach. Sort of visual commentary, if you get me. And a new venue, the King James."

The King James was a dive bar in Florence where townies divided their time between sharking quarter pool tables and harassing college students. It didn't seem like a good gig to me. I raised my eyebrows. "Really?"

"Mm-hmm," Olin said, comparing the labels of two champagne bottles. "Which picture do you like better?" he asked.

I stared at him. "I thought the idea was that we'd have the party for Dad and Doreen at your place after we all went to the Improv. Now everyone's going to have to drive an hour from here up to Cleveland."

"Uh, well . . ." Olin hesitated, cradling the champagne bottles.

"What?"

"Well, OK. Here's the thing. Sandy kicked me out. This morning, as a matter of fact," he said, shrugging as if amazed at the coincidence. "So . . . I was going to ask you anyway if I could stay with you for a while," Olin said, smiling hopefully. "You know, 'til I figure things out."

"Figure what out?" I said, a little loudly. Several people nearby looked my way. I ignored them. "What a cliché," I whispered. "You've already done that, remember? You made a bunch of money and you can do anything you want. Right? By the way, big Marilyn's going to have to find other digs."

"But I haven't really said anything, have I?" Olin said, ignoring the doll comment, setting both champagne bottles in the cart and picking out several more. "I've played the responsible kid for a while and truthfully, it's stressful. Besides, that's your department. This is my chance to make a mark, see?"

I shook my head slowly at him. I did not, in fact, see. I didn't understand how he thought I was the responsible one when I had failed at everything I'd ever tried.

Olin's expression turned serious. "Allow me to explain. I've been worried about Dad being alone all these years, and now here you come back and I find out he's getting married. So I feel like I can take some chances now. Besides, Elana says if you want to be free to pursue your art, you have to live the contemplative life and free yourself from the capitalistic machine."

"Elana?"

"I met her the other night—she's a drama student at Case. Very committed."

I was too annoyed to continue the conversation. "I'm going to go get some cheese. Please just try not to break anything."

As I headed toward the deli section, I tried to understand my irritation. Was it because he just assumed he could move in with me—sponge off a sponge? Was it because he seemed to go from one woman to the next without any apparent regret? Maybe it was how, in a more general sense, he could change plans and get kicked out and not worry about it; he just moved along, eternally comfortable, while I agonized over Camembert and Brie.

I was standing there, a cheese wedge in each hand, nearly in tears, when I looked up and saw Watson strolling along wearing a T-shirt and worn khakis, a Nikon on a strap around his neck and a grocery basket dangling from one hand, whistling a little tune to himself. He really hadn't changed—still rail thin, loose-jointed, melancholy but friendly eyes. He recognized me as soon as he saw me. He came toward me, hands shooting out of his pockets and spreading to hug me.

I smiled a stagey smile, a surprised game-show contestant. "Watson!"

We hugged, and he gave me a dry kiss on the cheek. I could smell toothpaste and the soapy warmth of his skin. "My God, Merle, it's been years!" he said. He stepped back. "You look great."

This was hardly true. I hadn't even combed my hair before Olin picked me up; my clothes were wrinkled and sagging, my sweater suddenly itchy and hot. I dug my fingernails into the palm of one hand to steady myself.

"I know you've been overseas . . . where were you again?" He seemed oddly perky, jittery even, one hand shooting through his spiky blond hair, and on that ring finger, a wedding band.

"England," I said. I knew I should say, *Oh, it looks like you've gotten married, congratulations, how nice,* but my throat seemed to be closing, my voice tiny and squeezed.

"That sounds neat." *Neat*—high up in his nose, flat as a field. I knew what was coming next, the question I had to dance around like a stripper's pole. "What were you up to over there?"

I sighed, the air coming out shaky. "Oh, low-end jobs, bad boyfriends, that kind of thing," I said. It was a little surrender, not trying to come up with a good story. Somehow it calmed me.

He laughed politely and shook his head. "You still have that great sense of humor."

My heart, shrunken and hungry, soared at this, even as he began telling me about marrying Ivy and starting the Lotus together to spread the mission of mystical vegetarianism, which existed at the juxtaposition of food and spirituality, and how they felt people in Florence were finally ready for this; there were even yoga classes at the Y now. All of which was to say that he was almost nothing like the boy I knew, who had made love to me once hidden among the heavy folds of the dusty curtain on the wings of our high school stage; we had tiptoed in after school, we had only just started and we were eager, fumbling to fit together, and he had said to me then, voice shivering with his pulse, that there was nothing in this world worth believing in except love and sex, everything else was a sham, our bellies sticking together, hot.

So I said, "I love those bee pollen-infused papaya-blueberry shakes." Watson beamed, and I asked, "What's with the camera?"

"Oh, I'm taking pictures for the Lotus newsletter. The mayor's breaking ground on a new shopping center on the southwest side of town, on known wetlands, very controversial, and I'm doing a story." Watson leaned to kiss me on the cheek again, which surprised me, my heart lurching in my chest. "And I better run. I have to drop this cilantro off for Ivy first."

I figured this was the developer's project my father had been talking about when we'd gone to dinner my first night back, and this meant the guy had gotten the approvals. I thought of the wet-eyed frogs on the environmentalists' wistful signs. I asked Watson to tell Ivy I said hi, which he promised to do, and which gave me a little thrill, the idea of reminding her that no matter what, I'd been with him first. Small of me? Maybe. Watching him walk away, I sank against the cheese display, sorry for myself. Maybe I had hoped that one day Watson and I would meet again and fall in love as adults, not as the jumpy, uncertain kids we had been. I mean, wasn't this supposed to be my dream? Marrying a sweet guy and starting a shabby-chic little restaurant in my cute hometown, where everyone I knew would stop in for herbal tea and a chat? OK, no; it wasn't my dream, but it sounded good, and it would have been nice to have a dream; almost any one would do. Fortuna had gotten it right; I had always lived life at the edges, and I probably always would.

I saw Olin waiting in line at the registers and joined him. He tapped his foot impatiently. "I wish these people would hurry up. I have flyers to make," he said.

I dropped the cheese into the cart. "Why don't you give me one?" I asked.

"Too bad. I said I'm out."

"Well, tell me about it."

Olin started unloading the party supplies onto the rubber rollers at the register. The light outside filtered in warm through the streaked windows, and our frizzy-haired, gum-snapping checkout girl seemed suddenly softened, beautiful. He smiled. "It's about someone you'll recognize. That's all I'm going to tell you."

18

ON APRIL 30, 1970, forty-six members of Students for a Democratic Society took over the Florence College Morris P. Alston education building to protest fascist, racist, hierarchical, Eurocentric, warmongering education. They yelled out a second-floor classroom window that they had taken two professors hostage—Peta Strimple and Langley Tubb, now retired—and that they had a bomb. The students listed several demands, including scrapping the four-point grading system in favor of self-evaluations, starting a counter-culture studies program, and serving vegetarian entrees in the cafeteria. Students milled outside on the carefully landscaped grounds, chanting and smoking pot and harassing the local authorities and ATF bomb squad that President Carruthers had called in.

The bomb, a shoddily made galvanized two-inch pipe deal, blew out all the windows of the second story on the east side of the building and tore chunks out of the walls. Many people outside and several inside were wounded by flying glass and debris, but fortunately none were killed. This was mainly because, although the students inside were tripping on LSD, they still had the forethought to drag the two professors with them as they ran to the other side of the building after lighting the cannon fuse that was stuck through a drilled hole in the pipe's end caps and held in place with chewing gum.

Five students, including one woman named Lilly Franklin whose arm was badly torn up in the blast, were later found guilty of masterminding the bombing plot. She got the longest sentence: fifteen years down in Columbus, released after eleven on parole. The four men got sentences ranging between eighteen months and eight years. To look at their faces in yearbook pictures, enlarged and framed in a solemn row at the campus historical museum, you would never imagine that they had threatened an entire town—the country even; they made the evening news. They look too happy and goofy with their bushy hair and floppy collars or beaded shirts. Their eyes are wide, eyebrows raised, smiles earnest and enthusiastic. Even in the shots where they are led in handcuffs from courtrooms, they look like they're about a year away from a haircut and a job at P&G.

Lilly Franklin was a twenty-two-year-old senior majoring in international politics and a big-time organizer of various clubs, initiatives, and interest groups, including Women Against Vietnamese Extermination, or WAVE; Initiative for a Bilingual America, or IBLA; the Society for Historic Review of Emancipated Women, or SHREW; and of course, the Students for a Democratic Society, or SDS, for which she had the illustrious job of photocopying flyers for the meetings that male leaders called. She had gotten convicted mainly for trying to take too much credit for her involvement, which basically consisted of buying some of the bomb-making materials. Even the guy who tossed the match got out after six years; he had pleaded not guilty due to LSD-induced insanity and later became an advisor to Nancy Reagan's Just Say No drug prevention program in the eighties. Lilly, who was great at project management but less effective in public relations, used her defense stand as a platform to justify the bombing; her apparent lack of remorse didn't play well with the jury, and they made an example of her.

My mother met Lilly in a pottery class that she was taking to try out college after having me. She was only twenty-one then (twenty-two according to her birth certificate), with a two-year-old daughter and a small house to manage. She was perhaps even more beautiful than when my father first saw her, her features more defined with motherhood. Next to her, my father seemed washed out and fast approaching middle age, though he was by then only twenty-seven. He had finished a degree in social work at Florence College and had gotten a job teaching overflow courses. He worked long hours and it seemed to be aging him, stooping his back and dragging down the corners of his eyes.

Tucked away in Guymon, Oklahoma, my mother didn't know that anyone was protesting the growing Vietnam conflict. But in this little college town in Ohio, things were different. Young men and women screamed antiwar rhetoric from bullhorns as my mother crossed campus to her class; they looked at her teased and styled hair and the nylons she wore with knee-length skirts and raised their eyebrows. But by the time her pottery class was almost over and my mother had become friends with Lilly, she had gotten rid of the nylons in favor of flare-legged blue jeans and gauzy Indian-print tunics. Sometimes she pulled the top of her hair back and wove it into a braid, emphasizing her high cheekbones and dark hazel-brown eyes. I learned later just how much she looked to Lilly for ideas of what kind of woman she might shape herself into.

On the day of the bombing, Lilly called my mother from

the professor's lounge phone just before the lines went dead. Her boyfriend, Charlie, had just screamed out the window that they had hostages. "You've gotta get down here, Joanie," Lilly yelled into the phone. "It's happening!"

It was a Friday. Beyond the milling students on campus, cashiers, parents, and factory workers just coming off shift stood on street corners or drove slowly by the police-blocked entrances to the college, talking about what it would take to get the students back in line. Some people said maybe the students needed to see a little real action, like our boys were dealing with every day in 'Nam. Storekeepers on Trade and River Streets cleaned up debris and ordered plate glass for windows broken the night before by bands of drunken students screaming speeches.

My parents had only one car, and my father had taken it to class on the far side of campus. We lived only a few minutes away from the north side of campus, where the Morris P. Alston building, a model of institutional fifties architecture, stood on a hill, so my mother put me into the stroller and started walking. It was my second birthday, and she had organized a party with some neighbors for that afternoon, which was forgotten in the resulting confusion.

Later, when my mother told this story, she always said she was on her way to warn my father of the disturbance, and that Lilly hadn't told her about the bomb, just that they had taken over the education building. But I think my mother was excited by the carnival atmosphere that had taken over the town, students her age dancing barefoot, girls barely dressed in muslin skirts and midriff shirts, boys with beads at their throats. I think she wanted to be part of it; maybe after running away from home at seventeen and having had a baby at nineteen, she was beginning to feel that adulthood had come too soon for her. The broken windows at Fortuna's reminded her that this wasn't just a town fair; it was real, because people were dying in the war, and it was time to do something about it.

My mother never made it to the philosophy and religion building where my father was teaching that day. She was crossing the street, heading for the Morris P. Alston building to see what Lilly was talking about at the precise moment the ATF agents swarmed it, and the blast blew a strong singed wind in her face. She stood still in the middle of Trade Street during the moments of shocked silence afterward. Then she picked me up and started running toward campus, thinking of her husband probably, or perhaps wondering if Lilly was OK. She left the stroller in the middle of the street. It didn't matter; all traffic had stopped anyway. Luckily she had not made it onto the hill; some of the students outside were just realizing they had caught flying glass in their skin. A student named Amelia Flink was blinded. People had started to scream. There were rumors for days that students had gone missing, killed in the blast, but later it was confirmed that fortunately, no one had.

These days, the *Daily Record* still covers the annual candlelit vigil on campus. Some years are better attended than others, and sometimes, usually at five- or ten-year increments, the *Record* includes a photo retrospective. There are the wounded in the hallway, the students' crazy-shocked faces, the kneeling girl clawing at her eyes, the frozen pandemonium. There's Lilly on a stretcher, tubes in her nose, straining to lift her head, as if trying to find someone. There's her boyfriend, Charlie, who caught a piece of metal chair leg in his left ass cheek, staggering out with the help of another shaggy-haired boy. Charlie served only eighteen months in prison; this is the photo he leads with when he scores a paid speech and slide show for college or high school history classes; I know, he spoke to my American Government class when I was a high school junior.

His scarred ass is his claim to fame; I hear he makes a pretty good living from it.

And there's the picture of me taken moments after the blast, mouth open wide, crying as my mother clutches me to her chest outside the building, her hair tangled in my fist, a blurry line of ATF agents' gas-masked faces like Fates in the background. Her mouth is open too, as if in surprise, her eyes narrow and fierce, and her free hand pushes up in the air, palm out and fingers spread, as if she's waving, or trying to signal someone to stop. Our photo never made the national papers, although you can find it in the museum on campus. It was too out of focus, too ambiguous. Was she trying to get Lilly's attention? Was she angry—at the students or the authorities? Was she just trying to make her way across campus to warn my father? This was the part my mother would never talk about, because it was ground zero of my parents' troubles—my father's repeated calls home when he heard the explosion, how he came running out of his classroom, his rage upon seeing the photo of us in the *Daily Record* the next day after my mother had lied about going to campus, maybe because she realized how crazy it was to drag a child anywhere near a place requiring a bomb squad. But she was impulsive, as was my father; they would never have gotten together otherwise, and then of course, I wouldn't be here, still asking questions.

Some say the Kent State shootings the following week could have been avoided if it hadn't been for the bombing of the Morris P. Alston building. Though the anniversary rarely makes the national news, the bombing did more than break a few windows and wound several students (Professor Peta Strimple was also cut badly on her upper left thigh). Some say it killed the student movement, too, that the sixties really ended on that day, and after that nobody thought of much beyond themselves. It forever changed our town, pitting townies and farmers against students, World War II parents against their boomer children. For years afterward, the town went into an unannounced but universally agreed-upon lock-down mode in the days leading up to the twenty-ninth, as if the stores on Trade Street still remembered the busted glass and overturned cars from the student riots the night before the shootings.

It was not a good day for a birthday.

After that, Florence College nearly closed; my dad, a new instructor and the husband of a suspected agitator, was among the first to lose his job for lack of students. My parents had to get an unlisted phone number because of my mother's picture in the paper, and people gave my mother dirty looks for years afterward, whispered "Communist!" and "Spy" behind her back in the post office, the produce section. It flipped a switch in my parents' lives, setting them off on different courses.

After that, my mother started to drink.

19

THERE'S ANOTHER PART of the story, and this is what I got from my mother during the one trip we took alone together. It was June 1979, and she and I flew down to Oklahoma City and drove to Guymon, Oklahoma, all of a sudden, after her father had a heart attack while trying to cut down the only shade tree he had. Practical, he'd started with the skinny lower branches, sawed them off, so that when he took an ax to the trunk, it would fall smooth, easy to cut for firewood. My mother said there had been no tree there when she'd left twelve years earlier. A tender-leafed tree like that was no accident; it had been nurtured once.

It was just about noon when we got there. I saw immediately how the tree in the back, even missing its lower branches, softened the chain-link fence around the patchy yard, the concrete patio slab, the small, low-roofed house. Beyond the fence was the Star-Lite Motel, now closed, on land my grandfather had refused to sell simply because he didn't like the rich developers who were building new houses with manicured yards and pools on former ranch lands. The smell of cows and chlorine mingled in the air. I had never even seen a picture of the Star-Lite; in my mind it had sparkled like its name, no matter how many times my mother had called it a dump. Now, it just looked shrunken—the sagging roof, peeling doors, blank window faces—ready to be folded into the ground.

Before leaving for the hospital, my mother introduced me to my grandmother—a slight woman with wispy white hair and deep-set eyes. She sucked her teeth, regarding me with the directness of a child. My mother had told me to use her given name instead of "Grandma," because her mind was shedding all things recent, her adult years an onion peeled, the shiny pale flesh of her childhood now exposed, fresh, and she was just herself, a girl, Irene.

I spent that first afternoon listening to Irene's stories; she talked constantly, raising her reedy voice to be heard over the TV that I turned on, hoping to distract her for even a few minutes. She pulled yellowed lacy slips from the backs of drawers and offered them to me as school dresses; she brought me a naked plastic baby doll, pink as a shell, and told me she had gone to school with a girl who got ill and shrank to the same size. It's not that I didn't want to talk with her. But hearing her swarming memories, caught like crushed beads on a string, made me stare at the mother-of-pearl clock face as if it could tell me more than the time.

On the plane, my mother told me Irene was so ashamed of her yellow Cherokee skin and angular face that she dusted it with pale powder. My mother said she always had a bottle of pink-white liquid makeup in her purse, might as well have been paint, it was a white woman's makeup, made for women in magazines, but she was not one of them, never would be.

Half-breed, the teachers called her without anger or irony in the schoolhouse. Even in 1979, maybe she'd forgotten she was a grandmother, but I could've said those two words to her and it would've been like firing a gun.

The Oklahoma I saw during that trip was just like my mother's descriptions—endless cattle fields and bright-tipped winter wheat waving under the flat, wide sky. Guymon was a bigger town by then, with a stubble of larger buildings in the downtown and a broad concrete highway replacing the two-lane road to Goodwell. Flying into Oklahoma City, my mother leaned across me to point at the land below, saying *There was nothing here before.*

Ms. Benetia from the kindergarten next door was with Grandma while my mother took me to see my grandfather. I was navigating; the piece of paper with directions to the hospital fluttered under an air-conditioning vent. My knees were chilled and my arms burned under the sunlight coming through the window. "Are you paying attention to where we are?" my mother kept asking me, voice cracking with exhaustion, fingertip stabbing the open map on my legs.

"Yes, we're fine," I said, trying to keep my tone low, patient. Something had shifted between us the moment we pulled into the driveway that morning; she stepped out of the cramped rental car and her posture was not so erect, her footsteps more tentative, not the heavy heel-toe I was used to hearing in the hallway at home. I thought of my mother alone in the house as a girl my age, eleven, shutters closed against the heat, wishing. I punched buttons on the radio, left it on a Spanish station, listened to the rapid speech, the high, tinny music. I felt as if I were on a different planet, everything unfamiliar—the wide sun, the dry air, the yawning horizon. I'd never been on so straight a highway, never seen my mother seem so uncertain.

"He may not know you," she said in the hospital, the green

light shadowing her cheeks. She reached for her purse strap, twisted it around one finger.

I sat with my grandfather for two hours while my mother conferred with doctors, harassed the nurses to check his temperature, bring clean pillows. I thought: You're the man who dragged my father across the hot-stoned parking lot? His body barely disturbed the heavy white sheets. I found his hand in the tangle of tubes and sheets and held it gingerly, felt the tough sun-scored skin stretched over bone. I wanted to ask him what he thought about the daughter he'd chased away coming back to care for him. He woke up and stared at my mother and me with pale green eyes. He fought to swallow. Somehow neither one of us thought to make introductions. My mother asked him what he thought he was doing in the heat of a too-hot day, chopping down a perfectly good tree. He blinked. "I couldn't see past it anymore," he whispered.

I noticed that the second joint of his right ring finger was crooked, just like mine.

One afternoon during that trip, I stood in the center of the Star-Lite parking lot and surveyed the fifteen rooms, five peeling turquoise doors to the left, five in front, and five to the right. Behind me, the wedge-shaped sign with the star over the *i* rattled on its spindly posts at the slightest breeze. To my left was the main office. From a distance the glass was a flat black, a mirror showing my stick legs, my sun-haloed hair. I pressed my face to the glass under a faded NO TRESPASSING sign, and I could see the dark wood of the front desk, the brown carpet, a narrow hallway off to the right.

I was systematic then, starting at the far left, trying each dented knob, counting how many steps it took me to arrive at the next door. The eighth door gave. I pushed it inward and a hot dark poured out. I stepped back, heart pounding. I heard a car turn into the gas station across the street, the scrape of the man's shoes on the broken cement as he walked around the side of his car to pump his gas. The air over the parking lot shimmered.

I turned back to the doorway and let my eyes adjust to the dark. The room was empty, which surprised me; I expected the beds and dressers and television to be there, preserved, but my grandfather had certainly sold the furniture long before. There was the smell of oil and something else, something like sweat. I saw the bathroom door at the back of the room, a dark spot on one wall, a scar, and I wanted to investigate, but I couldn't make myself go inside, imagining the door swinging shut behind me or something rushing from the shadows. I thought of my mother, maybe sitting at the table right then back at the house, leaning on one elbow, soda can hanging from her fingertips, staring out at the backyard where the tree's leaves lifted and settled in midday heat, not knowing she could lose me, and I felt terrified. I pulled the door shut and backed away from it.

Walking on the weedy path back to the house, I thought of my grandfather and the tree he'd tried to cut down. I remembered how my mother had told me he'd slept in the backyard nights when he was so drunk Irene wouldn't let him in. I wondered if one day, after the years of drinking had exhausted him and his daughter had left, and he couldn't look at his wife without hitting her, if an idea had pushed through his confusion, and maybe it was this: I'd like to have a tree, a tree would be nice.

He planted the tree and he liked having it, and after a while he started growing tomatoes, too. Years passed, and sometimes his daughter would call him and tell him how the girl and the boy were, and he sent money for presents because he didn't know what to buy for children, never had known. How did it happen that she came back? It was all her decision, never mind he had nearly killed himself trying to cut down that modest tree, the thought of it outliving him a gall.

At dinner the night before Grandpa came home from the hospital, we celebrated. I pressed a nicked white emergency candle from the silverware drawer into a ball of foil, lit it on the center of the table, helped my mother roll Irene's housedress sleeves. We dished the glistening chicken and gravied potatoes and beans onto plates, and I poured soft drinks into ice-filled glasses.

Grandma ate all of her food, nibbled at wing bones, her own hands like the naked bird wings. "Did he give himself a shave yet?" she wanted to know. "I hate those whiskers. Like an old porcupine." Her voice dipped low and edgy, eyebrows drawn up in silent mirth, tapping the table with one closed fist.

After dinner she napped while my mother and I washed dishes in the kitchen. We tried calling home but there was no answer. My mother bit a hangnail. "You want to get a Sno-Cone, quick, while Grandma's asleep?" she asked me. Her voice had changed; it seemed higher, a girl's voice, and her accent was lilting and broad like Irene's. She seemed to be turning into someone else, and I felt I needed to stay close to her, in case she changed beyond my recognition.

We walked to the corner, past the day-care center, the empty motel, the closed palm-reading shop. The Star-Lite sign drowsed in afternoon light. I felt like we were sneaking out, like my friend Tanya and I did one time when we were spending the night at her house, our bare feet wet with dew, the quiet yards and dark streets suddenly ours in a way they could never be during the day. We could see the house behind the motel, not fifty yards away, and I imagined my grandmother sleeping there, her breath stirring shadows.

We ordered our Sno-Cones at the Freezy Ice and sat at a concrete picnic table outside. Low clouds inched toward the train tracks to the west; a cooler wind bowed tall grass in the empty lot beside us.

My mother sighed. "I know this isn't easy," she said. Her mouth was stained red, shiny, her face freshly washed and hair pulled back, so she looked girlish.

"It's OK," I said. A week earlier we were fighting over whether I would be allowed to have boyfriends when I started middle school, and she had said there was no way. "When I was your age I thought boys were everything. I thought I'd need a man to save me, and I got married too young," she'd said.

"But it worked out, didn't it?" I'd said, defiant.

My mother bit her lip before answering. "Yes," she'd said. "Some things did."

We tipped our cardboard wrappers to catch the last of the cool, sweet juice, and I was thinking about that: *Some things did.* I took a deep breath. I was eleven years old, still stick thin and child-faced, but I wanted so much to be a woman. I could feel myself changing, the buds of my breasts hard under my nipples; I wanted to talk to my mother as an adult. "Do you ever wish things had been different?" I asked.

My mother looked at me over the rim of her wrapper, munching flakes of ice. "Like what?" A breeze coming from the direction of the clouds lifted wisps of her hair; the air smelled like water and freshly cut grass.

I leaned forward, tapped the plain gold wedding band on my mother's slim finger, so loose I could turn it with a touch. "What do you think things will be like ten years from now?" I asked. I'd heard Phil Donohue ask a guest that question, and it made me feel powerful, authoritative, to repeat it.

My mother looked up over my head, eyebrows raised as if she'd heard a sound she couldn't place. "I don't know," she said, eyes flicking to me and then away again. "I don't know," she said, and a thought got edges for me like a camera lens focusing: Life isn't decided and then lived; my mother didn't know her future, not even the basics, and this is the way I imagine her almost always now, uncertain, tracing the concrete table edge as if it could deliver direction. I took a deep breath and asked what I'd wanted to know all along.

"Do you ever think about leaving?" The question like a hammer hitting the soft indenture under the knee, the body moving without thought: reflex. I forced myself to meet her narrow-eyed gaze.

"I already left," she said. She meant from there—the Star-Lite, her father's rages, her mother's confused stories.

"No. I mean now."

"Don't be ridiculous," she said, flattening the cardboard ice wrapper and rolling it into what looked like a cigarette.

"I don't believe you," I said, shivering now in the warm, humid air from the act of speaking this directly, hearing myself as if it were someone else's voice. I could see my mother's jaw tightening, her eyes hard and angry; I wondered if she were going to slap me. We'd just been through another round in the papers, nine years since the bombing happened, my mother's and my picture once again in the *Daily Record* with all the others, the mention that she had been questioned about what she knew of the plans. My father had been on the phone to the editor, asking in his quiet voice tight-focused with anger, why they had to do this year after year, couldn't they leave his family out of it? But then he used the same voice when he spoke to my mother, and on the simplest things—like asking if he needed to pick Olin up after T-ball practice—his frustration blistering everything he said to her, and the drinking that smoothed the silences stretching through every evening, the way Olin, seven years old then, went in confusion from her to our father, wanting a connection he couldn't put words to.

"What do you want?" she asked me then. She leaned forward. "You're the reason I stay. You and Olin. Is that what you want me to say?"

I was too shocked to answer her. But then there was a thin, rising squall like a warning call from one of the stray cats I'd seen prowling the empty field behind the house, except at the top of its rise there was a coughing, crying sound, like a child, and we both realized the sound was coming from the house. We started running at the same time. I was faster; throwing open the front door, I found my grandmother in the middle of the living room, blanket clutched in both hands, one foot bare, sock trailing on the end of the other foot, face red. She kept screaming even when she saw me, then my mother, running in the front door.

My mother took her shaking hands. "Are you hurt?" she gasped, circling my grandmother, trying to find evidence of injury.

"Leaving me here all by myself," my grandmother breathed, eyes wide, chest heaving. And then I wondered if, as much as I wanted to be an adult, my grandmother wanted to be a child. It wasn't just the senility, it was something she had cultivated, maybe for her whole life, and that maybe it was that forced fragility, that trapped animal fear, that made her daughter run.

"It's OK," my mother said, standing behind Irene, stroking her shoulders, talking softly in her ear. "Nobody's left you."

"I was all alone," she said, tears following the deep lines of her cheeks, mouth quivering.

"OK, OK," my mother said. She walked Irene back to the bedroom again. "Run water for a bath. Lukewarm," she told me, and I was grateful to have something to do, to shake off the accusation in my grandmother's stare. Later, I held her wet, naked body, her arms trembling around my neck, as my mother gently dried and lotioned her skin. We dressed Grandma in cotton pajamas, dried her hair, put her to bed like a child.

After that I was exhausted, but my mother seemed calm,

rejuvenated. I found her in the kitchen, zipping her purse. "Be right back," she said, not looking at me, screen door slapping.

I don't know when she came back. I didn't see her again until the next morning, when, just as gray edged the blinds, I woke up stifled and hot in spite of the window unit blowing chilled air in my face. My mother was curled next to me, snoring, her breath alcohol sweet. I eased out of bed, pulled a blanket from the closet, and headed for the living room couch, so as not to wake her. I was almost asleep again when something, a breath against my face, woke me up. Grandma leaning over me. "Sugar?" she said.

"Grandma?" I said, catching myself too late. But she smiled, maybe she hadn't forgotten who we were to each other. Then she moved away from me, hugged her housecoat around herself. "It's gonna be cold out there," she said. "But those cows'll pop if we don't get to the barn, lickety-split."

I sat up on one elbow, my heart beating hard. I didn't know what I was scared of. But there she was, tugging on my arm, her hand light and cool like the glossy side of a feather.

"Come on, or I'll tickle you awake," she said, and then she started dancing, a little circular shuffle. She clapped her hands. Bare feet slapped on the floor in the next room, and I knew my mother was awake. She opened the bedroom door but Grandma didn't break her rhythm except to flip open a shade. Her cotton housedress swirled around her hips and ankles like a ball gown; she held her hands out to me, palms up for a moment, but I couldn't move. My mother and I stood on either side of her, nightgown hems lifting with the breeze of her footsteps. In two years I'd be the only one of us still alive. Grandma's smile was young and in the gray light her hair shone over her shoulders like a girl's. Call it a dream, a vision, I don't care. I know what I saw.

20

I KEPT THE APPLICATION I'd picked up at the Department of Social Services for a week before deciding to apply for the clerical position in client intake. It was a couple of days before Olin's gig at the King James; our father's wedding was that weekend. Olin and I still hadn't met Doreen, if you didn't count the few moments we'd seen her in her barge of a Cadillac, sailing down River Street. We couldn't even agree on what she looked like—Olin remembered her as platinum blond and heavyset; I thought she was dirty blond and lean. We didn't know what to expect; when we talked about it we caught ourselves whispering like two detectives comparing notes.

I was out of money and I needed a job, but I chose the DSS instead of some other square building with beige-walled offices because at the DSS I could imagine my father two floors up; in my mind he was floating there in his tiny office, with its narrow, crowded bookshelves and dusty window overlooking the parking lot, near enough to hear me if for some reason I decided to shout.

Marge Delinsky, DSS veteran, began our interview with an

overview of the importance of a professional persona when dealing with clients. I was wearing crumpled purple velvet pants and a red sweater, neither of which were in season; in my rush to pack, I hadn't coordinated things very well. Marge glanced from my clothes to my file and back again.

"So, you're Merle Winslow," she said in a contemplative tone as I sat across from her in an office not unlike my father's—cramped desk, low ceilings, except this room was windowless, the air hot and yellowish. "Hmm, senior editor for leading British publishing firm," Marge mused, resting her shelf of a bust on the edge of the desk as she scanned my application, eyebrows wiggling together, then apart, together, apart, like a pair of wrestling squirrels. She seemed to fill the room, straining the confines of her magenta suit, her thick fingers lightly cradling my file.

"Yes," I said quickly, wanting to avoid further questions. "That's me. My, uh, father—"

"I know your father, Miss Winslow," Marge boomed. "I hope you don't think that your celebrity status in Florence history or your connection to one of the Department executives will influence your treatment here in any way."

I raised my eyebrows, trying not to smile at the term "celebrity" applied to me and "executive" applied to my distracted, soft-spoken father. "Of course not. I just—"

"Fine, then," she said, setting my file on top of a precisely stacked tower of other manila file folders. "I assume you possess basic office organizational skills."

"That's about all I possess," I said with a laugh.

Marge Delinsky gazed back at me over her ornately gold-framed glasses in a way that could almost be called flirty except for the determined set of her jaw, the decidedly humorless expression in her eyes. She shoved the stack of folders across the desk to me. "Then let's see what you can do."

I stood, took the folders, which were heavier than I expected, and turned toward the door.

"One more thing, Miss Winslow."

I looked back and waited, trying to smile.

"Unmarried women of a certain age here often find themselves taken with the tragic yet occasionally romantic stories of our clients. I myself of course never have, but I've heard about it. If I had a nickel for every former millionaire who lost everything in the war or whatever and now lived on the generosity of the state, well, I wouldn't be here watching over you. You follow?"

"Certainly," I said.

"I'll keep an eye out for you. We girls have to stick together," Marge said, and then she allowed herself a small, pursed-lip smile. I smiled back, hugged my folders to my chest, and spent the afternoon in front of the squeaky black filing cabinets, alphabetizing people's tragedies.

Walking back to my apartment, I saw Frank coming out of the ACME Sparkle. At first I wasn't sure how I knew him; for one heart-rattling moment I thought he was some forgotten high school classmate who would remind me of how ridiculous I'd looked back then or point out how much older—and still ridiculous—I looked now. He cradled a bag of groceries in one arm and a newspaper pinched in his fingertips, which he tried to read as he walked, the breeze folding it over every few steps so that he had to stop and shake it out again. He was slightly ahead of me on the other side of the street, and I slowed down to stay behind him as he crossed to my side of the street, still reading. He was about ten feet ahead of me. I didn't know why I wanted to hide from him. When he stopped and shook out his paper again, I stopped too, but he noticed me. "So, do you normally follow people without saying hello?" he said, turning then, looking straight at me.

I flinched, startled, my face heating. "I'm not. You were ahead of me."

Frank raised his eyebrows, smiled. "It's OK, don't be embarrassed." He walked over to me, newspaper flapping like a trapped bird, grocery bag crackling. "How's Lettie?" he asked.

"Fine," I said, still irritated at his comment. "How's your plane?"

"She's a little cranky these days."

"Sounds like Lettie," I said, and he laughed.

"You definitely have her sense of humor," he said. And, apparently sensing that I wasn't sure how to read this, he said, "That's a compliment."

I shaded my eyes with one hand. "You hang out with my grandmother a lot?"

"When my plane needs work. She feeds me." This was odd; I'd never known Lettie to be much of a cook, but then, maybe she liked the company. The thought of her being lonely hadn't really occurred to me, and I felt guilty then, for all the time I'd been away. At the same time, I was happy to know that she had someone like Frank checking up on her, even if he had almost flown into her house. Compared to Terence, who couldn't take care of a cactus, it didn't seem so bad. I wondered what they talked about, if she had told him anything about our family, about me. The thought made me squirm. I also wondered what she knew about Frank, although there was no way I'd ask her. I'd never hear the end of it. "Well, I guess I'll see you around, maybe at Lettie's around mealtimes," I said. I started walking.

"So, where are you going?" Frank asked. I stopped, thinking he'd want to catch up with me, but he didn't seem to be in any hurry. "You want to get a cup of coffee sometime?"

I thought for a moment. "I'll be at the King James tomorrow night. My brother's got some kind of gig. In fact, the whole family will be there," I said. And thought, *What's left of us.*

"Lettie, too?"

"No, she's claustrophobic. Hates crowds." Maybe it was too much information, but I figured it would be a good start for him—my brother's performance-art debut, my father's mystery fiancée—whatever he was going to be to me; he could see it all for himself and decide.

21

FRIDAY NIGHT I met Olin at the King James an hour before he was scheduled to go onstage. Ernest's wedding was the next day; my birthday was the day after that. I had just started in client intake at the DSS. Olin had moved his few possessions out of storage and into my apartment—a futon, a dented chrome coffee table, a table and chairs—and suddenly the place seemed cramped. We planned to decorate the next day for the wedding reception.

The King James was just down the hill on Trade from the Iron, Florence's other college bar, though this one, possibly by virtue of being just a couple of blocks farther from campus, usually had more townies, leaning on the bar or menacing college kids at the quarter pool tables, just like this evening. It was early and the place was quiet except for the thrumping hum of the refrigerator behind the bar and the hollow click of billiard balls on the tables in the back. The decor was medieval meets Midwest gone wrong—plaster of paris gargoyle molds evilly animated with flickering neon beer signs, pointy Gothic rest room doors that featured a bishop and a nun, and since both wore long robes, newcomers often got confused, giving the townies at the bar a good show year after year. Windowpanes were painted purple, red, yellow, and blue for stained glass, and the floor was spray-painted in different shades of gray to simulate, I guess, a flagstone floor. Drafts: fifty cents and served in a cup like you get at the dentist when he hands you mouthwash and tells you to swish. It had been a long time since I'd been in here, and I hated to think how many hours I had given to the place.

Olin appeared from behind a dusty velvet curtain that hung from what looked like a shower rod suspended from the ceiling in front of the small stage near the front door, which was built apparently as an afterthought, because the three-foot-tall platform did not take into account the ceiling height, and Olin's head nearly brushed the cobwebbed ceiling—the cobwebs an inadvertent but authentic detail. I didn't remember the stage from my years as a regular, but then there were probably a great many things I didn't remember about the place, and it was just as well. Olin was wearing a black turtleneck and black pants; he didn't see me right away because he seemed to be measuring the width of the stage in paces, watching his feet and counting carefully. Behind him were two sets of black metal shelves, barely visible against the black walls. He looked back toward the area behind the tattered curtain, chewing a hangnail, eyes narrowed in thought. Fridays were usually reserved for karaoke, and the machine, monitor, and microphone sat on the edge of the stage. A hand-scrawled OUT OF ORDER sign was taped to the machine.

"Could you move that?" Olin asked the manager, who stood by, eyeing Olin suspiciously.

"The karaoke machine stays," the old man grumbled. The story on the owners was that they had opened the bar in the sixties after defecting from the former Soviet Union. The wife was famous in Florence for shining a high-powered flashlight in students' faces when they came to the door. The flashlight would go from the face to the ID, the face to the ID; it was like an Iron Curtain checkpoint. They'd never bothered to keep the place in good repair, but they'd managed to stay open for thirty years with rude bartenders and watered beer.

"Psst—Olin!" I hissed. The old man glared at me, faded into the shadows.

Olin hopped down from the stage and gave me a woolly hug. "Merle, so glad you're here. I want you to meet Elana. Elana!" He turned and shaded his eyes under the red and purple gels trained on the stage.

A serious-faced, petite woman emerged from behind the curtain, also in black turtleneck and pants, which accentuated her pale skin and large, heavily kohled eyes. She float-walked to the edge of the stage, where she assumed an attitude of patient waiting, eyes turned upward.

"Oh, sorry," Olin said, after we both waited with her for a moment, wondering if she would say something, like hello, for example. Olin went to the stage and helped her step down from the edge, where she landed in a kind of *plié*. She took his arm and walked with him duck-footed to where I stood.

"*Namastay,*" she breathed, bowing, palms together under the notch in her collarbone. I recognized her greeting from crashing Fiona's yoga classes.

I looked at her, then Olin, who shrugged, smiling benevolently. "Pleased to meet you," I said, trying to keep a straight face. "So, you're performing together?"

"Oh, no, no, no," Elana whispered with an indulgent smile. "I'm Olin's coach."

"And muse," Olin said, winking at me.

"And muse," Elana acknowledged, closing her eyes in

mock embarrassment. Olin gazed devotedly down at her hen-
naed hair.

OK, I thought. I'm game. "So, how did you meet?"

Elana looked at Olin, batting her eyes. He squeezed her
thin, pointy shoulders. "I was doing open mike at a poetry
slam up on the west side as a warm-up for the Improv—very
big names, a huge crowd—and I tried a little of the routine I
was working on—"

"And it was positively awful," Elana said.

"But she came up to me and—"

"Yes, I approached him and I told him he had true presence—"

"That means talent—"

"—But comedy just wasn't right for him. Especially at a
poetry slam," Elana said, with a giggle that suggested anyone
would know what she meant. "The truth is, your brother is
not a comic figure at all. He's dark. He's got this, this tension;
I'm sure you can see what I mean." She grabbed Olin's jaw
and lifted it, and as Olin tilted his head back I thought for a
moment she was going to show me his teeth.

"I see," I said, biting my bottom lip to keep from laughing.
But I was also worried for him, how he would be received.

"Come on," Elana said to Olin. "We have to begin our
breathing and vocal exercises. Remember, the body instrument!"

"Wait a second," I said, grabbing his arm. "He'll be right
with you."

Elana edged toward the stage, but waited there, tapping
one black-booted foot.

I turned to Olin. "Listen, are you sure you want to do
this?"

"Of course I do!" he said. "Do you have any idea how hard
I've worked to prepare? I mean, the set design alone took all day."

"You know how those townies are—they'll eat you alive!" I said. "Not to mention the pissy little college students buying beer with their laundry change."

"Merle, Merle," Olin said, smiling gently at me. "I've got to do this. Don't you see? She's all excited about it. I'm her repentant tycoon, her accidental capitalist. She's converted me to a higher purpose! OK, maybe it's silly, but I'm crazy about her."

"Olin!" Elana called from the stage.

"Wish me luck!" Olin said to me before turning and leaping onto the stage. He bent to lift Elana up with him, and she drew the curtain behind them.

22

I WENT TO THE BAR, bought two fifty-cent drafts, and, pinching the plastic cups between thumb and forefinger, found a wobbly table just as my father walked in. He opened the heavy, squeaking door and held it, but in the moment before he stepped out of the way, I saw a jumpy glow behind him, like sparklers burning just out of view. Then I saw her, the woman Olin and I had glimpsed in passing only a couple of weeks ago as she coasted by in the shiny Cadillac, throwing her head back and laughing as if she'd never known anyone funnier than my reserved father, owner of more brown ties than perhaps any other living man, who could go through an entire evening without so much as clearing his throat. She touched my father's arm as she stepped by him and through the door, smiling this time, too—what was so damn funny about the man?—the hand then patting the back of her teased and swirled and highlighted hair, smoothing its saucerlike shape. She was tiny-waisted and big-hipped and quite short— the highest peaks of her hair reached only to my father's shoulder—and she wore a silver sequined bustier with a black pantsuit and dangly sparkling earrings. So this was Doreen, my father's soon-to-be wife.

I was standing up to wave, clearing my throat to call out to them over the jukebox, which was playing Pink Floyd, and then I saw something that made me sit down hard in my seat. There were two Doreens—or at least another woman who looked like an exact copy of the first.

I threw back one of my beers and reached for the other one, grateful that I had thought to buy two as I watched my father help the first and then the second Doreen off with her jacket. He slung each over his arm and then scanned the bar, looking for Olin or me. I put my hands on the table and shakily pressed myself to my feet. I managed a weak wave until my father saw me. He smiled—that same broad smile that had made him flush from his neck to the tips of his ears when he told me of the wedding in the driveway just a few evenings ago—and waved back as he made his way to the table followed by the two smiling Doreens.

"Doreen, this is my daughter, Merle," he said to one of them. I was completely mixed up—I didn't know if she was the first one I had seen or the second. We shook hands, and I scanned her face and clothing for some detail that would distinguish her from the other Doreen, but there was nothing. Not one difference that I could find. I felt as if I had fallen into one of those puzzle books you could buy at newsstands where you had to circle the differences between two apparently identical pictures, like of a playground or a beach scene, except this was a dive bar with two middle-aged women dressed for a game show, their breasts jiggling in their itchy-looking sequined cups like four bowls of vanilla pudding. Then I noticed that Doreen sported a beauty mark just under one collarbone and I sighed with relief. I heard my father introducing me to Barbara and managed a smile, shaking hands with her.

"Let me get us one more chair," I said, taking one from the next table. We all sat, my father to my left and Doreen and Barbara next to him, wiggling to settle themselves like hens over eggs.

"I'll get us some drinks," my father said, and when he left us alone I decided I needed to be the one asking the questions. I was just opening my mouth, not really sure what my opener would be—the British, "I gather you're from abroad?" or the American, "So what do you do?" or the midwestern failsafe, "Nice weather we're having, isn't it?" But Doreen beat me to it.

"Well, I figure we should save each other some time, so I just want to say first of all that I certainly don't think that I can replace your mother," Doreen said, folding her hands on the table with a light click of her inch-long fuchsia polyurethane nails, which made me think of Chet, my former employer.

Barbara glanced at her and then at me, then reached across the table to pat my hand. "We both had a stepmother, too, and it turned out fine. In fact, I never would have made it into show business if it hadn't been for her—you ever heard of Priscilla Cashing, the great Broadway singer?"

Doreen cleared her throat. "More about you later, hmm? Now, things you probably want to know. I met your father while selling office supplies on commission and he very kindly offered to buy out my stock of sticky notes so I could make my quota for the day. We went to lunch, then to dinner, and then—well, we got along beautifully. Barbara and I have both been married twice, first to twin brothers who both had heart defects, then to business partners in Vegas who went out for pierogis and cigarettes—"

"Actually, to clarify, Doreen's husband went out for cigarettes, and mine went out for pierogis," Barbara said. "But separately and at the very same time that night, as it turns out."

"Not that it matters now. But Barbara has always taken care of me, even when I was left with practically nothing. She's smarter, good with money—the practical one, as you can probably tell."

I searched Doreen's face and found not the slightest hint of irony. I nodded and tossed back my other beer. "Do you mind if I smoke?"

"Not at all," they both said, at the same time, with the same flip of the wrist.

I lit up and drew deep and decided I didn't need to know more—about why they dressed the same, how they ended up in a small town in Ohio after the mysterious, simultaneous deaths of both their husbands, even whether they ever got confused in their pairings during the first marriages. I wondered if they realized there was just one of my father; he didn't have a brother or even a cousin that we knew about. What were they going to do?

My father came back with two glasses of cloudy white wine and two beers, one of which he handed to me, and I smiled gratefully at him.

He sat down, eyed my cigarette, decided not to say anything. "So, do you know what all this is about?" he asked me, gesturing to the stage.

I shook my head. "Nope. I have no idea!" Olin of course had told me nothing. There had been hints—he'd said it would be about someone I recognized, which was scary to think about, and he'd said it would be edgy and personal and probably the first performance of its kind in Florence. None of this was comforting.

Just then, I saw Frank come in, submit to the flashlight scrutiny. As he passed on the way to the bar, I ducked behind Barbara's hair. I was actually happy he had shown up, but I had changed my mind and decided he'd experienced enough of my family in Lettie. If he saw me as he passed again from the bar and found a table on the other side of the room, he didn't act like it.

23

ELANA CLIMBED ONTO THE EDGE of the stage, holding the curtain back with one hand. She brought the microphone to her lips and breathed in it until the room quieted except for the jukebox near the bar. "Could we cut the Pink Floyd, please?" she murmured.

The owner trudged to the jukebox and yanked the cord. "Hey!" someone yelled. "I paid for that!"

Elana smiled beatifically. "You are about to experience an art happening. The artist is Olin Winslow, a truly original and sensitive soul who, until this night, has lived completely hidden within the body of a businessman skilled in the cutthroat machinations of the money-driven world. We have titled the world premiere of this first, controversial work 'Marilyn Sings for Her Dinner,'" she whispered into the microphone.

Someone whistled low; there were a few giggles. "May your eyes and your minds be opened," Elana finished. She hopped off the stage, reached for the curtain, and, pausing for a moment, clutching the cloth, she dragged it aside, then ran to the back of the bar and took up her position at a slide projector near the pool tables.

On the stage, there were floating naked Marilyn Monroe thermometers—fifty, maybe sixty or more of them levitating at different altitudes above the stage, hanging from fishing line. They swayed slightly in the drafty, beery air, dozens of peroxide blond vinyl heads, wide red mouths, and busty, cocked-hip bodies, their digital read-outs glinting, thermometer tips jutting a few inches below their pink-toenailed feet like the jet streams of small spaceships. There was also a tall figure at the back of the stage draped in a black cloth; this I took to be Olin's life-sized Marilyn. I lit another cigarette and looked around; the place was completely silent except for the bar cooler's rattling motor and, next to me, the crackle of my father's thin plastic beer cup that he suddenly seemed to be clutching too tightly. My brother strode onto the stage, now wearing a black fedora in addition to his all-black costume, his face expressionless in concentration like a diver approaching the edge of the high board. He wove through the smiling Marilyns, a silver safety lighter in each outstretched hand. He paused, facing the audience for a moment with a cool gaze. Then, ceremoniously, he clicked both lighters on and held them under thermometer tips of the nearest two Marilyns. After a second or two they began singing, in unison, "Happy birthday, Mr. President, happy birthday, Mr. President," while he moved the safety lighters to the next two Marilyns, and then the next two, until there was a sort of ongoing, warbling round. Someone in the audience snorted; my brother continued to spark newcomers into the breathy chorus. A few people got up and went to the bar for refills. Olin, perhaps sensing that his audience's attention was fading, chose this moment to roll the life-sized Marilyn forward, and with a dramatic snap, he tore off the black covering.

Marilyn's hair flopped in front of her eyes; she seemed to smile just a little wider, her eyelids just a little heavier in front of the audience. She was naked except for Monopoly money Olin had taped to her breasts and crotch—gold $500 bills on top, blue fifties and green twenties below. He nodded to Elana; the slide projector clicked on. A side of uncooked beef appeared, a little fuzzy and off-center, on Marilyn's belly. Elana corrected the focus and positioning, and several people erupted into laughter. Olin kept the other Marilyns singing as more meat images appeared on Marilyn's belly—a rack of lamb, a pork chop, a sirloin steak. Probably thirty or so Marilyns were singing by now, and a few people at the tables in front of the stage were either singing along or laughing uncontrollably, holding their heads, leaning forward over their knees like schoolkids in a fire drill, their shoulders shaking. From the corner of my eye, I saw the owner stalking to the stage. "What is this?" he demanded.

Olin ignored him. The meat image series ended with a pair of dollar signs, which gradually faded away along with the "Happy Birthday" chorus. Olin stepped in front of the Marilyn, opened his arms, and prepared to speak.

"Hey!" the owner yelled, grabbing for Olin's pant leg. Olin stepped back, eluding him, and backed into the full-sized Marilyn. He whirled around to save her from falling, giving her what amounted to a splay-legged hug—which launched a round of whoops from the audience—and then, righting her, he turned back to the owner.

"Let me just finish, OK?" he stage-whispered.

The owner glared up at Olin but shuffled a few steps stage right, shaking his head. Olin stepped forward again, arms outstretched. He looked at Elana as if for assurance, and I looked back and saw her nodding encouragingly. I was aware that my fists and stomach were clenched; I couldn't imagine what would happen next. My father seemed equally nervous; Doreen and Barbara gazed at the stage with respectful attention, chins upturned, eyelids batting in unison every few seconds.

"Marilyn Monroe is the modern cave painting, the image of what we want—to own, to consume—the prize in our capitalistic hunt of life. We can undress her, buy her, make her sing for our dinner, and still she is only an entrance to eternity, to the unknown, the—"

"Throw me a doll!" someone yelled.

Clutching his lighters tightly, Olin continued, Elana mouthing the words along with him. "—the universe of our constant yearning. We created Marilyn, we carved her and cooked her for our feast of eternal gluttony—"

A nearly full beer flew past Olin's head, splattering against the back wall, and that was when he cracked. He grabbed the nearest floating Marilyn, yanked it off its string, and winged it in the direction the beer had come. Another beer glanced off his shoulder, splattering and beading on his turtleneck. He yanked two Marilyns this time and fired them into the audience, peroxide-blond heads over heat-sensitive toes. People were on their feet now, some shrieking as in-flight beers splattered them, others laughing hysterically.

"Get off the stage!" the owner screamed. "Get off!"

Olin ducked another beer and dragged the curtain closed as the audience continued to shriek with laughter. Several started crawling onto the stage, and the owner batted at them with a broom. He shook his fist at them. "For this I crawled on my belly for two days through the mud and ice?" he screamed, waving his arms in the air. I could barely hear him over the growing commotion. "I build a salon! For intellectuals to come and discuss art and philosophy and politics and religion, but no! I get millworkers and children of the bourgeoisie drinking pisswater!" He spat. "Damn this country! Damn you all!" He threw his apron on the floor like a baseball player slinging his glove and stomped out the front door, broom in hand like a rifle. His wife tried to stop him but he slapped her clawing hands away. Through the open front door I saw her chasing after him, her high-powered flashlight a winking star streaking, then disappearing on the wet street. Several kids, obviously underage, poked their heads in and then, seeing the coast was clear, folded themselves joyfully into the crowd.

By this time, everyone was on their feet. Someone pulled the curtain back. Olin and the life-sized Marilyn were gone. The remaining dolls were quickly plucked. I motioned for my father and Doreen and Barbara to follow me through the press of yelling college students. I thought I recognized the waitress from the Lotus, her nose ring flashing as she jumped up and down, screaming at a guy on the stage to throw her a doll like a groupie begging guitarists for picks. Someone was climbing the curtain. I looked around for Frank but couldn't see him. I decided I had to find Olin, to make sure he was OK. Someone plugged in the jukebox and Pink Floyd came on again, way too loud, even for a bar, making the crowd roar in surprise. It was impossible to hear individual voices anymore. I turned around to scream at my father to lead Doreen and Barbara the rest of the way out but I had lost them somehow. There was only a shoving wall of students and townies—flannel and baseball hats, cardigan sets and tattoos, paisley nylon blouses and brushed forward crew cuts, a weird mix of times, like no one could decide collectively which decade we were in. I threw myself into it, heading toward the back because I remembered there was a door and I wondered if Elana had gotten out that way. I saw her slide projector on the floor and yelled for Olin, knowing I couldn't be heard, couldn't even really hear myself. I opened the door and looked behind me for Olin and Elana and the life-sized Marilyn Monroe, any of them, but I couldn't see anything, and then someone grabbed me and dragged me out into the alley behind the bar.

It was dark and I screamed, hitting at where I thought a face might be, and the wet air smelled yeasty from empty beer bottles and something sharp, like motor oil. "Hey! Hey! It's me," Frank said.

I fell against him in relief, my face against his shoulder. He slid his arms under mine, half holding me up. "It's OK. You're OK," he said, the line of his jaw against my cheek. I turned into it, reaching for him, and then we were kissing, his face wet, kissing my throat, his hands on my ribs, the small of my back, pulling me into him, and I pressed my hands flat against his shoulder blades, held on.

He kissed my forehead. "You got lost in there," he said. His breath was still high in his throat. The streetlight shadowed his cheekbones and jaw. He smiled at me, and I pressed my lips together into what I hoped looked like a smile. "I was looking for Olin," I said, standing up straighter, trying to catch my breath.

"He's fine," Frank said. He led me out of the alley and around the corner toward the front of the building. We stumbled, blinking and deaf, onto the rain-slicked street. At the front door of the King James, a fire brigade of students had formed, passing plastic cups of pale, flat beer down the line to anyone who happened to be walking by.

I saw my father, Doreen, and Barbara near the corner. Doreen and Barbara were shimmying into their matching jackets and shivering. My father stood with his hands in his pockets, looking around nervously, and I knew that if it hadn't been for all the people around, I would've heard him jingling his change. I took Frank's hand and led him over to them.

"I haven't seen anything like that since Vegas," Doreen said, giving us a sparkly smile.

"It was odd," I agreed, looking back toward the students milling around the entrance. I was still shaky, dazed from the escape and the kiss. Everyone was looking at me, as if waiting for something, and I realized that people needed to be introduced. "Dad, Doreen, Barbara, this is Frank—" I looked up at Frank, realizing I didn't remember his last name.

"Bryson," he added, shaking hands all around.

"My, I love a man with a strong grip," Barbara purred. "What do you do for a living?"

"He delivers horse—" I started, but Frank cut me off.

"I'm a pilot," he said.

Everyone shook hands, smiling awkwardly. "I hope Olin's all right," I said, embarrassed.

My father's glasses were cloudy in the wet air. He pulled them off and looked at me, eyes rain-gray and irritated. "You put him up to this?"

I rolled my eyes. "Yes, Dad. I came home and said, 'Hey, Olin, here's a thought: Why not do performance art in dive bars?'"

Doreen took my father's arm, sidled closer to him. "Come on, it was fun, wasn't it? Everyone's excited. But then again, what does fun mean to a man who says brown is his favorite color?"

My father closed his eyes and laughed silently at this, his glasses still dangling from his hand, his head tilted back as if he might swoon into her arms at any moment. Watching this, I felt a little light-headed myself, because right then I knew Doreen understood him; she knew his singular self, and that was why he loved her, a love that was free of fear or secrets, as light as laughing gas, a silly flu.

"Olin's fine," Frank said. I felt his voice in my chest; I was still ringing with what had happened. "I helped him carry Marilyn out to his car. He said he'd meet us at the Iron after he takes her home."

"It's a doll," I said. *"It."*

Frank grinned at me. "He said *her.*"

"Let's just walk," I said. "It's not far."

Doreen shook her head. "I'm driving. I'm not leaving the Caddy around these kids."

"I'll go with you," my father said. He winked at me, in good humor again.

Barbara and Frank and I watched them walk away.

"Ah, isn't it nice when people find love later in life?" Barbara said as we walked up the hill toward downtown, Barbara and I on either side of Frank. To our left, the older campus buildings—Science, Music, Philosophy—receded behind black glossy ivy under the misty half-moonlight; the reproduction iron lampposts on Trade Street glowed, gilded under their amber globes. They were installed after I'd left, and now the tree-lined street seemed candlelit, a leafy-ceilinged room.

"Did you know those two are getting married tomorrow?" Barbara asked Frank.

"Really?" Frank said. "That's great."

"Yeah, she always liked older men," Barbara said. "Me, I prefer them young. How old are you, Frank?"

"Thirty-eight," Frank said.

Aside from being surprised that Barbara was making a play for Frank, I was also surprised he was only in his thirties. Even though nothing about him looked particularly older—his coarse brown hair was still thick and only the beginnings of a belly peeked over the belt of his jeans, but somehow the way his features fit together, the crooked nose, deep-set eyes, thin upper lip, could have put him at almost any age.

Barbara sighed. "Are you married, Frank?"

I heard our shoes scraping gravel on the sidewalk edge. "Nope," Frank finally said.

"Well, you still have time. Thirty-eight's young for a bachelor," Barbara said, deliberately not looking at me, the dots of her earrings winking. I said nothing. Frank didn't either—he was trying to pretend the conversation wasn't happening. I was thinking about time, how you could live in several layers of it at once, how as a child I had walked on this street with Tanya and figured out you could use lipstick as a blusher if you had to, then as a college student trying to reinvent myself among kids from other towns who didn't know me and couldn't even remember the Morris P. Alston building bombing. I thought of how my mother had walked this street maybe imagining years in her future that she wouldn't actually experience, and now, what would I call now? I was asking myself this when I felt something warm and dry brush my hand. I caught a distinct scent of heated metal and realized Frank was sliding his fingers in between mine.

24

THE SUMMER OF 1981, a woman moved in next door. Our neighbors the Spritzes had divorced, moved out, put the house up for rent, and, it was said, agreed to split the profits. It sounded like something out of a soap opera—foreign, exotic. Florence was a small town, and the only other divorce I had heard of in my thirteen years was between my friend Tanya's parents.

My mother considered any house on our street within her hospitality air space and usually brought a well-intentioned but overcooked casserole or pound cake to new neighbors. But she didn't even mention going over to see the woman next door, and neither did my father. It joined a list of things my parents weren't discussing that summer, along with why my mother's work as events coordinator for the Florence Ballroom Dance Society was taking up so many of her evenings, and why, since spring, my brother and I had often found my father asleep on the couch in the morning before school.

It was early June, but already so hot the pavement never

really got cool at night, the bare patches in our yard jaggedly lined like Lettie's china. "Crazed," my mother called it, and that was exactly how I felt. I slept later and later. Olin was away for two weeks at Camp Bear Trail learning useful things such as how to make hollowed-out canoes and start fires with human hair. Often I woke in the middle of the night to check on our father and found him there on the couch, sleeping in his clothes, a blanket over his knees, one arm tucked under his head as a pillow. After the woman next door moved in, he slept on the couch every night for a week.

I saw her the first time through our kitchen window, which looked into her backyard. There was no fence, just a few bushes and a couple of maples, and then the slope of land down toward four houses facing the next street. She was sitting in a lawn chair drinking a beer, smoking a cigarette, and talking to her cat. I could see her lips moving slowly, her eyes cast downward and half-closed, as if talking in her sleep. I opened the back door and followed the hedge as close to her yard as I could without being seen. Now I could hear her and just barely see her through the dark lace of the bushes. "It's been a long time since we sat outside together," she said to the cat as it arched its neck and back under her hand. "So now we can start over."

She was small-boned, pale-skinned, and dark-haired, slightly heavy around the hips. She was in her thirties, maybe, my mother's age. And beautiful in a way that made my chest ache with a want I couldn't describe.

I snuck back to the house. I wasn't doing anything important enough to tell anyone, even a cat, and I knew it. My project that day had been to pack away my stuffed animals. I'd had it with dolls now that I sprayed clouds of my mother's White Shoulders perfume and walked through them, listening to 45s in the afternoons, dancing slowly in front of my mirror and pretending I was Olivia Newton-John. The summer stretched ahead like a flat, hot piece of metal. I wanted something more.

Later that day I met my friend Tanya at Finch's Drug on Trade Street. Tanya thought she was Diane in John Cougar Mellencamp's song "Jack and Diane." She wore tight jeans, white T-shirts, and black boots, even in the summer. I mean, she was obsessed. Except her Jack weighed less than she did and was into Dungeons & Dragons. We stood around on corners and watched high school and college kids drive by, free as birds. All we bought at Finch's were candy bars and Bonnie Bell lip gloss because our mothers wouldn't let us wear makeup. It was a make-believe time; we had pimples and flat chests but we pretended things weren't so bad.

"I saw our new neighbor smoking and drinking a beer," I informed Tanya as we strolled down River Street, sharing a bag of potato chips and a grape Super Slush. I was wearing a fabulous new hot pink and lime green terry cloth halter top and shorts ensemble, which she didn't appear to notice.

"So?"

It had seemed so important somehow. I had never told Tanya about the single scotch and soda my parents drank every night that lasted until my mother walked slowly down the hall, hand on the wall, to bed, and my father fell asleep on the couch. I knew even then that other people didn't drink like my parents did. One way I covered for them was to be shocked at any kind of drinking, as if it were something I had never seen. "So, it was right in the middle of the day."

"Well, what if a man did that?" Tanya was really into women's lib, and I was too, although neither of us understood it very well. We'd seen ERA marches on TV, we'd seen old pictures of women burning their bras, and we wanted to join in, though we were late to the cause and could hardly find bras small enough to fit us. We didn't know whether to kiss men or kick them; at thirteen, there seemed to be no in-between. We'd cut out an article called "Catch His Eye, Catch Him" from one of her mother's *Cosmo*s that said to attract a man you had to put yourself in his field of vision as much as possible, looking beautiful, of course. "It's not necessary to speak," the article advised. "Only to be seen."

"Well, what if you did that?" I asked.

"Duh, that's different."

"Whatever." Still, I wanted to know what my neighbor meant when I spied on her in the backyard, talking to her cat about putting the past behind her. I wondered what she thought about when she leaned her head back and let the smoke escape from her mouth, as if it were too much trouble to blow it. Back then, I was jealous of problems like hers, the ones I imagined she had—a baby out of wedlock? A divorce like the Spritzes? It was hard to guess.

My main problem was that I wanted to skip eighth grade, so I wouldn't have to finish my last year at Cleaver Middle School, where the fat Hatcher twins harassed me constantly for being tall. "What, you stretch yourself at night?" they screamed in the cafeteria.

But my parents, when I could get their attention long enough to talk about it, were against me skipping. Issues around my brother's and my upkeep seemed to be the only topics they could safely discuss without quick arguments—a couple of snapped sentences followed by long silences. "What's your rush?" my father kept asking. "You'll be glad you waited," my mother said, which is what she said about every-thing. They agreed on this so much they almost shouted.

Tanya and I headed first to Jack's house, Tanya's fantasy boyfriend. In reality he ran whenever he saw her, because their conversations consisted of her making fun of his skinny arms and legs, and often she tackled him to emphasize this point. His bedroom filled the entire basement of his house. In the middle of the room was a huge bulletin board where he plotted his next moves in Dungeons & Dragons. We crouched on either side of a dirt-sprinkled basement window and watched. We heard his voice through the glass, "Once again, I've anticipated your simple-minded maneuverings, peasant!" he shrilled.

"He's talking to himself!" I whispered, giggling.

"He's just really into it," Tanya said, defending him. She wanted him to be someone else so much. When we fantasized about what we would do on dates, she talked about taking long hikes to the top of a mountain and having a picnic from an old-fashioned wicker basket. But Jack didn't even like to go outside, and his arms were blue-white all year round. Tanya and I were good friends; we'd memorized the entire *Grease* album together, but I never knew what she saw in him.

The next evening my mother had a meeting with the Florence Ballroom Dance Society events planning committee and she wasn't in the mood to talk. She always had projects, charting her biorhythms or learning how to macramé; I think there was a businesswoman in her somewhere, curled and dreaming. On dance nights she ate fast and changed into heels and a circular skirt that swayed from her hips like a bell. She wore extra eye shadow and sprayed perfume in her hair.

My father didn't like to dance and had refused to join the club. If he'd thought this would discourage her from continuing, he was wrong. Nights when she was gone, he stood on the back patio and stared into the trees. He drank more than usual; when I came out to join him, he put his arm around me and swayed side-to-side. He'd heel-toe with one foot and say, "Do you think this would impress her?"

I wanted to know who she was practicing the cha-cha and fox-trot with, but I also knew this wasn't a good question to ask. She came home sweaty and flush-faced after dance nights, and if she came to my room to kiss me good night, her damp skin smelled like overripe fruit. All I knew was that something had changed between my parents; an agreement had been reached. But it was an unsteady peace, a pile of slick black dance records in the middle of the room that trembled with every step.

The next weekend I had just finished packing away my Winnie the Pooh collection, the Barbie summer house, the talking baby dolls, when I heard a knock on the back door. My mother was at the grocery store; my dad was napping in the living room. I'd stuffed everything into two boxes, scrawled CHILDHOOD TOYS on the sides with a fat marker, and slammed the boxes on the floor so hard my picture frames rattled, hoping my father would hear and come in to ask me what was wrong. My mother and I had just had another discussion about grade skipping and it hadn't gone in my favor.

The knock was so soft I stood up and listened for a moment, thinking it might be just a breeze thumping the screen door. But then I heard it again, and this time I was sure.

The woman from next door stood on the chipped gray paint of our cement back steps holding an unlit cigarette. She was short and slightly overweight, but her wrists and ankles were delicate, making her seem smaller. Her shoulder-length brown hair was straight on top, and the bottom half hung in frizzy waves from a bad perm. She was barefoot and wore cut-off jeans and a white tank top. She didn't have on a bra; I could see her nipples, a faint shadow, through the fabric. One hand was tucked in her back pocket; I wondered for a moment if she were hiding something. "You got any matches?" she asked, squinting up at me.

For some reason her question shocked me. "You shouldn't

be smoking," I said and immediately felt prissy in my Keds, cuffed shorts, and Izod.

She cocked her head and smiled. "Your mom smokes."

"What? No she doesn't."

"Yeah, she does. Listen, your mom and me—" Then she stopped, as if realizing a mistake.

We stared at each other. Her nasal O's and bad grammar rang in my ears. I thought she looked familiar, but I wasn't sure.

She smiled, touched the rim of her glasses. "Oh, it's probably my mistake. I thought I saw her out there in the garden one night. So, you got any matches?"

I held the door open for her. "I don't know, maybe in the drawer," I said, leading her into the kitchen. I found a half-used book of matches from Pizza Hut in the junk drawer right away but pretended to still be looking. I thought they were only used for the candles on our table at dinner, but now I imagined my mother standing in the garden, the hose spilling silvery water in the dark, the mushroom smell of earth rising around her and mingling with blue smoke ribbons in the muggy night air. "I'm Merle," I said, keeping my back to her.

"Lilly," she said.

I turned around, matches in hand. "Are you from around here?"

"No. Not really."

I handed her the matches. When she reached for them, I noticed a web of white lines in varying thicknesses, scars snaking from her left wrist to her shoulder. The pinkie finger on that hand was gone, the small stub delicate and exposed, like something private. On the other fingers there was pale lavender nail polish that had mostly chipped away, and again I felt a tenderness for her like a pressure in my chest. "Hey," I said. "Would you like to see my room?"

"Sure," she said, smiling again, the same slanted, surprised tug of her lips as she gave me on the back steps, telling me my mother smoked.

"This way," I said, leading her down the hallway. I thought my room was pretty adult with the double canopy bed in dark wood and the matching dresser and desk and chair with a typewriter on it, even though we didn't have to type papers in eighth grade. I was getting ready for when I skipped to high school, for when I finally wore my parents down and got my way.

"Old toys?" she said, looking at the boxes. She was standing in the doorway.

I wanted her to come and sit down on my bed and listen to my records, an eclectic collection—Lionel Richie, the Beatles, John Cougar Mellencamp, Pink Floyd, Squeeze, the Cars. I wanted to offer her an ashtray. "Oh," I said, "That's just stuff I'm getting rid of." And suddenly my scrawled label seemed petulant, whiny.

"Can I see?"

"Sure," I said. I tried to think of an appropriate record to play while she pulled open a cardboard box flap. She pulled out my Belinda doll with green eyes, a pink bow mouth, straight red hair, a barrel chest, and pudgy arms and legs. In between her pink lips was a round hole for a bottle that appeared to drain when you tipped it, which I had lost.

"I had a doll like this," she said. "You getting rid of it?"

"Yeah. I don't need that stuff anymore."

"Oh." She held it in front of her and then cradled it. "My gram said you should always hold a doll baby like a real baby. Otherwise it's bad luck."

"Really?" I thought of all the times I'd dragged the doll around by her hair.

"Yeah."

"That's wild," I said, trying to sound grown-up. "You can have it if you want."

Her eyes flicked to me and then to the doll. They were hazel green, with a dark rim around the edges like a shadow. "Well, I got to go before . . . well, anyway, thanks." She was walking toward me now, and I knew she was ready to leave, and I couldn't think of anything else to keep her, so I let her pass.

I followed her down the hallway and to the back door. "Could I visit you sometime?"

She turned back to me, still cradling my Belinda doll. "Sure. Anytime. Thanks again." The half-smile again and then she was on the other side of the bushes, gone.

I went to the kitchen window and watched her walk back to her house. She stopped to light the cigarette, and that made me think of my mother again, this new secret. There were a lot of larger questions I couldn't answer right then—why my father was sleeping on the couch, why the Florence Ballroom Dance Society took up so much of my mother's time, why my parents seemed to step around each other carefully, as if sudden movements might touch off an explosion—so when it came to the details, I wanted to know.

I walked down the hall to check on my father, who was still snoring on the living room couch with the paper on his chest, Stan Getz's sax whispering on the stereo. Then I went to my parents' bedroom and kneeled in front of my mother's dresser, slid each drawer slowly open and groped to the back. On the bottom drawer, plastic wrapping crackled under my fingers. I pulled out the pack, shook out one, then two cigarettes, put it back and patted the socks and cotton nightgowns into place. I held on to the open drawer for balance and thought of Lilly— what had she said? *Your mom and me.* And why were my parents pretending she didn't exist? In the sunlight streaming through the open shutters, tiny floating dust particles gleamed like gold flecks. I blew them away from me in a wave. Certain details were coming into focus—the long strips of chewing gum packs my mother bought each week at Finch's, the evenings she decided to water the garden after it was already dark, my father pretending to be already asleep when she came home— but nothing fit together yet.

I walked on invisible spike heels past my father, who was snuggling a throw pillow on the couch, shut my bedroom door, and sat on the bed. I imagined leaning against a cracked brick wall, wearing a leather jacket and smoking a cigarette, ignoring Tom Melba, the guy I was currently in love with, as he walked by. I fake inhaled and blew. "What are you looking at?" I asked the quiet air. Actually, Tom was another reason I wanted to skip eighth grade, because he was a year ahead of me and would be at the high school in the fall. I had gone to see Mr. Percy, the school psychologist, a fat, balding man with a shiny face and watery eyes, because I was so in love with Tom that I was getting stomachaches every morning. When Mr. Percy asked me what was wrong I told him I thought I was going crazy. "You're not crazy," he whispered, looking like he might start crying too. He didn't seem convinced.

I bit my lip. Was I crazy? I was pretty sure of it that past May, but only seeing Tom once a week at church had cooled me down a bit. I would see him next at a church barbeque coming up the following weekend, a fund-raiser for a new wing for the youth center. My father had found an architect who had recently moved to Cleveland, an old college friend of his from back in Oklahoma, and he had offered to design the wing and oversee the construction for free. Everyone at church was excited about it. I imagined offering to introduce Tom to him, his eyes widening with instant respect. "Tom Melba," I would say, "This is Hall McLendon."

25

WE FOUND OLIN in a booth in the Iron, head in his
hands. He'd changed into a gray T-shirt and Indians baseball
cap, bill forward, unusual these days, and even the Indian
laughed sadly on his forehead. He was alone.

I sat down across from him and patted his arm. Frank was
getting beers and Barbara had gone to discover the wonders of
the rest room. "Olin," I said. "Don't feel bad. You were terrific.
I mean you made an . . . interesting point and you entertained
people—"

I heard a groan from under the bill of the cap. "Oh, that's
not it," he said.

"What, then?"

"Elana's pissed and I lost every single one of those
Marilyns. I mean, I had no idea what I was up against!
Marketing's so easy. You just offer a free sirloin coupon on the
packaging and, boom, you make a sale!"

Barbara sat down next to Olin in the booth. "I actually saw

some promise," she said, tucking a highlighted strand of hair behind her ear.

"Really?" Olin breathed.

"Absolutely. Some real range, pathos even." She patted his cheek. "Maybe I could coach you a little, help you with projection and things?" She was almost baby-talking him—I couldn't believe it.

"I don't know," Olin said, shoulders sagging.

Frank brought a pitcher and four glasses and sat down next to me. He poured Olin a glass and set it next to Olin's almost empty whiskey glass. "I think you did great. You took a risk, and most people never do."

Olin glanced at Frank, drained his whiskey. "Yeah. Thanks for the help."

Barbara clicked the ends of her nails on the wounded table and scootched a little closer to Olin to regain his attention. "Listen, I'm serious about the coaching. I've got connections around here."

"Oh, yeah?" I said. "What kind of connections?"

"Oh, producers, soundmen, you know. I was a screamer for a long time."

Frank cleared his throat and took a long drink of beer. Olin and I looked at each other as if to say, you wanna take this or me? Olin shook his head.

Frank bit first. "Screamer?"

"You know, for the movies? *The Man with the Bronze Face, Doctor Dringle Doubled, Naked Spacemen* ring a bell? I was in big demand in the late seventies. Anyway, I can make some calls if you're interested. I think you could go places with your comedy act."

"Art happening."

"Whatever," Barbara said, and then she did something to Olin under the table that made him sit up very straight.

"I'm going to go look for Dad and Doreen," Olin said, squeezing past Barbara.

"Oh, I'll go with you, honey," Barbara said, checking her lipstick in her compact mirror. She pursed her lips, smiled, and clicked the compact closed. "See you two later," she said.

Frank and I watched as Olin, closely followed by Barbara, faded through low-lying clouds of cigarette smoke before disappearing through the doors. We sipped our beers without saying anything for a while. I watched the groups of college students huddled in the other booths, clustered around the jukebox, waiting at the rickety bar for Angel to get around to them. It was hard to believe I had once felt part of this. "Come on, drink up," Frank said. He stood up.

"Wait! We can't leave Olin with that nutty . . . I mean, with Aunt Barbara."

Frank smiled at me and held out a hand. "He'll be fine. Let me take you home." I took it, tucking my fingers into its dry, folding warmth.

A few minutes later, we were sitting on the stoop in front of my apartment, sipping the last two beers of Olin's microbrewery sampler—Frank with Blackened Voodoo from North Carolina and me with a Raspberry Blonde Wheat from California. I couldn't read Harold's sign for the day; it was already lying in the grass, slapped down by the woman across the quad.

"So, thanks for rescuing Olin. And me," I said.

"No problem. He's got a funny thing about that doll, doesn't he?"

"It's not a doll. It's a life-sized replica of Marilyn Monroe. It's a collector's item. The Cleveland Hard Rock Cafe offered him five thousand dollars for it."

Frank chuckled. "You're a good sister." He tapped out a

rhythm with his feet, blew over the top of his bottle. "So he told me you took off all of a sudden. Why's that?"

I took a deep breath. "I had a list of reasons at the time. But really, I think I just needed a change of scene." And this: Because I thought leaving would make me something other than what I was.

Frank leaned his forehead toward mine, and for a moment I thought we were going to touch foreheads, but then he tilted his face up again and kissed me, dry lips against mine, rough skin of his fingertips light against my neck. We kissed slow and calm, deliberate this time, and I drank in the eroticism of the straight kiss—no leather, no toys, no dirty talk, maybe just a little tongue.

I rested my head in the curve of his neck, thinking right then of buying warm bread, reading the newspaper—thinking I could do these things with this man, so relaxed, but then my foot slipped off the step, knocking over my beer. It clinked down the steps, rolled onto the grass. We both watched the spilled beer fizz and bubble, sinking into the concrete.

I heard a door opening down the row and looked over Frank's shoulder. It was Harold, peeking around his open front door. "I thought I heard something out here," he said. "You kids smooching?"

"Yep," Frank said.

"Well, break it up or go to bed. You're too old for pussy-footin' around." He slammed the door, and something inside clattered to the floor.

"What a sweet old bastard," Frank said.

"That's Harold. Wonder if Lettie'd like him," I said.

"Hard to say . . . these things are tough to predict," Frank said.

We let this thought float in the humid darkness. I didn't

want him to leave, but I didn't want to invite him in. A feather-light breeze moved over us, and I sat very still.

After a while, Frank stood up, pulled me to my feet. "I gotta go," he said. "Early delivery in the morning. The horses are raring to go."

"Who buys the stuff?"

"Horse breeders who like Nelson."

"Nelson."

"The quarter horse who won a few races in the nineties and lives well at the Sugar Bush Farms. He eats and gets whacked off all the time. How's that for a schedule?"

It sounded like one of the straggler books in the X Publishing list and the thought made me grimace. Frank laughed, probably thinking I was just grossed out at the general idea of it, which I was.

"How'd you get into this work anyway?"

Frank was standing on the step below me so we were almost the same height, resting his hands on my hips. "It was my father's plane, his hobby. Flew it on weekends and scared my mother to death, then one morning a few years ago he had a heart attack in the kitchen and that was that."

"I'm sorry."

Frank shook his head as if to say it was OK. "My mother, if you asked her, would have preferred more time with him. But you've got to admit that it's better to go like that, making coffee with your wife, than sticking around suffering."

I nodded and thought of Joanie in her car that night, how she hadn't been alone and how maybe in some way I could be glad for it.

"Anyway, here's to happy endings," Frank said, kissing me on the forehead. I watched him walk away, hands in his pockets, shoulders forward in a sleepy slouch, and I stood there for a while after he'd gone, wondering if he'd just asked to die with me.

Inside, I decided to write back to Fiona. I picked up a package of Silk Cuts she'd sent, pulled out one cigarette, and popped it in my mouth, looking around for a blank sheet of paper. I could smell the tobacco and, still, the slightest hint of talcum powder. I went through both of my duffel bags until my hand hit the cool spiral of my mother's sketchbook. I flipped through her pencils and watercolors—a self-portrait of her gazing down at the viewer from shadowed eyes, a drawing of the Star-Lite Motel on the edge of a glassy lake, a study of reds and purples like the inside of a lightning-fired cloud. And the page she used to practice the night she altered her birth certificate and decided to become a different person. After that, the pages were blank; as far as I know, she never tried to draw or paint again after those classes she took as a young girl in west Oklahoma, trying to record the world as she saw it or wanted to.

Also, of course, I had her birth certificate, which my father gave me when I finally confronted him with everything I knew about my mother, her secret life a bloom of smudged ink on the scraped parchment. I kept the certificate in a plastic sheet protector, tucked between the sketchbook pages. The crinkly paper with its tiny, italic type seemed too small, thinly official; it was hard to believe it marked the beginning of my mother's life.

I found a clean sheet of notebook paper and headed for the living room, where I settled into Olin's sagging couch, cigarette still unlit in my mouth, bitter all of a sudden. I pulled it out and stared at it, rolling the thin paper between my fingers. It seemed pointless to smoke it, really, when you consider a cigarette doesn't give you much of a buzz. And it seemed a holdover from a previous life that to my relief was already drawing away from me, faster than I had expected or hoped. I dropped the cigarette into one of the empty beer bottles I'd brought in from the stoop and tossed the rest of the pack into the trash. "Dear Fiona," I wrote:

> OK, I am at this moment deciding to quit smoking, at least until morning. I just kissed this pilot who flies an unreliable plane and I'm not practicing my breathing, I'll admit it. Did you know there are people who pay—a lot—for horse sperm? Sorry if I'm jumping around here. My brother just got into performance art and frankly it's gotten me a little scattered. Also, he's moved in with me. Listen, I hope Terence is OK. Tell him I'm really sorry, if you don't mind. Tell him I'll try to write.

I looked up at Marilyn, her cocktail waitress smile a frozen sexual offering, and decided to save her for another letter. I chewed my pen, and my thoughts wandered to the party the next night and whether we should stand the coffee table on its end to accommodate more people in the room. I thought about Terence—I really did want him to be OK—and I wondered whether Olin had gotten rid of Barbara and made up with Elana. I wondered if my father was curled around Doreen the way I used to find him with my mother before he started sleeping on the couch and practicing dance steps by himself on the back patio under the moonlight while my mother fell in love with Hall McLendon.

I folded the letter up, once, twice, three times. The fifth fold got harder. I'd read somewhere that you couldn't fold any piece of paper more than seven times, no matter how big it was. I had never tested this rule extensively, but it held true in this instance. It was physics, simple and unavoidable; there were limits to things, to how many atoms could fit in a space and whether the bustling quarks would allow you to put another crease in a sheet of paper or love someone in spite of yourself or come home without regret or know things that you would never completely understand no matter how much you went over the facts: those were just the rules.

I leaned back, dropped the letter on the floor, balanced Frank's empty beer bottle between my breasts, and breathed deep, thinking of it.

26

BY THE SUMMER OF 1981, it had been years since people had called my mother a "commie" or a "pinko spy" in the grocery store, or whispered loudly behind her back while she waited in line at the bank. As children, Olin and I had simply ignored it as she did, following her lead, standing straight-backed and silent. We knew it hurt her, how she wanted to explain that she'd had nothing to do with it; it was just chance. One time a woman walked straight up to her in the fabric store—it was always women who did these things; I grew up wondering why we sent men to war when women were far more cruel—and she asked how my mother could stay in this country after what she had done. I was with her that time, and I stepped in front of her and said this: "Get away from my mother." The woman backed away from me like I was a coiled snake, and that is one of the proudest moments of my life, still. I remember my mother's hand squeezing my shoulder, thanking me. Later, I heard her crying quietly in her bedroom.

Eleven years after the bombing, no one seemed to remember anymore. It was as if getting over the ten-year hump was all we needed. The Morris P. Alston building had long since been repaired; there were already students enrolled who didn't even remember seeing the event on television. People had moved away, moved in from other towns. Trade Street had been widened to accommodate the increased traffic.

Other people may have lost interest, but at age thirteen, my interest had just begun to grow. There was Lilly, our new next-door neighbor who knew things about my mother. There was my father, sleeping on the couch, pretending not to wait up for my mother the nights she stayed out late at the Florence Ballroom Dance Society events. I was certain there was more to the story. I'd already searched through my parents' bedroom—every drawer, closet shelf, and attic box, looking for letters, photos, the kinds of things Nancy Drew would find—and found nothing. I had decided Lilly was my only hope.

I slipped out of my bedroom window one night in slow motion, so as not to rustle the bushes, and tiptoed to Lilly's house. I had to step quietly, because her windows were open. I saw a lamp and a couch and a blue TV flicker in the living room and not much else. The walls were white, freshly painted over Mrs. Spritz's faux paneling.

I made my way around the back of the house to the bedroom window. The long grass tickled my ankles; wet heat seemed to radiate from the ground. I had to stand on tiptoes to see in because the fall of land behind the house made the windows in back higher up. Balancing on my sneaker toes, I could see Lilly stretched out on a twin bed next to a fan, which sat on two cardboard boxes. The overhead light was on, harsh and yellow. She was reading a book. She wore shorts and a man's undershirt, and every few minutes she sprayed herself with a water bottle. Her belly showed, pale and soft between the band of her shorts and the hem of the T-shirt. My Belinda doll sat near her head on the pillow. I wondered why she'd rented a whole house when she had almost nothing to put in it.

She placed the book on her chest, closed her eyes, and rubbed her left arm, the one that was lined with jagged white scars that seemed to flash in the light, and that's when I recognized her. I had seen her in the newspaper photographs over the years—Lilly being carried out on a stretcher, her hair a dark cloud around her head, her arm already wrapped. She'd shown up not far from me and my mother in photo retrospectives years later. She was Lilly Franklin, one of the bombers of the Morris P. Alston building, and she had hardly a stick of furniture because she'd been in prison since 1971.

I took a step back from the window to catch my breath and saw Lilly's head jerk up from the pillow. She'd heard me. She jumped up and moved silently out of the room, hitting the light on her way through the door. The room went black and I froze, trying to figure out which way to go in order to avoid her in case she came out to investigate. I decided to sneak around the other side of the house from where I'd come, but Lilly met me, rounding the corner with a baseball bat clutched in her good hand.

"Hey!" she said.

I held up my arms and she stopped. "It's me, Merle."

"What the hell are you doing?" Lilly demanded. She was barefoot. She let the bat drop so that it was sticking out from her hand like a sword.

"I just—I just—" I stuttered.

"What? Tell me." Her voice was low, threatening. I could see in her anger a fear that must have come from her years in prison, always standing guard.

I took a deep breath. "I know who you are."

Lilly twirled the baseball bat and regarded me suspiciously. "Yeah?"

"You're Lilly Franklin, right?"

"Who told you that?"

"I just put it together," I said. I gestured to her arm and she pressed it against her ribs reflexively.

"You must be very proud of yourself."

I stuffed my hands into my shorts pockets. "Can I come in?"

Lilly sighed and turned around, and I followed her. She let me in the kitchen door. "You want something to drink?" She opened the refrigerator. I could see several bottles of beer, a hunk of cheese, and a leftover pizza.

I nodded, wondering if she might offer me a beer, which I half-wanted her to do, even though I knew I didn't like beer from stealing sips from my father when he wasn't looking. Instead she reached in the back and pulled out a pitcher. "All I have is water for you. But it's cold." She poured it into two jelly jars and handed one to me.

"Thanks," I said. We sat in the living room, Lilly on the couch, me cross-legged on the floor. The cat came in from the bedroom and settled himself at Lilly's feet.

"So," she said. "What do you want to know?"

I was taking a sip of the water, and it was so cold it hurt my teeth. I coughed, cleared my throat. "Uh, well." I tried to think. I had dozens, maybe hundreds of questions, but they were so crowded in my head at that moment that it was hard to think of just one. "Why'd you come back here?"

"Well, my folks live in Shaker Heights and they wanted me to come home, you know, move in for a while until I could get a job, get back on my feet. But I know how it was for them after—after it happened. My aunt told me. They lost all their friends. No one would talk to them. They don't need that all over again, people peeking in their windows and stealing their mail." She stopped and sipped her water, and I thought she was finished, but then she tapped her glass and shook her head. "So I came back here because your mom told me about this place." She looked at me then, a level gaze, because she knew she was telling me that she and my mother had kept in touch somehow. I couldn't believe it—I thought of the searches I'd done of the house and how I'd found nothing.

"How?" I asked.

"We wrote letters every once in a while. Well, a lot at first. But then only once every few years or so. Christmas cards, that kind of thing. She wrote to me when you were born, and then when Olin came. To let me know. A lot of times she didn't write me back. But she did find this place for me, because she understood why I wanted to come here. I guess I needed to live in this town again, since this is where I left off. So when I got out, I cleaned out my bedroom and picked up Che, and now I'm here." Lilly settled the cat in her lap and stroked him.

"What's his name again?" I asked.

"Che. As in Che Guevara."

I was drawing a blank. I shook my head.

"The Cuban revolutionary?"

"Oh."

"What are they teaching you in school these days, anyway?"

I shrugged. I still couldn't believe that Lilly and my mother had kept in touch all those years, however tenuously. "You were right, by the way," I said. "About the smoking."

"Sorry. I shouldn't have said anything."

"It's no big deal. I don't know why she wants to hide it." I took a deep breath. "She drinks all the time." I kept my eyes on my legs, traced a finger from freckle to freckle. Lilly was the first person I had ever told straight out. Just like that. I didn't know then that other people had noticed, that it was just something no one talked about.

Lilly stood up. "Would you like some more?" she asked, pointing at my jar. I nodded and she refilled it in the kitchen, came back, and sat down across from me again. "Listen, you need to know something. About the bombing."

"What?" I could hear the kitchen faucet dripping, the cat purring, the fan whispering in the bedroom, frogs outside croaking like someone calling from far away.

"Your mother didn't plan it, you know? She knew a little because she hung around my apartment—you, too, in bunting and lace, and we'd get together, sometimes just a few of us, but sometimes there'd be maybe twenty of us crowded in the room, and she'd stay in the kitchen, holding you, pretending not to listen. We talked about what we wanted to do to stop the war. And when it started to get heated, when we got into details, I invited her in. There were five of us—she could have been six, no one would have suspected her, and maybe we could've gotten what we wanted. But she said no. She said, 'I've got a baby, I can't get involved.' I didn't let her come back after that. But sometimes I'd see her stroll by with you—I was angry at her for being weak, that's the way I saw it then—but I was in love with her, too. She was so beautiful. I didn't want to let her go. I felt like a child next to her. But did she know what was going to happen and when—that it was really going to blow? No, I don't think so."

Lilly sat back then, as if she'd practiced this speech in her head for all those years and had completed a mission in delivering it.

I stared at her, wanting her to go on, but she was holding on to her glass of water tightly, looking at her lap. I felt dazed from it, the image of my mother cradling me, wanting to be a mother and a girl again, free, wanting both, but choosing. I tried to fit it in with the woman she was now, remote, full of secrets. "So, do you . . . why don't you talk anymore?"

Lilly smiled. "What would we say? She wanted to help me, but you have to understand, that bomb blew a hole in both of them." She finished her water, tapped the glass. "When I was in prison, I used to imagine I could float up through the ceiling, and I could see the whole earth underneath me. Sometimes I'd imagine being in my parents' house, watching them getting ready for bed. Sometimes I'd pretend I was right here, watching your mother with you and your brother, reading you stories. I still miss her." She bit her lip, as if realizing she'd said too much. She stood up, motioned me toward the door. "You should go, you know. It's late."

She walked me to the door, and I asked her if I could come over again. Lilly pinched the bridge of her nose between a thumb and forefinger, her scarred arm tucked shyly behind her. "Just be smart about it, Merle. I don't want to cause trouble for you."

Sneaking back into my bedroom that night, I didn't know how I would fall asleep. But I did, almost immediately. I dreamed I skimmed starlight from the surface of dark water and spread it on my skin, which lifted me from the ground, until I could see streetlights and campfires and fireworks flickering all over the globe, and I felt the cool pressure of space on the top of my head, sliding between my fingers as I swam upward, thinking it was just a little farther to see what I wanted to see, but I never got there. I woke up frustrated, sheets tangled in my legs and fists, my conversation with Lilly a heaviness in my ribs.

A couple of weeks later my mother confronted me about the cigarettes I'd stolen from her dresser. She cornered me in my room, sniffing the air, right before we left for the church barbeque. "It smells like smoke in here," she said.

"Oh, I was lighting these," I said, holding up the Pizza Hut matchbook in my other hand. "I like the smell."

My mother considered this. She lifted her chin like a deer

listening for wolves and walked the perimeter of my room, running her fingers over furniture, glancing from spot to spot. "And why," she said, perching on the edge of the bed, "are you suddenly into the smell of matches?"

"Why?" I repeated. My palms were getting cool and damp.

My mother surveyed the room again and looked at me. "Enlighten me." She could be very sharp during the day, before she had that first drink.

"OK," I said. I took a deep breath. "I found your cigarettes."

My mother's expression didn't change. "You were snooping," she prompted.

"Well, actually I—well, yes, I was. I'm sorry."

"And did you smoke any of them?"

"No," I said, shaking my head, "I promise."

"And you know you will never . . ." My mother waved her hand as if directing traffic forward.

"I will never smoke," I said.

The hand waved for more words, but I dug in. "You know, maybe you shouldn't be keeping secrets," I said.

"Like what?" my mother demanded, her eyes narrowed, challenging me. I couldn't meet her eyes; I stared at the floor, defeated. She held out a hand for the matchbook, which I gave to her. "I would like you to consider how we are supposed to treat you as an adult when you pull stuff like this." Her voice even, bell-like with reason. She never explained the secret smoking, and in fact I never caught her at it. I still don't know why she needed to hide it; maybe it wasn't so much the habit itself, but a need for something hidden. Some people kept diaries, and she had once kept a sketchbook, but maybe at that point, already in love with Hall McLendon and feeling trapped, maybe dreaming of escape, the cigarettes marked minutes that were hers alone.

"I'm sorry," I said. I kept a solemn expression but I knew something had shifted between us. I had caught her at something; I'd seen further into her life than she'd expected, and we both knew it.

My mother stood up. If she were excited or nervous to see her lover, she didn't show it. She looked at me from the doorway, hand on a cocked hip. "Get your stuff and let's go."

Of course, I didn't know Hall McLendon was my mother's lover at the barbeque. Maybe what was happening between them was just starting then. My father introduced me to Hall, and when I think about that evening, the one evening I saw them together, I can't remember any tension between them. Did my father know? Had he decided it was something he could live with?

The tables for the barbeque had been moved inside because of forecasted rain. There were tents over the grills. Thunder rolled outside; a storm had been moving at the edges of the sky for hours, and you could feel it more than hear it, like getting close to the ocean.

We were in the undercroft, a beige-carpeted room with high windows and a draft. People milled around, spreading paper tablecloths and putting out stacks of cups. Kids played chase, their screams echoing in the large room, excited by the humming air, the storm shifting, folding over itself. I saw Tom Melba and his parents arrive and barely allowed my eyes to flick in his direction, a mysterious half-smile on my face (practiced from the in-depth article "How to Smile Like Mona Lisa"). Also, I had piled my hair on top of my head with what I had planned to be soft, flowing curls, but I wasn't that good with my mother's curling iron yet, so there were crimps here and there. Tom, I managed to notice in my carefully nonchalant half-second glance, was wearing a white Polo shirt, which showed off his tan and made his shoulders look broad and adult. I wanted to rest my head against one of those shoulders, feel his lips pressed to my hair-sprayed curls.

My mother led the way into the room, and Hall McLendon came over to greet us. She carried a bowl of potato salad against her hip, which swayed her step and made her seem girlish, awkward. Hall leaned to kiss her on the cheek, then shook hands with my father, then turned to offer a long-fingered, bony hand for me to shake, which impressed me, to be greeted as an adult.

My mother held the bowl of salad in both arms now, hugged it to her, as if she weren't sure what to do with it.

"Can I take that for you?" Hall asked, gesturing for it.

"Oh, no thanks; I can take care of it," my mother said, and her accent right then was wide open and twangy, like Hall's, like it had been during that trip we'd taken to Oklahoma two years earlier when she became a young girl and told me she didn't know where she'd be in ten years. Something about his offer to carry a bowl and her saying she could manage it sounded even then like the niceties adults used to mask whatever was happening that couldn't be discussed. She left us, carrying the bowl to the other side of the room, where women were stocking the tables with chicken salads and casseroles.

We sat, Hall at the end of the table, my father between us on the side. Hall tipped his folding chair back at a dangerous angle, slowly rocking back and forth. I noticed he wore cowboy boots with his khakis. His legs were so long that his knees poked up higher than his hips. He had thinning hair and the beginning of a beer gut, but a handsome, tanned face and very white teeth. He looked completely relaxed in his body, draped in the chair, one long arm dangling, a cup of iced tea dwarfed in his other hand. I remember being slightly distracted as we talked, trying to track where Tom was in the room.

"Did you know I'm the only living witness to your parents' marriage?" Hall said, winking at my father.

"Really?" I said. I scooted forward in my folding chair.

"You about killed yourself the night before," my father said.

"That's true. That was back in my wilder days," he explained to me with a wink. "I still miss old Clink Johnson," he said to my father, who nodded and smiled, but his attention was elsewhere; maybe he was looking for my mother. Outside, it had started to rain, drumming the roof.

"Excuse me, Hall," my father said, "be right back." We both watched him walk away.

"You know, you look just like Joanie," Hall said, slapping one knee. He had this direct way of speaking to me that was different from other men, the fathers of my girlfriends. I guess it was because he didn't have children, hadn't developed that gentle, patronizing tone. It surprised me, how he said her name instead of referring to her as "your mother," the way most adults did. I was in that adolescent no man's land, neither child nor adult, and I didn't know how to react.

"Tell me about how they met," I said, urgent then—I was hungry for information, I wanted to know how they had started, what they were like together back then, as if that would help me understand the mysterious present, in which my parents moved through the same house and yet seemed to be in two totally different universes.

"Well," Hall said, tilting his chin up, looking at the ceiling, remembering. "It all happened kind of fast. One day your dad and me's staying up all night in the studio or drinking beers and shooting off firecrackers, and the next he's handing over his T-square and telling me he's getting married."

"What was—what was she like back then?" I asked.

Hall smiled, shook his head. "She was beautiful. She

seemed to move in slow motion. One day, Ernest and I were in the park just shooting the—relaxing after class, and there she was. I saw her first, and I wanted to ask her out, but I was too—well, Ernest beat me to it. And then one other time—"

My father was testing the microphone at the podium, tapping it with muffled thumps.

"I better go on up there," Hall said, leaning forward so all four legs of the chair were on the floor again.

"Wait," I said. "Just tell me, tell me about the other time."

Hall looked over at my father, who was scanning the room, maybe looking for my mother. "Well, I went to see her where she worked at that cockroach motel. I tried to ask her out myself," he said. "It was only a couple of days after Ernest and I'd met her. I figured may the best man win. But she turned me down, said she was already spoken for." He smiled, shook his head, and I could see him then, fifteen years younger, standing at the Star-Lite's glass door, wishing. I was shocked by it, how with a simple choice everything could have been different. I thought of my mother, pursued by two men, but choosing—the romance of it made me light-headed and, I'll admit, jealous.

Reverend Phil came to the podium, and my father waved Hall over to introduce him. Phil was a long-haired, redheaded hippie and forward-thinking environmentalist fresh out of divinity school. Pretty much everyone except my father disliked him, but no one snored during sermons anymore.

I watched my father and Hall McLendon standing on either side of Reverend Phil as he led us in prayer. Neither one of them seemed to be listening, both of them staring off in different directions, preoccupied. "Dear Lord, we are gathered here to celebrate the beautiful world you have made, and we ask for your support as we make more room in your house to do your work. We thank you for the earth and the rain, the food and drink. We ask you to forgive us our competitive, materialistic natures and look forward to the simplicity of heaven." Several people cleared their throats, jingled change in their pockets. "Furthermore," Reverend Phil continued, "we ask you to forgive our destruction of your planet through the use of poisons and Styrofoam, and we promise to recycle wherever possible today."

"Amen," everyone said firmly. Reverend Phil looked up from his folded hands, as if not quite finished.

Everybody stood to fill their plates. I managed to orchestrate running into Tom Melba in the coffee line. There was Kool-Aid for the kids, but I noticed he took a cup of coffee, which he loaded with cream and sugar. I decided to pour myself a cup, black, and we waited for our turn at the powdered doughnuts. I stood so close to him my sundress brushed against his khakis. I waited for him to say something first, but he didn't. I leaned forward to get into his field of vision, but he just slurped his coffee and stared out the window.

"Tom," I finally said.

He looked at me. We were exactly the same height. His lips formed a friendly upward curve, like the smiles you give to cashiers and waiters.

"Did you know that my dad got the architect to design the new wing for free?" I said.

"No," Tom said, unimpressed.

"You can meet him if you want to. I'll introduce you," I finished, breathless. I sipped the inky coffee and nearly choked, hot bitter liquid high in my throat.

"Yeah, like I give a crap," Tom said.

My face heated and I turned and walked quickly away.

Across the room, I saw my mother flicking a piece of lint off Hall's shirt, my father off to one side, watching them over the rim of his Styrofoam cup.

A week later, Lilly told me she was moving. I saw her coming back from a walk when my father was mowing the lawn. I ran next door when he was mowing away from the house, back turned. My mother was picking up Olin from camp.

"Where?" I asked.

She turned her head to check on Che, who was hunting, weaving through a bed of creamy yellow flowers. "My sister's out west. I think I'll stay with her awhile."

"Why?" Through the bushes in our front yard I could see my father cut the mower; I heard the wheels crunch over gravel as he rolled it into the garage. A breeze skittered over treetops, birds beaked Lilly's front yard for worms.

"You know, I used to be so concerned about what people thought of me," Lilly said. "I wanted to be good, so as a child I joined the church choir and volunteered as a candy striper. I wanted to be beautiful, so I spent a lot of time trying to figure out what men liked—you'll get what I mean someday. And I wanted to be loved, so I said and did a lot of things I didn't mean. I just need to be someplace fresh."

I looked at Lilly, who gazed serenely at our crisply mown lawn. "Don't leave," I said.

"I'm packed, hon. I'm leaving at six tomorrow morning, if you want to see me off."

That night at dinner I wanted to tell my mother that Lilly was leaving. I thought she'd want to say good-bye. But Olin had just gotten home and was regaling us with stories of raccoons trapped in the latrines and a kid who'd broken his collarbone falling out of a tree, and there wasn't an opportunity. Plus, I wasn't sure if she'd want to know, or what she'd say.

The next morning the sky was a watery gray when I helped Lilly put the last of her bags into her light blue Rabbit. Che glowered in his travel box on the front seat. "Tell her I said good-bye," Lilly said, hugging me, quick, her hair still wet from the shower and smelling shampoo-sweet. I wished my mother could be there; I felt Lilly deserved it, after all those years.

"I will," I said. I watched her drive down the hill toward town, and then saw something, a flicker at the edge of my vision, a bird taking off. I turned and saw my mother in the garden, across the yard, half hidden by the bushes, filling bird feeders. She curled closed the top of the bird feed bag, held it against her ribs, and looked over at me, and I realized then that she had known somehow, and she had wanted me to say her good-byes for her, because she had chosen to put things behind her, and there was no in-between.

She walked into the house barefoot, dark hair sleep-tangled at her shoulders. I felt I could see a great deal at that moment—my father curled on the couch, breathing deeply, Tanya snoring softly and dreaming of riding a Harley with Jack, Reverend Phil in his garden rolling a joint, Tom pulling on rubber boots to go fishing with his father, Hall McLendon drawing designs on our church and my family, my mother alone in the kitchen, remembering, our town and the river golden under the rising sun—all of us dreaming.

27

THE MORNING AFTER Olin's gig at the King James, I woke slowly from a dream about my mother—I often dreamed about that last time I saw her, the bias-cut green dress she wore that seemed to float at its scalloped edges, her hair shining and swept up, her lips glossy, red, too alive for the picture.

I closed my eyes to bring the image back, hugged myself to contain the pressure in my chest, the ache that comes from sensing something just out of reach. I knew I was dreaming about her because of how much I had been thinking about her since I'd come home, with my birthday coming up, not to mention the Morris P. Alston building bombing—the photo retrospectives, the vigils, the students looking not very different from Lilly Franklin and her friends—the Mod Squad meets the bomb squad, with the floppy collars and long hair and halter tops and flared jeans. I thought about what it must have been like for them—for Lilly in particular—when it all became real, when they had to live with it as a terrible act instead of just an idea that made them feel briefly powerful.

202 ~ QUINN DALTON

And for my mother, making that split-second decision to pull me out of my stroller and start running toward the noise instead of away, maybe to check on her friend, maybe to find my father, and to have it all misunderstood—would she still have been alive if she hadn't gone there that day, if we'd never been frozen into the grainy forever of that photograph?

I made coffee with Olin's state-of-the-art espresso machine, an artifact from his thermometer past, and washed my face and combed my hair, wondering where Olin was. I shook my head to rid myself of the image of Barbara groping him under the table at the Iron. I stretched out on his futon, waiting for the espresso machine to finish hissing and spitting, thinking of Frank, and also about the day to come: my father's wedding to a woman he'd known all of two months, whose sister seemed to have the hots for my brother.

What to do at a time like this? I poured a cup of syrupy espresso and got dressed so I could fix up my next-door neighbor with my grandmother. Humming to myself, I blew on my espresso, tested the temperature, and tossed it back, shotlike. The caffeine hit the backs of my eyes first, then my forehead, then moved back toward the base of my skull in a powerful though not altogether pleasant way as I opened my front door. But what I saw next made the caffeine completely unnecessary. There, standing on my front stoop wearing round purple shades and smoking a cigarette, was my ex-boyfriend Terence.

I stared, speechless.

Terence blew out a long stream of smoke and regarded me coolly. He gestured in a general way to everything behind him. "This is what you left me for?"

The caffeine high was quickly turning to nausea. I held on to the doorknob and bit the inside of my cheek to steady myself. "What are you doing here?" I breathed.

Terence ignored the question. He looked up toward the

roofline of my building, dramatically cast a sweeping gaze at the rest of the quad, then glared at me. "More to the point, this is what England fought for? What a godforsaken wasteland! What total lack of aesthetics! How could you leave me for this, this unimaginative squalor?"

He was starting in with the terribly correct, elevated boarding school syntax he often adopted when upset. Somehow, the familiarity of it was both soothing and disturbing. "How did you find me?" I asked.

Terence waved the question away. "Oh, Fiona finally gave in. I told her I just wanted to make sure you were OK, which is true, so she gave me your father's number. Then I called him and pretended to be your employer, asking where to send your final paycheck," he explained, obviously pleased with himself. "He seemed a little short on the phone. Did you tell him all about me? And was he scandalized?" Terence was hopeful.

I was starting to recover from my initial shock. I had almost forgotten how hot he was, his sinewy arms and full mouth, his chest muscular but wiry. "Look, this is a nice and interesting surprise," I lied. The truth was, I was angry, shocked, and a little ashamed—pissed at myself for mistaking his weirdness for originality all these years and ashamed of my current circumstances, which were, all told, no worse than I had left in Clerkenwell, but the fact that Terence had made a point of being unimpressed had somehow gotten to me, which also made me angry. "But I'm busy right now, OK? You'll have to figure out some way to amuse yourself." I stepped onto the stoop and Terence stepped theatrically out of my way.

"Well, that's all right with me. I just need a place to crash."

I stared at him. "Not here."

Terence stared back, truly shocked. "Your boyfriend of

204 ~ Q U I N N D A L T O N

seven sodding years and you can't let me stay for a night or
two? This is unbelievable," he said, dropping his cigarette in
the grass and tapping another one out of the pack. "This place
has made you harsh and insensitive, like Scarlett after the War
Between the States," he said, referring to one of his favorite
American movies.

I took the cigarette out of his hand and, remembering I'd
decided to quit, crumpled it in my fist. "I know you, Terence.
That's what you told me the last time around, remember? And
you never moved out. Rent a room, why don't you? Or better
yet, go home." I threw the crushed cigarette at his chest and
hopped down the steps, proud of myself for standing up to him.
I headed down the row to Harold's unit, Terence following.

"Do you really not care about me at all?" Terence asked,
already wheezing from the effort of keeping up with me. "You
can just cut your man off, leave him stranded with no home
and no date for the big surprise weekend he'd planned just for
you?"

I stopped and turned around so quickly Terence nearly ran
into me. I wagged my finger inches away from his long, freckled nose. "Don't even pretend that anything you did in our
relationship was just for me, OK? Now, if you feel short-
changed because you didn't get broken up with in person,
then here it is. My decision to come home was not designed to
get your attention. It was not a 'cry for help,'" I said, holding
up bunny ears around the phrase and immediately feeling stupid. I waved my hands to rid us both of the gesture. "Look, I
have things to do. My father's getting married today. My
brother has just moved in after deciding to quit his job and
become a performance artist, something you would understand perhaps better than anyone else I know. I've just started a
job, a real job, which you may not understand, and I need to
get some decent clothes." We were standing in front of

Harold's door by then, and I was turning to knock when Terence grabbed me by the waist, pulled me toward him, and kissed me hard on the mouth.

Harold's door flew open. "What's all the racket out here? Well, well."

I pulled away from Terence in time to see Harold's amused smirk. "What the hell is wrong with you?" I said.

Terence shrugged. "Just kissing the woman I love."

Harold laughed. "You're not the only one, pal."

It was Terence's turn to look indignant. "Have you been cheating on me? Is this the reason you left me?"

"She left you?" Harold asked, leaning against his doorframe to listen further.

"All right, both of you!" I yelled. It seemed absurd to introduce the two of them, but I didn't think there was any other way to regain control of the situation. "Harold, this is my ex-boyfriend—"

"Ex-boyfriend?" Terence repeated, tapping out another cigarette. "That's a bit harsh."

"Terence is visiting for a *brief* time," I said, glaring at Terence. "Terence, this is Harold, my neighbor."

Terence extended his hand bedecked with a mood ring, university class ring, and bracelet with pink and orange plastic charms that looked as though it had come out of a cereal box. Harold regarded it suspiciously, then gave it a brief shake. "Say, you a limey?"

Terence rolled his eyes. "Yes, and I presume you're a Yank."

"Damn straight. Well, I was there in 'forty-four. D day. Saved your asses."

Terence opened his mouth to respond, but I beat him to it. "And they are all very thankful, I'm sure," I said. "Now, Harold, I wanted to ask you, are you free this evening?"

"Now you're asking the codger out?" Terence, indignant.

"Shut up!" I said to him.

Harold eyed Terence briefly, then turned to me with a smile. "I'm kind of up to my ears in women right now but I always have time for a lovely lady like yourself."

I sighed. "Look, it's not for me."

"Oh, come on, don't be ashamed that you like a lot of men. I mean, I'm not threatened by that at all. Really, I'm flattered," Harold said, bushy eyebrows raised as he grinned.

Terence giggled, but I pressed forward. "We're having my father's wedding reception here tonight and I thought you might like to meet someone."

"Who?"

"Well, my grandmother, Lettie. She's funny, a good cook, has aged very well—"

Harold's smile turned to a glare. "You know, I don't need this guff from you. I've gone through more hearts than you have condoms. Take Sandy across the way there, who vandalizes my signage? I took her skeet shooting and then straight to the sack. Thought she could just bag me, but I'm an independent man! All those years I tried to get a woman to marry me, catch-as-catch-can during the war, having to pay for it in Streetsboro, and then finally, the sixties. Sex everywhere! I grew my hair and it's been a dream ever since." He pointed a knobby finger at me. "Fixing me up with your damned grandmother, what the hell do you take me for?" He slammed the door, and I could hear him banging around and muttering.

Terence seemed to have been stunned into a kind of suspended animation by this exchange. He smiled in admiration toward Harold's door. "That old man is quite the firecracker, isn't he? It gives me hope, you know? For the older years."

Just then Harold threw his door open again and brushed past us, carrying a sign, which he planted in the grass after picking up the sign our neighbor Sandy had stomped down the previous morning, apparently still miffed over her breakup with Harold. The sign read, WHY WORRY ABOUT TOMORROW WHEN THERE'S ALWAYS TODAY? Harold swept past us again, slamming his door.

"What's with the signs?" Terence asked.

"Public service," I said.

We watched in silence as Sandy, still in her robe on this Saturday morning, emerged from her apartment across the quad, brown hair rumpled, a determined expression on her round face. She crossed the grass, pulled the sign out of the ground, broke the slim wooden post over her knee, dropped the pieces on the ground, and marched back to her apartment.

"That is quite bizarre," Terence said, taking a long drag on his cigarette.

I looked at him as if to say, you're in no position to call any-one bizarre, and he looked back at me, shrugging as if to say, I know. I felt a tenderness for him that seemed dangerously like sympathy, and I folded my arms and pinched my rib cage until the emotion passed. "Terence, how did you get here?"

"I rented a car," he said, gesturing toward a pale purple SUV in the parking lot not unlike my brother's. "I love it. It's so huge, so powerful. Quite a thrill."

I looked at Terence and he smiled back at me sheepishly. He couldn't help who he was any more than I could. I tried to think back to childhood, tried to imagine what could have set me on the course that put me on the front stoop of an old sex fiend next to my ex-boyfriend younger version of same. "Let's go to breakfast," I said.

Terence followed me toward the pastel truck. "Really? That sounds lovely. You're coming around, aren't you?"

I turned to him and smiled. "Yes. Now, let me drive. You were never any good even on the left side of the street."

Terence looked at me, suspicious, but handed over the

keys. I got in, hit the powerlock, and drove away, leaving him waving his slender arms and screaming. I had to admit to myself that it was a little bit too easy, but I was due for that. I turned and headed north, toward Lettie's house, toward where my mother was buried nearly twenty years ago.

28

TWO WEEKS AFTER Lilly left town, during that muggy summer of 1981, I argued with my mother about makeup, specifically, my not being allowed to wear it. We were standing in the bathroom, where my mother had mounted a magnifying mirror over the sink, next to the medicine cabinet mirror, so she wouldn't have to bend as far to apply her makeup. I wanted to use that mirror the way my mother did, to inspect myself closely and spread on eye shadow and lipstick. Except now the looking was no longer satisfying; it pointed out my freckled, pale skin, my nearly white lips.

When my mother put on makeup, she pulled inside herself and became someone else entirely, perfected, contained. Talking interfered with her concentration and her accuracy. It slowed her down, and on dance nights she didn't want to be slow.

"What dance are you learning tonight?" I asked, testing the air.

"Rumba," she said. She plugged in her hot rollers. At the time she was wearing her hair teased and piled high on her head like a coppery helmet. I remember thinking it glamorous, but now, in photographs my father took of my mother in dresses she had bought or made specifically for those dance nights, the hair looks faintly goofy, a presence all to itself. I wonder what he thought about taking those pictures, if he knew how important it was to her, if he ever regretted not going with her.

I sat on the toilet seat and watched, elbow propped on the cold edge of the sink, where I knew I was almost in her way, wanting to annoy her probably, trip her up, keep her from leaving. I imagined the flashing dance floor, the handsome men, her freedom to dance with anyone.

She layered on the concealer, base, and blush, all of which she mixed herself from tubes of red and white and brown and even green creams. She mixed them in a white plastic bowl I'd eaten cereal from as a toddler. I knew that when she was through she would rinse the bowl in the sink and leave it to drain on a tissue on the counter. I knew every step but I loved to watch. I sat there, the toilet lid shifting to the side under my weight, bouncing one knee, wanting to ask her if I could start wearing lipstick now that I was thirteen, officially a teenager, trying to determine the moment that would most likely get me a yes.

My mother started on her eyes, first spreading on a beige cream meant to keep the eye shadow from creasing. Then she lit a match from the kitchen to heat her eyeliner so it would spread evenly over her upper lid. Then she chose the eye shadow shades, matching them to the dress she'd selected—usually three shades, a pale cream or pink, a dark charcoal or brown, and a bright accent.

That last night she chose a silvery white, a deep, almost black green, and a frosted lilac. These colors came from the jungle pattern of the fabric of her dress, where toucans poked their heads from behind a field of thick greenery. Sewn onto the toucans' feathers and the jungle flowers were iridescent sequins; she'd added them one by one while watching television on nights she stayed in. The dress hung on the outside of the closet door, a flag for a country I might visit someday.

I watched her brush on the colors, pale for the inner corner of her eye and right under the brow, dark green on the outer corner, and the lilac on the edge of her lid so that it flashed when she blinked like a signal.

Time was running out. I slipped a bright coral lipstick from her makeup basket and spread it on, using a mirror that had once been one half of a compact. I turned my face from side to side, admiring how it made my whole face seemed brighter, as if I had been out in the sun. My cheeks looked flushed like the girls in the JCPenny catalogue.

"How does this look?" I asked, smiling up at my mother.

My mother glanced down, one eye in progress. "Too old for you."

"I think it looks good," I said.

"It looks like a girl wearing makeup she has no business wearing." My mother plucked a tissue from the box. "Here," she said, dropping it into my lap. It tickled the tops of my thighs. I left it there and looked back at the mirror, sucked in my cheeks. I remember my face clearly, my freckled nose, my ribbon-braided barrettes hanging down with beads on the end.

"I know what looks good on me," I mumbled.

"Sure you do," my mother said. She tilted her head back, surveying her work. Then she put down her eyebrush and slid out a set of false lashes. The look she gave herself in the mirror was innocent, friendly, like the woman on the Clairol commercial, but her voice was edgy.

I dug another color from the bag. I wiped off the orange lipstick and replaced it with a pale frosted pink. "How about this one?"

My mother did not look this time. "Cheap." Her tone was definite. She didn't want to talk, she wanted to leave.

"How come you don't look cheap in it?"

"Because I'm a grown woman."

"Just let me wear this light pink?"

My mother didn't answer. She had squeezed the clear glue gel onto a fake lash and was placing it carefully on her lid.

I stood up, heart pounding. I wanted to scream, to scratch my face off. I was tired of my shiny nose, my pale cheeks, my flat eyes. I was tired of boys, older boys who went to the high school and whose names I didn't even know, hunching their backs and calling me Murkey, a punishing variation on my name, and every time they said it I felt as if I were falling off a bridge. It was too humiliating to discuss. I felt certain my mother had never been made fun of in this way. There were only a few more weeks until I had to face the kids at school again, to walk by the guys on the school bus, trying to pretend I hadn't heard them. I scrubbed a tissue over my mouth and face, orange and pink lipstick smearing. "You want me to be ugly!" I screamed. I turned for the door, banging my shin against the toilet. I shrieked in anger and ran down the hall to my bedroom. The night stretched ahead. I was a prisoner, trapped. I put my face in my pillow and imagined not being able to breathe, dying from suffocation. I thought of how they'd cry for me. I imagined my mother saying she wished she had let me wear makeup.

After a few minutes I heard my mother's footsteps swishing into my room, nylons against shag. She sat carefully on the edge of the mattress, and I knew that meant she had put on her dress and didn't want to wrinkle it, crush the sequins.

I rolled onto my back, arms over my face, but I could still see a fuzzy shadow of her face and hair, now pinned up, spit curls at the base of her neck. She rubbed my belly and then turned her back to me, pointing to her zipper.

"Can you fix me?" she said.

I sat up and pulled the long zipper to the top. Then she stood and smiled, her mouth wide and generous, and she looked as if she could have appeared from a fashion magazine. "How about mascara?" she said then, and it took me a minute to realize what she meant. She gestured to me to follow her, and I did, back to the bathroom.

"Wash your face and I'll show you how to put it on," she said. I splashed cool water over my face, rubbed a bar of soap over my cheeks and mouth, rinsed. My mother handed me a towel.

"Here's what you do," she said, pulling the wand from the tube.

"I know how to do it," I said. I had watched her for years. I knew how she used even strokes from the base of the top lashes to the tips, how she used the tip of the wand to dab on the smallest lashes at the corner of the eyes and at the lower lid. Still I was shaky with it, and on the second eye I let her apply it. I tried to look at her as she stroked it on, her face open with concentration as it was when she did her own eyes.

"Now," she said.

I stood and looked in the magnified mirror. I looked like a child movie star, a soap opera child. Then I took in the whole effect in the regular mirror. I imagined walking past the boys on the school bus, watching their mouths drop in surprise at my transformation. I couldn't wait.

"It's beautiful," I breathed.

"Mm-hmm," my mother said, looking at me in the reflection. I looked at her reflection, and in the mirror it seemed we were looking past each other. She caught herself, distracted. "Now, I've got to find my clutch." She turned, but I continued staring at myself for a moment and then ran after her.

She found her purse and I followed her out the back door,

watching her balance carefully as she touched down on each paint-flaked back step in her spiky heels. My father was in the living room reading the newspaper. I turned around and called down the hallway to him. "Dad!" I yelled through the screen door. "Get the camera!" I wanted to preserve my first moments as child beauty queen; I wanted to stand next to my mother, who was looking through her small sparkly purse, checking for lipstick, powder, extra hairpins. "Dad, take a picture of me and Mom!"

Olin was outside, too, where the yard rose to a small hill. He was making a fort like he'd learned at camp, sitting cross-legged and barefoot in a shallow hole he'd dug, dirt smudged on his face and creased in his hands and the backs of his knees. He glanced up at my mother and me as I came outside behind her. It was still light out, a summer evening, and the trees were a shadowy dark green at the trunks, sunlight glossing the top leaves. Olin had been busy leaning branches against his fort walls, but when he saw our mother, he stopped.

"Mom," Olin said, pointing at her dress. Everything was still except the slow lifting of leaves in the evening air, lightning bugs blinking on and off under the trees.

She looked down, hunting for stains, rips. "What?" she asked.

Olin pointed where the sunlight caught on the sequins sewn to the pattern of yellow and orange toucan feathers on her dress, the fuchsia flowers peeking from the leafy background. The sequins winked as she looked down and straightened and bent to look again, just in case she'd missed something. "You've got fireflies on you," he said. "All over you." He grabbed his hair with both hands and twirled it around his fingers, something he did when he was nervous.

I was ready to laugh at him, turn to my mother to commiserate with her about what a child Olin was, how he didn't understand what was possible. But my mother had looked down again and spread her arms, and the sunlight on her shoulders was orange, and her dress seemed to recede into the green air so that she was part of the shadowy trees, the leaning grass, flickering with light, there and not there, and it seemed she could spread the glow on her skin, on me and Olin too. We could have floated away from the triangle we formed right then, Olin in his rickety fort, me touching my new, stiff eyelashes, our mother looking down at her dress and wanting to believe what Olin had seen. But we stayed where we were, gazing at ourselves and each other, waiting for something, until my father came outside with the Polaroid, squinting in the low sunlight, the slapping screen door like a finger snap, awakening us.

"So what's different about me, Dad?" I asked, standing next to my mother while he fumbled to turn on the camera.

"Uh, I don't know," he said. He peered over the camera at me, searching my face for clues.

My mother hugged my waist. "Don't worry about that, Merle. Men never notice anything." Then she laughed, and my father smiled back at her, and maybe in that moment he couldn't help but admire her, in spite of whatever had gone wrong between them, because she was so beautiful. After the pictures she got into our dark blue Buick that she called the spy car, and she drove away, and I went to bed wearing my mascara because I was so happy about it I didn't want to take it off, and I never saw her again.

29

THE FUNERAL WAS ON a Saturday at the Fredemeier and Thigtree funeral home. I know that my father had taken me and Olin to stay with Lettie the same day that I woke to find her sitting on my bed, a look on her face like she used to get when it hadn't rained for a long time and she was staring at her dry fields, except more resigned, as if she'd realized it would never rain again. I know my father packed our suitcases with as many clean clothes from Olin's and my dressers and closets that he could find and told us we would stay with Lettie for a little while, which turned out to be the rest of the summer. I know he also gave our TV to Goodwill, complaining of bloodthirsty journalists. But I don't have specific memories of anything between seeing Lettie sitting on my bed and the day of the funeral. The first thing I remember is putting on a dress. It was a sundress, dark pink with red and white flowers, with darts at the bust that made it look a little poofy and created the illusion that something was actually there, which it wasn't. It came with a jacket and a round-brimmed straw hat with a band of matching fabric. My mother had picked this outfit out for me only weeks before, but the hat was missing. I remember kneeling on the floor of the front bedroom upstairs in Lettie's house, dust bunnies in the corners turning slowly on the dark wood floor with the hot breeze from the three open windows—Lettie was never much of a housekeeper—and I was looking through my suitcases for that hat, even though I knew it wasn't in there unless it had been flattened. I was sweating, my hair sticking to my neck, the air outside buzzing with heat and bugs and thirsty birds. Lettie knocked on the door, waited a second, opened.

"OK, hon. It's time," she said. She was wearing a black cotton long-sleeved dress with white cuffs and a Peter Pan collar, which made her look like a nun. She wore hose, which I'd never seen her wear before, and black leather pumps, which looked new, but which she later told me she'd worn for her husband's funeral and my father's graduation from Florence College not long after he and my mother had arrived with their wide, desperate smiles and dusty clothes.

I could see a few hairs along Lettie's shins, pressed flat under her hose, little squiggly lines on her skin like the crazing on her china, the clay in our dry, patchy backyard, and I felt my throat tightening. I didn't know whether I was going to cry or throw up. "I can't find my hat," I managed to croak.

"We'll find it later," Lettie said, clopping a couple of steps into the room, hand outstretched to me. Her footsteps sounded like the horses on the new farm next door when they stepped carefully down the metal ramps out of their owners' trailers, bobbing their heads in deep arcs as if they were saying Yes! Yes! Yes!

I can remember her taking my hand, helping me to my feet. I can remember standing up and realizing we were the same height. It had happened all of a sudden—one day I was looking up at her and still half-believed she could pick me up, and the next our eyes were level, and I no longer felt I knew my own body.

We walked downstairs, where my father was waiting with Olin, and I remember Olin looking up at us as we came down the stairs. His face was round and serious and pale against the dark fabric of his suit. Lettie had let out the hem of his slacks, and you could see the ridge of the previous fold still, a faded line around his ankles.

I started sweating through the arms of my dress jacket as soon as we walked outside. Bees flew in lopsided circles and fell out of the air in exhaustion. My father drove us to the funeral home in Lettie's car, a used gray Caprice; Lettie in front, Olin and I in back.

The visiting hours started at two o'clock at the Fredemeier and Thigtree Funeral and Cremation Services, on Archdale Street. It being a Saturday, there were a lot of people. That was the reason Lettie gave me when I asked why there were cars parked all the way down the street. She said, "It's Saturday. People don't have anything else to do around here." This was her way of comforting me, downplaying the real reason—people always turned out for untimely deaths, murders, suicides. She couldn't give the reason most people would offer: *So many people loved your mother, dear, that's why they're all here.* Because not many people in this town loved my mother. I knew that. I'd heard the whispered comments. I know now there had been letters to the editor about spies in our midst, terrorists, plotters who wanted to destroy the American way, letters that had once or twice mentioned my mother's name.

I remember sitting in a private room before the funeral with my father and Olin and Lettie. There were Bibles on two matching side tables perched next to an overstuffed mustard and green-striped couch. The couch faced a pair of dark wood armchairs with green upholstered seats and backs and little pads on the arms. The carpet was the same green.

I realized that I would never be this close to my mother again, in the same building with her. Always she had been within view, or I knew she was just in another room, or at the grocery store, or out at one of her many meetings for the events committee of the Florence Ballroom Dance Society, and that she would be back, and whatever mysteries she carried with her she would bring back, so that even if I didn't know the details of her secrets, I would at least be near them, and for pretty much all of my life, that had been enough.

Outside, murmuring voices swelled and receded. I could see from the corner of my eye Olin's shined dress shoes flicking back and forth as he swung his feet. I could see my father and Lettie across from me on either end of the couch, looking at their folded hands, the angle of their narrow shoulders almost exactly the same. I knew they had been here before, to bury my grandfather. My father had been eight years old then, a year younger than Olin, and I wondered if he was thinking of that as he looked up at my brother, gazed at him, really, with a confused, expectant expression. I studied the landscapes on the walls, all of the gauzy pastoral scenes, the fake plants anchoring the corners of the room, the plush green carpet that matched the chairs and the sofa and was supposed to make you feel as if you were in one of those landscapes, probably, loping along with the big-eyed deer, the sun warming your back. I could hear Lettie tapping the leather-bound Bible.

"What dress did you pick?" I asked no one in particular.

Lettie looked at me, then at my father. Neither of them said anything. But I knew they understood what I meant.

"Well?" I asked.

"The blue one," Lettie said, as if that would be enough for me to know which one she was talking about. But my mother had a lot of clothes, and she liked blue, so it could've been anything. The off-the-shoulder evening gown? The soft sweater dress with the thin silver belt? The silk sheath?

"Which one?" I asked. I needed a picture.

My father looked at me. "Please," he said to me. He cut his eyes to Olin and back again as if to say, *Don't upset him.*

But Olin didn't even appear to understand what we were talking about. He was still swinging his legs and blowing little spit bubbles. He knew Mom was gone, and he understood what death meant. He'd buried some goldfish in his day. But it seemed he hadn't put it all together yet; he was just waiting for everything to get back to normal, like taking off the 3-D glasses after you leave the theater.

My hands were balled into fists in my lap. "Which one did you pick?" I asked him, saying each word slowly, staring at him. Maybe this was where the trouble between us began— my questions, his refusals.

My father clenched his jaw, looking at me and then past me. His face was tight as he stood up and walked out of the room, closing the door quietly behind him.

I expected Lettie to be angry with me for upsetting him. I expected her to shake a bony finger at me, to say I needed to know when to hold 'em and when to fold 'em—lines she often used from her all-time favorite Kenny Rogers song—but she just patted the seat cushion next to her. I came over, and Olin, jealous, followed, worming between us. We sat huddled on the couch, the three of us, hip to hip. Lettie bent forward to bite a thread off the hem of her skirt, fished the thread out of her teeth. "It's the one with the ruffle around the neck, the one you can pull down around the shoulders if you want," she said, looking straight ahead, talking matter-of-fact, as if she were giving directions.

I could see my mother then. I imagined the dress framing

her slim shoulders, her long neck, the way the muscles formed
a line up to her high cheekbones, and I imagined her hair was
up, maybe a silver choker at her throat. My stomach ached
from it; I felt a pressure behind my ribs, something rising, like
the dough Lettie left out on the still-warm stove every
evening, ready for baking in the morning. I felt as if my bones
would crack from it.

Later, I remember standing in the main room, a few feet
away from the casket, my father facing us, as if welcoming us
to a party. I think he was trying to appear calm, but his face was
red, and his glasses were slightly crooked the way they got
when he lifted them to wipe his eyes during pollen season. I
tried to look at him without looking at him. He stood there
with his hands in his pockets, nudging a worn spot in the carpet with one foot. He didn't seem to really be there; I felt I
could see him receding, like in those space movies where people got stuck in an air lock and then it opened and you watched
them fall away from you, screaming. The awfulness was in
seeing it, that's what I thought then, watching my father
quickly pass a handkerchief under his nose, as if it weren't
grief but allergies that made his nose run. It made me want to
comfort him—somehow I thought he needed it more than I
did at that moment—but then he was heading for the double
doors. He opened them, and people began filing in like a rush
of water. They stopped to shake his hand, talked to him with
low voices, bowed heads. They signed the book on the white
podium in the corner. I recognized a lot of them—parents of
my friends, coworkers of my father, families from our congre-
gation.

I felt as if the air was leaving the room. Olin must have felt
it, too, because he went to Lettie and grabbed her arm, pressing his face against her dress sleeve. I thought of Lilly, wishing
she would appear among all the faces. I figured she had no idea

what had happened, and of course I had no way to let her know. She was the only person I wanted to see there besides maybe Tanya. For all I knew, Lilly was out west by then, and I wished I could be with her, wherever she was, rather than in that close, filling room.

For one moment between greeting guests, my father turned and seemed to be looking at Lettie and me, but not with any real focus; it was as if he were interested in a spot just above our heads, looking for something that wasn't there, but that he thought might appear at any moment—he looked anticipatory and confused at the same time, and this was the expression I would come to associate with him in the years remaining before I told myself I was leaving Florence forever.

30

A FEW MINUTES after ditching Terence and stealing his rental car, I was sitting beside the low granite marker, which said, simply, "Joan Madison Winslow, December 8, 1948–June 17, 1981." The day I'd gone to confront Lettie about withholding the fact that my mother had died with Hall McLendon, I had stopped here first. It was June 1990, nine years after her death. This was also my last stop in Florence the next day, after picking up my tickets at the travel agency, before driving to Cleveland Hopkins International.

I sat cross-legged at the edge of my mother's grave. The grass was neatly trimmed; the narrow roads through the cemetery were a new, liquid black; small flower beds stitched borders around granite benches shaded by thick-trunked maples with new green leaves. It was a perfect spring day; the earth damp and cool, sunlight warming the lifting air. The cemetery had acquired or cleared more land back toward the train tracks that met the river in town and followed south toward the green fold of the Cuyahoga Valley; from where I sat, I could see nothing but lawn dotted with white. The road was hidden by a low brick wall.

I touched the cool stone, ran my fingers over the letters, as if to find her in the uneven surface. It was hard to imagine that what was left of her physical life was here; that anything else of the person she was existed only in memory. At times like this, I wished I were religious, that I believed in an afterlife, but even after years of listening to Reverend Phil's offbeat sermons, it hadn't sunk in, so I was left with the smell of the soil and the damp ground seeping through my trousers.

"Joanie," I said, "I miss you and I feel guilty about this. But Dad's happy. And that's something we both want, right?"

I could hear wind, birds protesting from the treetops. I thought of that morning nearly twenty years earlier when I woke with Lettie sitting on my bed. I'd had one of those dreams that started after Lilly told me about my mother taking me in a stroller with her to meetings at Lilly's cramped apartment, listening but not really listening to whispered plans, pot smoke gathering at the ceiling, Crosby, Stills, Nash, and Young on the radio, Neil about to get famous for singing "Ohio." Lilly told me how she used to lie in her prison bunk and pretend she could float through the ceiling, float to the windows of her parents' house, or of our house, and see us getting ready for bed. After that I dreamed of floating, too; I dreamed of night air streaming between my fingers like dark water, of the cool pressure of space on my head, of rising and turning to see campfires and lamplights and the flickering movements behind curtains. I'd had a couple of weeks to think about what Lilly had said, and I'd seen my mother out in the garden the morning Lilly left, a ribbon of silvery water falling from her hose, and I was sure then that she'd known somehow that Lilly was leaving; it just wasn't in her to say good-bye, to close that long loop of their friendship teased open again by Lilly's return.

On that morning when I woke to Lettie sitting on my bed, it took me a few minutes to remember that I was still wearing the mascara my mother had stroked on my eyelashes the night before. I raised my fingers to one eye, felt the stiff lashes, now a little clumped. I was looking at Lettie—it still hadn't quite dawned on me how weird it was that she was in my room at 8:30 in the morning, which was earlier than I normally woke up, it being summer vacation. But maybe I'd felt her weight as she sat on the edge of the mattress, maybe I'd heard her breathing. She looked different then—thin, but more muscular from years of working the farm alongside the hired help, her hair gray instead of white and cropped over the ears like a man's. She was looking at me as if I were sick, her lips pressed together in a grim line, her eyes steady on me.

I don't remember saying anything to her, but I must have asked her a question—maybe what was wrong—because I can remember her voice, she was answering a question. She said, "Your mother was in an accident last night."

I don't hear my voice in this conversation. Was I asking where she was? If she was all right? Or maybe nothing at all. Maybe I was just lying there, a fingertip brushing the tips of my mascara-stiffened lashes, still groggy with sleep, waiting to hear more.

When Lettie said the next part, she pressed her hand against my forehead, as if checking for a fever. She said, "She's gone, Merle," and leaned toward me, to hug me, I guess, to take my hand, her eyes reddened, and what I noticed first was that her lashes were gray, dark gray—she'd never worn makeup except for phases when she liked to wear bright pink or orange lipstick, just to make people stare—and the wetness at her lids pressed her lower lashes down like crushed spider legs. That's what I noticed, and I remembered thinking how glad I was my lashes weren't gray, and how I was scared to get

old, and then I was sitting up in bed and I think I was screaming.

But there was something else. Something Lettie said that I
had both remembered and not remembered all this time, and
standing there in the smooth green cemetery, a breeze thread-
ing the warm air, I could hear it: Lettie's voice, her breath
against my hair as she held me, rocking me, how then she'd
said, "She could have turned the car, she could have turned it,
God knows." Her own desperation was what made her say it
before she could catch herself, I understood that now.

I stood up and kissed the top of the stone, the granite
smooth and cool as a forehead, grabbed a clump of grass and
stuffed it in my pocket as I walked away.

Driving along in my stolen lollipop-colored rental SUV,
bass thumping, I felt tears prickling at the corners and backs of
my eyes, but I just kept going along slowly until the feeling
passed. People sped by and swerved around me, honking, but I
didn't care. I knew where I was going, but it had been a long
time since I'd driven and I wasn't going to make any mistakes.

31

IN THE SPRING OF 1986 I had just turned eighteen—my mother's and my picture included in another round of *Daily Record* retrospectives covering the Morris P. Alston building bombing—and I was about to graduate from high school. I was planning to go to Ohio State for at least the first year, my idea of getting away, if only by a couple hours' drive. I had recently visited the police station, read my mother's file, and had decided Ohio State was just the first step—I was getting away from Florence forever, as soon as I could figure out a plan. But then one morning after I had just finished blow-drying my hair and spraying my bangs into a startled-looking crest, I found my father doubled over on the floor.

He ended up in the hospital. A heart attack, the same thing that had killed his father. There was an emergency surgery and several weeks of recovery afterward. For the next week, Olin, then thirteen, and I spent the evenings after school sitting with him, doing our homework or watching the clear liquid drip into my father's arm, the flower of bruise where the intern had inserted the needle wrong.

I thought of the last time I'd been in a hospital room, on that rushed trip with my mother to Oklahoma after her father had a heart attack. I thought about what I'd read in her file, the photographs of the curve of road where she had died, where I'd driven many times since I'd gotten my license, and never without remembering it: the thick trees, the pale wrinkle of road, the broad shoulder, plenty of time to swerve, the gash of tire marks in the mud where there was a dip. Even when it had been dry and hot that summer, that place was cool and wet, near the river. But something was missing; nothing in the file explained why there were no skid marks on the road, when as fast as they were going they would have laid rubber if they'd tried to change direction at the last second. Maybe the coroner missed that in the photos; maybe he thought it didn't matter, that my mother had been too drunk to know how fast she was going.

On my father's last night in the hospital, he was awake but not talking very much. The pain medication kept him pretty addled, and several times when he talked, eyes half-closed, I wasn't sure if he was awake or talking in a dream. He was so drugged I couldn't make out any words. He kept blinking and trying to focus on the ceiling, as if expecting something to appear at any moment.

Olin was asleep in a chair near the window. I pulled my chair closer to the bed. "You want to watch TV?" I asked him.

He blinked, sighed. "That woman next door," he said. This time, I understood him clearly.

"Mrs. Pitcher?" I asked, thinking he meant the older couple with the yapping poodle who at that time were living in the Spritzes' old house, waiting for their Florida condo to be finished.

My father shook, or rather rolled, his head from side to side. "She's a criminal," he said.

It took me a moment, then I got it. He meant Lilly Franklin. He said, "You brought her here; you tell her to go."

I realized he thought he was talking to my mother. Because she had invited Lilly. And that was probably why my father had started sleeping on the couch that summer, a form of protest, even if he didn't yet know about her affair with Hall McLendon.

I took a deep breath. I asked the question I had wanted to ask for years, even before I found out about how Hall McLendon had died with my mother in the spy car. I didn't care if it was cruel, dishonest to pretend. I felt my father had been pretending for years—punishing my mother with his distance, refusing to acknowledge her drinking, her loneliness, her friendship with Lilly, who was perhaps the only woman my mother had counted as a friend. I wondered why his mind had turned to Lilly rather than Hall; maybe Hall was still too painful to remember, five years after the accident.

Now that he was sick, I knew I would stick around for my brother's sake, but I had already decided that when I left, I'd never come back. As for what happened next, if I had it to do again, maybe I would've just touched his shoulder, shaken him lightly, tried to draw him out of it. Instead, I took a chance. If he thought I was Joanie, alive again and with him, maybe he was remembering everything—the late nights with the Florence Ballroom Dancing Society, Lilly's reappearance, his former friend Hall McLendon. I leaned in close and gave Joanie her voice again. I asked, "Did you know I loved him?"

My father squeezed his eyes shut, pressed his lips together as if bearing down on a pain. It didn't seem that he was even breathing. "Yes," he said, and I saw a tear slide from the corner of one eye, and then another. Not long after that, he fell asleep. I watched his chest rise and fall, watched my brother shift positions, try to curl up in his chair. I leaned forward, pressed my forehead against the edge of the mattress next to my father's hip, and stayed there until a nurse came in and sent us home.

I waited four years to tell my father what I knew. I didn't even bring it up to Lettie, because it wasn't her story to tell. I waited until I had graduated from Florence College with honors, until my brother was ready to go off to Miami University. I did it with a question. We were sitting at the rusty iron table on the patio, drinking a cup of coffee after dinner. Olin was inside on the phone with his girlfriend, I can't remember her name now, but she looked like Joanie with her high cheekbones and dark reddish hair, and I remember my father didn't even like to look at her. My father had propped his feet on a yellow plastic footstool that had been around since Olin and I were kids. It was a nice moment, there in the backyard, and I knew I was going to shatter it. I asked my father, "When did you find out that Mom had faked her birth certificate?"

My father stopped in mid-sip. He placed his coffee cup on the table carefully, as if it might break. The evening seemed suddenly quieter—the green shadows deeper under the still trees, a car moving down the street hushed and slow. I figured my father had a lot of questions right then—how long I'd known, how exactly I had found out, why I was bringing it up now, so many years later. I wanted him to have these questions, to feel what I'd felt for so long, locked out from what should have been known and put to rest long ago.

He didn't answer me, though. And if he had any questions, he didn't show it. He shifted in his seat. He asked me only this: "Would you like to have it?" He didn't wait for an answer. He walked slowly into the house, leaving me alone in the patchy backyard with the weed-choked garden and slumped birdhouses my mother had once maintained. It didn't take him long to find it. Perhaps he'd kept it in his middle desk drawer within easy reach; perhaps he'd looked at it often. He placed the yellowed paper on the table next to me, patted it gently, a good-bye.

I understood then that we would never have the conversation I wanted to have, about what had led my mother to her affair and what he wished he'd done differently. There would be no spoken apologies or regrets. I didn't even know why I wanted it anymore, what satisfaction it would bring me.

I stood up and thanked him. I called out a good-bye to Olin through the open windows. I got into my car and drove back to my apartment, the birth certificate on the seat beside me lifting and falling on currents of air from the cracked windows. I started packing and left a week later. I didn't see my father again for ten years.

This is what I thought about, driving from the cemetery to my father's house, the last time I'd seen him, and that night in the hospital when, in drug-addled half-sleep, he told me he knew his wife had been in love with someone else.

All the shutters were closed at my father's house. I might have just kept driving by at my funereal pace, but there was no Cadillac in the driveway so I figured I wouldn't be interrupting anything. I parked at the curb and knocked on the front door, not the door we normally used when I was growing up, since the back door was nearest to where we parked our cars at the top of the driveway.

My father came to the door in a velvety navy terry-cloth bathrobe, the kind of thing a new wife-to-be might have bought him, his white pajama legs sticking out underneath like bed sheets. "Can I come in?" I asked.

"Sure," he said, surprise lighting his gray eyes. He swung the door back and walked toward the kitchen, where I could smell coffee like a sharp chocolate brewing. "Doreen's out shopping," he said. I followed him and sat down at the kitchen table.

It was strange to hear the casual fact of her, to see her orange silk robe thrown over a chair. The kitchen linoleum was more yellowed than I remembered and curling like an old newspaper at the edges—even the appliances seemed stooped and geriatric, the toaster and can opener huddling on the crumb-dotted counters. "Coffee?" he asked.

"No thanks," I said. "I went to the cemetery," I blurted out, maybe from nerves, at being there after so long.

"I was just there the other day," he said mildly as he opened cabinets.

This surprised me. I guess I hadn't thought of him visiting her, but of course he must have, over the years. He poured himself a cup and came in and sat down across from me, black coffee in a blue cup in one hand, a bright grapefruit in the other, which he began to peel.

"You're the only one I know who eats grapefruit like an orange," I said, watching him try to peel it in one piece. He did it in two.

"Really? How do they do it in England?" he asked, which made me think of how he had never been out of the country, not even to Canada, as far as I knew. There was a whole flotilla of continents around us, green and unknown.

"In halves," I said. I watched him bite down on a fleshy pink grapefruit section and purse his lips at the sourness, juice sprinkling the tabletop with little orange drops. I said, "My ex-boyfriend has shown up."

My father finished chewing. "Are you getting back together?"

"No, but I wondered if you'd mind if he showed up at the reception."

"That's fine," my father answered. "You have to be open to the unexpected." He bit into another section and winked at me as he chewed.

"You're right," I said. "I mean, I think so, too." I wanted to say that I knew he'd done his best. I wanted to tell him I was happy for him, but I didn't trust my voice. I stood up, jingling my keys. I blew him a kiss and started for the front door.

"Hey," my father called after me, following me to the living room, his toes peeking shyly from the hem of his pajama bottoms. I had forgotten about how he never wore slippers, how his bare feet shuffling on the kitchen linoleum first thing in the morning sounded like sandpaper rubbed on wood, how that summer before my mother died I could lie awake in my room and hear him walking in there to make coffee after sleeping on the couch. "Hey," he said again. "Once you get to know Doreen, you'll like her."

I took a deep breath. "I think so, too" I said, more confidently than I felt. I walked outside and waved to him, the sunlight bright and hot on my hair.

My father's quiet certainty felt like that, a warmth on my scalp. I wanted to feel it from my mother, too. I was crying by the time I stopped by the liquor store across from the car dealerships and bought a cheap tequila and margarita mix combo for the wedding reception, the kind where the tequila is shrink-wrapped to the yellow mix with smiling limes in sombreros dancing on the label. The guy behind the counter took a long look at my puffy eyes but shrugged and sold me the stuff anyway. Then I drove past the apartments, expecting to see Terence on my doorstep, but he wasn't there, so I doubled back and parked. I rushed to my apartment, expecting him to leap from behind a corner or a bush, but he didn't appear.

Inside the apartment, I cracked the seals, found an empty water bottle, poured in the tequila and mix and shook up the concoction, thinking of when I used to dye my hair. I tipped back a sip, closed my eyes, and imagined the polite glass of wine with Joanie somewhere in the cosmos and started crying again.

I was stretched out on the slippery couch, arms folded across my eyes, when Olin came in with two boxes balanced in his arms. I sat up. "Olin, don't you think you've stuffed this place enough with your junk?" I said.

Olin put the boxes down on the floor. "This is the last of it. And some decorations for tonight." He sat down next to me, eyed the bottles. "Are you drinking?"

"Listen, if your ex-boyfriend of seven years just showed up on the day of your father's surprise wedding, wouldn't you want a drink?"

Olin grabbed the bottle from me, leaned back, and took a long gulp. "Your ex-boyfriend?"

"Terence."

Olin considered this, twirled the bottle from his fingertips. "Well, if your girlfriend broke up with you because your aunt-to-be offered to get you on *Cleveland Tonight* if you went away with her for the weekend, you'd probably want a drink, too."

I took the bottle back from him and set it on the coffee table. "Elana broke up with you?" I asked, ignoring the other part about Barbara.

Olin looked at me for a moment. "She was already pissed about the art happening." He pulled out a string of multicolored lights. "Here, help me hang these."

It could have been Christmas. We'd skipped a few; I was happy to make up for it.

32

BY NOON, we were almost finished decorating when there was a knock on the door. "Shit, it's Terence," I said. "I have to hide."

"You want me to get it?" Olin asked, grabbing the couch for balance as I ran past him to the bedroom.

"I don't care, just make him go away!" I shut the bedroom door and waited. I heard some talking, then some laughing, then footsteps and Olin stuck his head into the room.

"What if it's Frank?" he asked.

I closed my eyes, sighed with relief. In the living room, Frank was wearing a beaten leather jacket and jeans. The room smelled of heat, of clouds cut in half. "I have to make a delivery. Want to come?"

"Oh," I said. "I really don't like to fly."

Olin stepped from behind me, put his arm around my shoulders, and shuffled me forward. "You flew across the ocean. Surely you can make it to—" He looked at Frank questioningly.

"Sandusky."

"—and back. Right?"

I didn't say anything, and neither did Frank. He was checking his watch, looking out the window, perhaps calculating the
amount of wind and sunshine we'd need to move through. I
felt that this was some kind of test—not that Frank was testing
me specifically, but that it was a larger kind of test, more related
to fate and opportunity, and I wanted to pass. "OK," I said.

A half hour later, I was sitting in Frank's white twin-engine
Baron with the red stripes on the wings like war paint. The
runway wavered in the afternoon sunshine and seemed to
float against the velvety green field of horseshit-fed grass. I
glimpsed Lettie's house through the trees. Frank walked
around the plane, flipping up the ailerons, checking the gas
and tires. A satisfied-looking horse gazed at us drowsily from
behind a fence a few dozen yards away.

"That's Nelson," Frank said to me on the copilot's side
through the open window, pointing. I nodded. It bothered me
that you could open a window on something that flew—it
seemed to be inviting danger. Frank climbed in, pulled out a
frayed logbook, and made some notes. He flipped a couple of
switches, and the cockpit dials lit up. "Put this on," he said,
handing me a headset.

"What, am I going to have to help you fly?"

"It's so you can hear me. And buckle up."

I laughed. "You don't really believe that will help."

Frank didn't answer. He pushed in two plungerlike things
and pulled them out again. He started the engines, and we tax-
ied down the strip. The engine and the rushing air filled my
headset; my teeth vibrated. "Don't you need to talk to someone
on the radio or something, let them know we're going up?"

Frank shook his head. "We're flying visual."

"Meaning?" I prompted.

"Meaning that we're flying west at an even altitude plus

five hundred feet. Probably forty-five hundred or something."

"Or something," I said.

"Whatever feels good."

I decided then to try pretending that this was actually a movie I happened to be in. We lifted off the ground, and the grass and trees fell away slowly, like a dress floating to the floor. I could see Lettie's house and the highway, colors bright and crisp like model train set props. It was a beautiful, clear day, but I realized I had started pinching the inside of my arm very hard. I tried to do the Walrus Belly breathing exercise but couldn't keep the rhythm. I settled for a lot of deep breaths. Frank pulled the throttles toward him and the plane lifted sharply.

"How old is this plane?" I asked, trying to sound unconcerned about the smallness holding us in all that high blue air.

He thought for a moment. "Twenty-five years, I think. Are you hyperventilating?"

"Isn't that kind of old?" I asked, ignoring the question.

"Well, middle-aged."

"And you're comfortable with that? Middle-aged?"

Frank glanced over at me. "Yes, in fact, I prefer it."

We flew to Sandusky, looped around the shiny amusement park, the glinting lake, and landed on a seemingly too-skinny airstrip in a field in the country. I stood in the shade of a low white building with benches and a vending machine inside that apparently served as the passenger waiting area, and watched as Frank unloaded small brown plastic cylinders that looked like large travel coffee mugs into a faded green pickup truck driven by a round-bellied man in overalls. Then we took off again, and the lake got flat and small and glassy, and I couldn't help asking if he was sure we had enough gas.

Frank pinched the bridge of his nose with his thumb and forefinger and smiled. "Merle, you're so refreshingly paranoid. It's funny, it calms me somehow."

I wasn't going to be put off. "Don't you remember when we met, and you had to borrow Lettie's phone to call for repairs because you had almost crashed into her maples?" I thought of that low buzzing, the plane a drunk bug flying into a spider web.

"Of course I remember. That was only two weeks ago," Frank said, but he didn't seem to feel the need to explain further.

I looked at the land beneath us, the blue rim of atmosphere on the horizon. There was the sunlit lake to the left, and the billowing green-and-yellow-checked farms to the right. After we'd been flying close to an hour and banked to the south, I figured that we had to be over territory I had driven and walked on for years, but from above, nothing looked familiar. "We're close, aren't we?" I asked.

"Yep. There's the college down there. Look for the radio tower. Three o'clock."

I leaned closer to the window to look. I saw the tower and tried to find other buildings that I knew were nearby, like my father's office and the Morris P. Alston building. "I don't recognize anything," I said.

"Everything looks different up here," he said. He smiled at me. "You get used to it."

"I'm still trying to get my bearings on the ground," I said, and it was true. As we descended, I looked down at the miniature trees and streets and realized this lack of recognition was what I'd been living with ever since I got back; I'd been looking for things that had long since disappeared.

"So tell me, Merle," he said after a while. I didn't look at him, even though my heart pressed hard against my ribs at the sound of him saying my name, a hopeful criminal leaning against bars. "How are things coming with the party?"

I thought about Terence, his lavender rental car, his purple sunglasses, his presence a bruise. The plane lurched, and I forced myself not to comment on it. The engine sounded like a strangled lawn mower. I decided this had to be normal. "There's something you need to know," I said.

Frank smiled at me, and he looked very handsome then, his crooked nose balanced by the steady line of his jaw. "I know, I know, it's a family thing. Anything could happen. It might be embarrassing, right? It might be funny. But I was thinking we could—"

And then he stopped talking because it had suddenly gotten a lot quieter, like when you've been driving for hours and you stop the car. I could still hear the engine but it seemed far away somehow. The relative quiet filled the plane like water; I could hear my own breathing. I looked to my right. The prop on my side of the plane had stopped, and it seemed we had begun coasting in a very long arc to the ground.

"Frank?" I asked, but he wasn't saying anything; he was flipping switches and messing with the throttles. But then I heard his voice, low and echoey. "OK," he was saying, almost lovingly, as if trying to comfort the plane. "Got an engine down, that's all."

"Frank," I said.

He shook his head. "No oil pressure. Probably the cylinder. Or the crankcase. Damn it. I'm shutting down so it won't seize and taking us down a bit."

Right then I could hear everything—my heartbeat, his breathing, something rattling in the fuselage, and I thought of my father as a young boy coasting toward that irrigation ditch, crawling over his father's limp legs, and then of my mother as the tree spread itself in her vision, headlight-pale and deep, a room she could never leave. My head felt heavy on my neck.

Frank was looking at the left engine and back to the oil gauge, back and forth.

"What?" I demanded.

He didn't answer.

"Frank, damn it."

"Just watching the temp on the other cylinder head, if you must know," he said. He reached for my hand. "So, you want to get married?" he said then.

I stared at him, then back at the receding sky. There was that strangled lawn mower sound again, now coming from the other engine. Things were getting bumpy. "What?" I yelled. "Fly the plane! Make it fly!" The ground seemed too close now, the trees no longer broccoli-like and safe, but huge, leering and grabby.

Frank was looking straight ahead now, determined. "We're OK, trust me," he said. He got on the radio. "Baden Center, this is Baron-seven-two-seven-five-golf at 3,500 feet en route to Florence. I've lost an engine and request permission to land."

"Baron-seven-two-seven-five-golf, are you declaring an emergency?" a man's voice barked across the static.

"Seven-five-golf no, but request landing as soon as possible. Request preferential handling."

"There's no emergency?" I shouted.

"Seven-five-golf, you are clear to land straight on runway one-eight," the voice came again.

Frank looked at me. "Merle, I mean it."

"No, goddamnit! Don't ask me just because you feel bad for me because I'm so uptight or because you're going to kill us or because my father's getting married and I'm not!" I realized I was scooping armfuls of air toward myself while I screamed, as if I could pull us further along, swim us off the ground.

Frank shook his head, flipped another switch. "We're going to be OK," he said. "We're going in, nice and easy." The landing gear clunked out. The trees were now close enough that I could see shocked birds scattering like blown pieces of paper, and beyond that, the small airport and the pale runway, rising toward us. I closed my eyes halfway, enough so I could still see but my eyelashes were blurring everything a little. I could feel my lungs swelling, my ears popping, my fingertips vibrating, and then something else, something like the quiet of sliding beneath the surface of a warm bathtub of water, the lift of the hair from the scalp, the sound of squeezing veins and sliding blood cells everywhere. It was the feeling of letting go, the moment before you open your mouth and let the water in, before everything that you are becomes everything else. I relaxed into it, this new, other place. I thought of Joanie and wondered what it had been like before, if it had been pure terror, or if she'd had time, in those last slivers of seconds, to see anything but that widening tree, to say something like good-bye.

We landed hard. I kept my eyes closed even after it was clear that we hadn't crashed, that we were moving slowly along the bumpy runway. The plane came to a wobbly stop.

"Come on, take a look," he said.

I opened my eyes. We were parked in front of a white wood-sided building with a window near the top where someone had propped a fake owl.

"Welcome to Baden County International," he said, smiling. He hugged me, pulled off my headset. "We're fine."

I let my forehead rest against his neck. The heat of his skin felt like a just-driven car; I could feel him clicking and cooling. "I'm not going to marry you," I said.

He was breathing deep, as if he'd been running. "OK," he said. "Given the situation, I can understand that."

"But, it's not because I don't like you," I said, feeling his chest rise and fall under his leather jacket. "I mean, I do like you." I wanted him to tell me why he'd popped the question and if he'd really meant it, or to at least admit he could understand how one could see the whole thing as a little odd. I wanted him to say I made him desperate, but he didn't seem desperate at all, just very calm, a man who'd avoided disaster and was trying to pull himself together. Meanwhile, I was dazed, tingling with adrenaline. It was all rattling around in my head—the lilting plane, what seemed like death sailing up to me like a huge green blanket, and then the idea of marriage, like the thing you have to pick out of a list of objects that doesn't belong—square, square, circle. Cold, cold, warm.

"Listen to me," he said, letting me go. He looked through the windscreen as if we were still in the air. "At some point you're going to have to believe that people are looking out for you."

I sat up straight, fumbled for the door handle. "Yeah, well, thanks for the attention," I said. "That's just what I needed."

A guy named Earl, a mechanic friend of Frank's, drove us back to the farm. In the distance I could see Nelson dozing in the tree shade, nose dropping toward his muscled chest and jerking back up again as if waving to us. We got into Frank's car and he drove me home through town, past the cemetery, past the high school, turned and crossed the bridge, past Fortuna's and the Lotus and the Iron, all looking cleanly washed in spring sunlight. We passed the college, the Morris P. Alston building hunkered down on the hill, looking almost like a place where interesting things could be said, and then he pulled into a parking space in front of the Baden Lake Apartments. He cut the engine, leaned to kiss me on the cheek, but I stopped him.

"So do you always propose that way?" I asked. My legs still felt weak and heavy from the scare in the plane, so I figured it couldn't make me any more nervous to bring it up now.

Frank looked at me, his brown eyes calm. "No, it just came to me," he said. "I make my best decisions under duress."

"That's funny," I said, feeling his hand close over mine. "That's when I make my worst." We smiled, and I caught myself thinking that this man, who seemed unable to fly a plane without an emergency landing, might be good for me.

I didn't even notice Terence and Harold coming from the other side of the quad, arms around each other's shoulders; I had totally forgotten about him. "Merle!" Terence called.

Frank and I turned, watching them through the windshield as they approached. Terence and Harold each held a hasher in their free hands, smiling idiotically. I didn't want to have to handle introductions, so I kissed Frank quickly on the cheek and slid across the seat. "I have to go," I said. "You'll come tonight, won't you?"

Frank nodded. I shut the car door and watched him drive away. Terence and Harold came up behind me, giggling.

Harold took a long drag of his hasher and wagged his head slowly. Terence beamed at me, eyes red and puffy.

"I had no idea," Harold said, pausing, the sentence swirling almost out of his reach before he managed to pick it up again, "No idea how wonderful this stuff was!" he said. "All these years!"

"Oh, yeah, a real thrill," I said. I shoved my hands into my pockets, looking for my house key, and felt something cool and silky, like a lock of hair. I pulled it out. It was the grass clump from my mother's grave. I turned it in my hand, studying it. This seemed to claim Terence and Harold's deepest attention. I headed for my apartment, Terence and Harold following. They watched me as I pressed it into the ground in front of the front steps. By the time I'd climbed the two steps to the stoop it was impossible to tell it apart from the other grasses; it might as well have disappeared.

33

WHEN I OPENED THE DOOR to my apartment, leaving Terence and Harold outside, where they had decided to lie down on their backs and observe the clouds, I found Olin in the living room wearing a charcoal gray suit and sail-white shirt, pacing. "Man, you are late," he said. He was a dark pencil line, dividing the room. The multicolored lights winked on and off where the walls met the ceiling; the coffee table leaning against the wall next to the window reflected him, a fuzzy, glowing double. A sign hung from the top of it, CONGRATULATIONS ERNEST AND DOREEN, lifting from the breezes sliding around me from outside. In the other corner, Marilyn stood draped in a toilet-paper veil and revealing dress, Olin's signature touch.

I stepped inside and shut the door behind me. "I was nearly killed," I said, but Olin wasn't listening. There was a knock on the door. I opened it to find Terence leaning against the frame, Harold behind him on the grass, stretched out like a flung scarecrow.

I rolled my eyes. "Fuck off, then," I said to him in my best

BBC accent, flinging the door closed again. "That's Terence, by the way," I said to Olin.

Olin was all business. He waved me toward the hallway. "Come on, get dressed, we have to go!" he said.

Terence opened the door again and came in, flopping down on the sofa. Olin and I stared at him. "A fine visit this has been," he said. "And you must be Olin," he said, extending a hand. "So very pleased to meet you. Love the doll," he said, gesturing at Marilyn.

"It's not a—whatever. Thanks," Olin said, shaking his hand. He grinned at Terence. "So you're the old boyfriend," he said.

Terence shook his head. "I'm the current one. She left me because I wanted to take her on that swinging ferry—"

"Terence, where's Harold?" I said. The interruption worked; he was too stoned to maintain a train of thought. He stared at the ceiling, tapping his chin, a "Where-was-I?" look on his face.

"Swinging ferry?" Olin said, smiling at me.

"No, a plane, like the one I nearly died in today," I said, trying to change the subject. I grabbed Terence's hand and dragged him to the door. "Come on, you have to go."

"No, stay! We have time," Olin said. "Want a beer?"

"Now that's more like it," Terence said.

I squeezed Terence's hand tighter, opened the door. "I thought you said we were late!" I yelled at Olin.

"Hey, if you have all day to fly across the state and back, I have time for a good story," Olin said, open beer in hand, waving Terence over.

"It's a small, shitty plane, not a time machine!" I yelled at him. "Now get out!" I said to Terence, shoving him out the door and locking it. I spun around, chin jutting, to find Olin in a "What, me?" pose, shrugging, hands up. I grabbed the beer from him and stalked down the hall to get ready for the wedding.

I stood in the bedroom and stared at my rumpled clothes, rifled through duffel bags curled on the floor like two sleeping campers. It occurred to me that I hadn't even thought about what I was going to wear. I only had one dress, a black, nearly see-through number that Terence had bought for me, with built-in, removable bra cups. I didn't even know if I had brought it with me in my hasty packing, and I knew I didn't have any shoes, just the clunky black boots I'd worn on the plane and every day since. "Well, fuck it, I'll make it work," I said to myself. I took off my clothes and put on the dress and pulled a black sweater over it, shoved my bare feet back into my boots, my sweaty toes searching the seam of the soles. Checking myself in Olin's big square mirror that matched his bed, I pulled in my stomach and folded my shoulder blades into the backs of my ribs, watching my breasts lift and fall with my breathing. My hair, pulled back into a twiggy ponytail, was ribbed and tangled. I shook it out, smoothed it with my fingers, felt the ridge where the rubber band had crimped it. I hunted around in the side pocket of one duffel bag and found three bobby pins.

"Merle?" Olin called down the hall, sounding so much like our father it made my chest ache.

"Almost ready!" I called back. And maybe it was then, as I stood up, holding my tiny metal bobby pin bouquet, that something shifted in the room, maybe a cloud sliding away from the sun outside, which threw a slant of light on the wall and made me look at the mirror again, layers of myself lifting in and out of focus—my child face peering out from under too-long bangs, my teenage self hiding beneath hair glitter and stage makeup, and the face of me now, a woman who hadn't looked at herself in a long time, cheeks pale against the dark smudge of her wrinkled clothes. I kneeled to feel around in the duffel side pocket again, still watching myself, and found a tube of lip gloss. Leaning close to the mirror, I held the gloss in my teeth as I pinned up my hair, then pinched my cheeks the way I'd done as a girl when my mother was still alive and not letting me wear makeup, not wanting me to smear on that mark of womanhood, wanting me to stay young and safe, even as she drank herself away from me. I pulled the lip gloss from between my teeth and gently bit my bottom lip, then my top lip, color blooming from the marks. The lip gloss was waxy and thick and smelled faintly of vanilla. I thought of my mother on the morning of her wedding, the sky probably the color of faded cloth as she quietly packed her bags, slipping into the best dress she could find on such short notice. I pressed my forehead to the cool, repeating glass, my knees burning on the carpet, and then pushed myself to my feet.

The wedding was at the courthouse across from Tony's Choice Cuts—a butcher shop, not a salon, I realized, as Olin and I passed, leaving Terence and Harold in the quad, contemplating blades of grass. The courthouse was small, Georgian, square white columns sticking out of the brick. Doreen's mint green Cadillac was parked out front, almost as long as the building.

Doreen, Barbara, and my father were waiting in the lobby. My father was very contrasty—black suit and white shirt, hair darkened from being slicked back while wet, skin pink against his collar. Released from his usual browns and beiges, he looked like a photograph of himself. He smiled when he saw Olin and me and hugged us both.

This time, fortunately, Doreen and Barbara were dressed differently, but not by much. Doreen wore a floor-length white tulle skirt like the bottom of a cake and a glossy leather bustier that laced up the back, and when I hugged her, my fingertips ran down the raised diamonds of skin that pooched between the laces. A constellation of pearl-tipped pins poked from the swirls of her hair. Barbara wore an ivory suit, cleavage grinning from the neckline V, rhinestone buttons glittering. She tottered over on very high spike heels from where she was chatting up the guard working the side door and hugged us next, shrouding us in an atmosphere of perfume and hairspray.

After the hugs, we all stood around, our waiting echoing off the marble floors.

"Lettie should be here any minute," my father said.

"I should have asked her if she wanted to be picked up," Olin said.

I kept checking to make sure I wasn't standing where the setting sun coming through the windows could shine through my flimsy skirt. I felt as if I were in one of those dreams where you're suddenly naked and no one has noticed yet, but you know that they will.

Just then Lettie came through the front door in a flare of red, sequins on her pantsuit flashing, her hair a nodding cloud on top of her head. She tapped her foot as the guard checked her purse, then grabbed it back from him. Olin and I stepped back to widen the circle for introductions as she approached. She scanned Doreen, then Barbara.

Doreen smiled like a schoolgirl, dipped a hint of a curtsey. "Pleased to meet you, Mrs. Winslow."

Lettie raised one eyebrow. "I didn't know you could still wear white at your age."

Doreen looked as if a strong wind had hit her face. My father stepped forward, took Lettie by the elbow, and began leading her toward a side chamber, possibly a little faster than Lettie usually walks. "Let's find you a place to sit," he said.

Doreen was breathless. She looked as if she needed a place

to sit, too. Barbara patted her arm and glared in Lettie's direction. "I'm sorry," I said.

"Yeah," Olin said. "She's kind of got a mouth on her but, really, she's very nice."

Doreen and Barbara didn't seem convinced. Just then, the judge swept into the room from another side door, robes swaying. He was very tall and white-haired, the skin taut over his sharp cheekbones. "I'm ready for you now," he said, his voice seeming to come from high in his nose. We all streamed after the judge like magnets drawn to the dark metal of his robe.

We crowded into the tiny chamber. I was expecting something a little more official looking, but it recalled a doctor's waiting room—bare floor, a line of plastic-bottomed stacking chairs against the wall with angled metal legs like the landing gear of Jetson's cartoon spaceships, a dark, fake wood desk in one corner, and some framed official-looking documents on the walls. We stood between the row of chairs and the desk.

"I'm going to get comfortable," Lettie announced, settling into a chair. No one said anything.

"Will the two who are to be married approach?" the judge intoned.

Doreen and my father crowded closer to the end of the desk where the judge was standing. My father pulled the license from his pocket and handed it to the judge, and I thought of my mother with her razor and some diluted Clorox, shifting her birth a year back in time. A notary public, a prim, small-featured woman, slipped soundlessly into the room through a "secret" door made to look like the paneling. The judge handed her the license and she smoothed it under her hand before she began to write in a ledger while we all watched. The judge cleared his throat. "And who will be the witnesses?"

Barbara stepped forward, wedging herself between Doreen and the desk. "Right here, honey," she warbled, waving, then, cowing a little under the judge's glare. "Your Honor, I mean."

The judge barely looked at her. He waited for a moment. "There must be two witnesses."

My father turned to the three of us—Olin, Lettie, me. He obviously hadn't even thought of this detail. I saw him struggling to decide. Lettie would have been the easiest choice if it hadn't been for her fashion commentary, because then he wouldn't have to choose between Olin and me. His eyes moved back and forth between us, and right then I thought of when he asked me to dance nights when Joanie was learning to cha-cha with other men, when he'd told me to come back to him safely that summer when my mother and I had gone to Oklahoma to nurse my grandfather after his heart attack. I watched him looking at us and knew he didn't want to choose, and I was opening my mouth to say it was OK with me if Olin wanted to do it, to make it easy for him as a kind of thanks for all the times he tried to make things easy on me, even if it didn't always work, but then I saw my father reach for me and at the same time I felt Olin's hand on the small of my back, nudging me forward, and I took his warm, square hand and stood beside him and called myself his witness.

A few minutes later, we walked out into the purple-gray evening light, Ernest and Doreen leading us, Barbara giggling and tossing handfuls of rice over them dug from her beaded pocketbook.

"They're both tacky," Lettie whispered to me.

"Shh," I whispered back, lacing her thin fingers in mine. Then I caught a glimmer at the corners of her eyes and I realized she had been crying, maybe happy to be able to see her son get married this time. Olin brought up the rear, whistling, and I thought of how it must have been for my father that first time, driving away from Joanie's drunk and raging father, his children as unknown as flowers yet to poke through the soil.

34

AFTER THE WEDDING we drove in a short procession to the apartments, Doreen and my father leading in the Cadillac, Lettie alone in her faded used Volkswagen Golf with bumper stickers for PETA, and Barbara riding with Olin and me in the backseat of the Bronco, leaning forward close enough to nibble Olin's ear and telling off-color jokes. As we pulled into the parking lot, I remembered that Terence and Harold were probably still strung out on Moroccan hash, and worry gathered into a hard little disc behind my sternum. I didn't want them messing things up. It was getting dark as we parked, and I couldn't see them as I went ahead of the group to open the door. Olin was helping Lettie find her way down the bluish shadowed sidewalk, while I plugged in the string lights and pulled out refreshments.

Barbara was right behind me. "Can I help you with anything, honey?"

"Yeah, get me a drink and cut the Vanna act," Lettie yelled from the doorway as Olin led her inside.

"Easy, Lettie," Olin said. He shot me a tired glance as Barbara and I climbed the steps behind them.

"I hope you kids don't mind, I invited some friends," Lettie said, checking her hair in the chrome trim of the upended coffee table.

"Your pinochle partners, I presume?" Barbara asked with a sneer-smile.

"Strip poker," Lettie shot back.

Ernest and Doreen came in and Olin popped open a bottle of champagne. "Here you go," Olin said, bringing them two foamy plastic cups.

"Cheers," my father said, lifting his cup to us. He was beaming that smile that made the top of his forehead and tips of his ears red and shiny, Doreen glowing at his side, the red and green and purple and yellow lights breaking apart in the layers of her skirt, fragmented rainbows. I was happy for them, but I had to admit to myself, jealous too. I wanted a love like that to push my blood to the inside edges of my skin, to make me swell with color.

There was a knock at the door. I was certain it would be Terence or Harold, probably delusional by now, worshiping crystals and singing medleys from the *White Album,* but the knock was too measured, too polite. Olin opened the door to Marge Delinsky, my thorough supervisor at the DSS, who balanced a pot of fuchsia impatiens over a tray of cookies. The smell of flowers and warm sugary dough filled the room, which suddenly seemed crowded with people, Doreen and Barbara twin ivory screens for all the reflected hues, Marge's teal suit vibrating energetically with Lettie's tomato red as they shook hands at my father's introduction.

Olin crouched by his stereo on the floor, slipping CDs into the changer, and the room was filled with Stan Getz's hushed saxophone, a live recording. I could hear the floorboards squeaking under Stan's feet, the dusty air over the stage, lifting the felt-wrapped gold tones toward the ceiling. I filled two more cups of champagne, emptying the bottle. "Here, you need one, too," I said to Olin. We leaned against the wall to make room for Lettie's friends, who were just walking in, three wispy women with hair rinsed into variations of gray, all of whom would probably have looked simply gray by themselves, but together told on each other, the pink hue informing on the blue, the blue a narc for the gold. Lettie yelled for someone to open another bottle of champagne, and we watched my father work his way toward the kitchen to take care of it.

"He looks happy, doesn't he?" Olin said.

I nodded but didn't say anything. Olin elbowed me. "And how about you? You going to snap out of it?"

I was trying to think of what to say, and I was watching Lettie handing out plastic cups of champagne to her pastel friends, gazing at the half-open door, and then I saw a mood-ringed hand push it open all the way, revealing Terence and Harold behind him. Terence was still wearing the same outfit but Harold had changed into a blue suit that hung unevenly from his shoulders and was too short in the arms. "Shit," I said.

Olin looked to where I was looking. "Ah, time to hear about the dangling ferry, or whatever!" he said, starting toward them.

I grabbed his arm. "Look, it's none of your business."

"Hey, hey, I was just kidding," Olin said. He looked a little scared.

I let him go and watched him greet Terence and Harold. He introduced them to everyone as if they were honored guests, smoothly moving through the room with drinks for them and refills for everyone else, and I thought he had turned out the best of all of us, with his natural grace, his laughing confidence.

It didn't take Terence long to find his way over to me. "I recognize that frock," he whispered, leaning against the wall next to me. I felt his hand, rising, reaching for me, and I pushed off the wall.

"I don't even know why I brought it," I said. I didn't want to look at him.

"That's simple. You're still in love with me!" he said, gloating smile dulled by the stoned drape of his eyelids.

"Why don't you get some rest. You look awful," I said, and I caught a glimpse of hurt in his expression as I walked away, since he hated the idea of not looking wonderful, his smile now drooping, too, almost enough to make me feel bad, but not quite. I bit the inside of my cheek and did a quick Walrus breath, just to make sure.

I found Doreen outside on the stoop, smoking a cigarette, white dress yellowed under lamplight. She looked a little forlorn, a prom girl whose date hadn't shown up. "You don't have to smoke outside," I said. It was chilly; looking at her bare shoulders made me shiver.

"Oh, I don't mind," she said. She seemed distracted, pearl-tipped pins in her hair trembling.

"Are you OK?" I wanted to put a jacket over her shoulders, something with pearls and spangles.

She tossed her cigarette into the bushes. I could tell from the way she turned to me, the way she took a deep breath, eyelids fluttering, that she had something to tell me. When she started, the words came fast. "I wasn't really selling office supplies when your father and I met—I mean, I had some sticky pads and mechanical pens with me, but I'd just bought them at the art store down the street, and I was trying to get people to write me checks for this, uh, business investment opportunity—anyway, I told your father I was trying to raise money for some charity, and he believed me and wrote a check." Doreen had woven her fingers together and pressed her hands down so that the palms were flat, parallel to the ground, polished nails so long they dug into the backs of her hands.

"And?" I asked, thinking of her two previous husbands of the heart defect and midnight pierogi run, and I wondered for a moment if she was going to tell me their deaths hadn't really been due to ill health or bad luck.

"Well, I was walking down the street to go meet my ride, and I had your father's check in my purse, and I had a little time, so I stopped in this sandwich shop for a meatball sub. Then, the weirdest thing happened. This old guy who was running the place—he'd had a stroke or something because half his face was dead—he told me I'd stopped there for a reason, because I had a decision to make. I sat down and ate my sandwich—I was eating kind of quick because the old guy made me nervous, and I started thinking about your father. All of a sudden I couldn't get him out of my mind. I was thinking of his gray eyes and his brown tie, and how serious he'd looked when he gave me the check, and I started thinking that there's a difference between gullibility and faith—I'm Catholic, see, and I know. And I was thinking that your father had faith in me, and that if I turned around and walked back to him, I could change my life."

I leaned against the cool brick next to the front door. Doreen was looking at me, waiting for my reaction. "Does my father know?" I asked.

"Yes. But I guess it makes me sad that he didn't tell you anything about me. I mean, I could tell you had no idea what to expect last night."

"Oh, don't feel bad," I said. "Everything I know about him I've heard from someone else." I patted her soft shoulder, and she hugged me, and I breathed in hairspray and perfume and the ironed plastic smell of synthetic clothing, the tulle dress crunching against my legs. I took her hand and led her inside.

On the stereo, Etta James was singing about her funny valentine when, across the room, my father cleared his throat—I heard it easily over the crowded room chatter, I was tuned to it, like a mother who can recognize her baby crying, except the opposite. "A toast!" he said.

We all lifted our plastic cups.

"To Doreen and our new life together!" he said.

Someone clapped, and a few other people followed suit, the clapping like stray firecrackers popping around the room. "And to my son and daughter, and to the past, which has brought us all here," he continued, and this time no one clapped, maybe because they weren't sure if he was finished, or maybe because they couldn't really tell if the last part was leading to a happy or sad ending. My father waited, cup balanced lightly on his fingertips, the quiet moment stretching out too long. I started clapping loudly, and then everyone else clapped, and then he drank, head tilted back, his throat pale, the Adam's apple knobby and exposed like a child's knee. He held out a hand to Doreen, and she twirled into it, wrapping herself in the inside of his elbow, and they began to dance. I watched and thought of Joanie at the Florence Ballroom Dancing Club, whirling away from us.

After a few minutes, Olin stepped up to them to cut in, and my father held out a hand to me, pulling me to his chest. His eyes were smiling, bright as buttons, and we danced a slow, simple box step. I closed my eyes and drew in his gray woolen smell, the smell of whiskers and cotton undershirts and something else, sawdust, maybe. "I'm happy for you, Dad," I said.

He kissed my forehead and smiled at me, his eyes only slightly above level with mine. Over the years I had forgotten that he wasn't a tall man; my memory had pegged him from the child's perspective. "Thank you," he said.

Other people joined us—Harold and Marge, Terence and Barbara, who made an oddly attractive couple, I noticed, Terence still a little pouty, his smooth white jaw pressed to Barbara's rouged cheek. Olin dipped Doreen and they both laughed.

"I can start paying rent here next week," I said to my father then, and immediately I felt juvenile, absurd. I was trying to say that I could take care of myself, that I was going to stay, to be in his life with him again if he still had room for me.

"Whenever you're ready," he said. We turned again and I saw Olin's Marilyn, wistful in her toilet-paper veil, her shoulders bare and glowing under the string lights. I pressed my forehead against my father's neck, felt a scratchy spot where he'd missed shaving. I'd spent most of my life trying to be different from my parents, my tight-lipped father, my impulsive mother; I'd told myself I would choose a man not because I was trying to escape something, like my mother did, and the man I chose would be fun-loving and bright with emotions, unlike my father. But I had run away as surely as Joanie, and I was beginning to think I had misread my father after all, his stoic lack of tears after his father's death not a sign of fear, but of a gentle restraint, survival with grace.

I closed my eyes and let him lead me, step step, step step. I felt like a child being carried to bed, entirely loose, arms and head heavy, bending to whatever cushioned them. The music ended and someone opened the front door, cool air streaming into the warm room. I smelled a sharp hint of engine and I lifted my head; Frank stood in the doorway, scanning the room, a bunch of yellow daffodils in his fist, their heads nodding like a choir.

My father and I stepped apart and he took Doreen's hand, Doreen in her sparkling hair and dress gazing up at my father with a tiny, secret smile, not the woman I'd first seen cruising by with her shout-laugh but love-glazed now, a shy princess, and my father her awkward prince. "I think we'd better go," he said to Olin and me. "It's a long drive to Florida."

I kissed him good-bye on the slant of his jaw and walked with him and Doreen and Olin to the door, sliding past them as they said their good-byes so I could greet Frank. "Hi," I said to him. Behind us, Barbara was throwing rice again.

"Quit that, you're just making a mess," I heard Lettie say.

Frank handed me the flowers, which smelled faintly oily, but in a good way, like a gas station on a summer morning when you're on the way to the beach. "I'm sorry about earlier today," he said.

I wanted to ask, which part? But I didn't. "Thank you," I said. I waved to my father and Doreen as they walked to their car followed by Olin and Barbara. From that distance, they could have been a pair of kids going to a formal, my father stiffly leaning to open the Cadillac door for her, the tentative way she took his hand, except of course she was in the driver's seat when they pulled away, honking and waving.

35

A BLUES TUNE CAME on next, a boat rocking slow. Frank followed me to the kitchen and watched while I filled a stray Corona bottle with water and threaded the daffodils in. I held up the bottle to check the water level, and we both watched the stems float and sway in the bubbly, beer-laced water.

"Hello," Terence said from the kitchen doorway. He held out a not very steady hand to Frank to shake. "And who might you be?" he asked, boarding-school syntax sneaking up on him. Frank looked at him, then at me.

"Frank, this is Terence," I said, sighing. "Terence, Frank."

Terence glared at Frank. Frank gazed back, not aggressively, just in an I'm-keeping-my-eye-on-you kind of way. And I guess if I ever thought human males were somehow different from males of other species in territorial disputes, seeing Terence and Frank stare at each other silently, shoulders slightly hunched, chins jutting, I had to admit I'd been wrong. Women would at least feel they had to make conversation.

We stood in a quiet triangle, Terence accusing, Frank watchful, me embarrassed and flattered.

"Terence is here on a surprise visit from England," I said. I might as well have been talking to a pair of offended cats, so instant and self-contained was their mutual dislike.

But Terence broke first. "I work in the sex industry."

Frank nodded. Then, biting his lip to suppress a grin, "Me too."

"Oh, really?" Terence said, a little breathy now, eyes flicking to me and back to Frank. "And what's your area?"

"Sperm delivery."

Terence rolled his eyes. "Oh, how original."

Frank, clarifying: "Horse sperm."

Male disdain floated above our heads, squirmy and whiptailed.

I heard a crash in the living room and rushed gratefully to investigate. The toilet paper–adorned Marilyn had fallen against the leaning coffee table, looking drunk and swoony now, veil askew. Lettie held the pot of impatiens Marge had brought over her head in both hands, like a basketball player ready to shoot. "YOU UGLY OLD BASTARD!" she shrieked at Harold, who was cowering on the other side of the couch. Her friends were gathering by her side, pastel thugs.

"I didn't do anything—will someone calm her down?" Harold quavered, backing away.

"YOU GRABBED MY ASS!" Lettie roared.

"All right now," Olin said, coming from the side, scoring the flowerpot. "Everybody just calm down."

Harold was working his way to the door—the room was so crowded people couldn't get out of the way. I noticed that Marge was right behind him. Lettie flung herself at him as he got near; her friends held her back. "THAT'S RIGHT, RUN!" she commanded. Harold was sliding around the door-edge now; Marge managed to follow, working one breast at a time around the turn. She glanced over her shoulder at me, sheepish, blinking, flushed-faced and nervous. I couldn't believe she was the same woman who warned me about falling for former millionaires in client intake. I raised my hand close to my chest and gave her a little, secret wave just from my fingertips, and she beamed back at me before closing the door behind her.

"GODDAMN MEN," Lettie said, shrugging off her whispering friends, lighting a cigarette. I assumed she wasn't thinking of my father when she said it. "Someone get me a drink."

I followed Lettie and her friends down the hall with a bottle of champagne and a cup. Lettie sat on the bed, her friends settling in around her, landing birds, their combined weight barely dipping the mattress. "Here, take this," I said. "And calm down," I said, laughing to myself at the chance to say it for once rather than hear it.

I felt a buzzing warmth behind me; it was Frank, concern crowding his eyes. "Want me to beat him up?" he asked Lettie, and then he smiled. I'd forgotten that they knew each other, that they might even call each other friends.

Lettie poured champagne into her cup, handed me the empty bottle. She was barefoot, her ankles blue-veined and papery next to the ruby sequin–scattered pant leg, and I could tell she was tipsy, her cigarette drawing shaky little circles in the air. "Let me tell you something," she said. "This thing between men and women, it's messy. It just makes a clutter. It's sticky and bloody—it makes my head hurt to think about it." She took a big gulp of the champagne, shook her head as she swallowed. "And now you two are going to play it out, I can see. Well, good luck to you."

The woman I was when I left would have been mortified, twenty years old, scared of myself, living close to my skin because the depths of me were too frightening to explore.

Maybe I would have walked out of the room. Maybe I would have stood there and argued for the sake of arguing, or decided I felt sorry for her so I wouldn't have to feel sorry for myself. But now, there was so little I needed to do—reach for the warm tips of Frank's fingers, lean to kiss Lettie's dry, soft cheek, link my past and future by my mouth and hands.

Walking outside with Frank, I didn't feel like talking at all. The music was behind us, the glowing lights a pressure on our backs. We were almost to his car when I heard a rustling in the hedge, giggles like a bird bustling to flight. It was Barbara and Terence, holding on to each other for balance, Barbara with her arms around Terence's neck and her head on his shoulder, laughing. When Terence saw me he straightened, smile fading. I wanted to tell him it was OK, that I wanted him to be happy. I touched Frank's arm. "Wait just a second," I said. "Terence, I've got something for you," I called, running back to the apartment. I thought of my mother searching the shadowy brown lobby of the Star-Lite for her sketchbook. Inside, I saw Olin dancing with Lettie.

"I thought you were gone," Olin said, grinning.

"That's one way to put it," Lettie said, but she smiled too, and winked at me. The room was nearly empty now, just Lettie's friends and their thin chatter in the kitchen.

"I forgot something," I mumbled. I looked around in the bedroom, opening drawers, feeling through my empty bags. Back in the living room, I felt under the couch and found what I was looking for—my still-unsent letter to Fiona and the peekaboo shorts. I grabbed my purse too and stuffed both inside.

Outside I found Barbara and Terence and Frank chatting awkwardly in the quad, Barbara reminiscing about a movie where she had to stand under a wind machine for three hours while the crew dumped gelatin on her for *Slime Men Are*

Coming. "I thought I'd never get that goop outta my hair," she said wistfully, twirling a frosted lock around one finger.

"Terence, could I talk with you for a minute?" I said.

He looked at Barbara and shrugged an I-can't-help-it-if-everyone-wants-me shrug, and followed me a few feet away.

I pulled the peekaboo shorts out of my purse, took his hand, and folded them into it. They flashed, watery pink, in the moonlight. Terence looked at them, then at me. "You don't have to keep them," I said, and all of a sudden, it seemed pretty absurd, giving him underwear when it was clear we had both moved on to other things, the kind of thing you'd think was appropriate if you'd watched way too much TV growing up, as I had. I was glad my face was shadowed and the moonlight was hitting Terence instead, his skin paler, the shadows of his eyes liquid and deep.

"You don't want them anymore?" he said, cutting his eyes over to Frank and wiggling his eyebrows like Chaplin. He tried to smile then, but ended up biting his lip, and I could feel his disappointment, brittle in the air.

"I wanted to say good-bye," I said. "I mean, I don't know how long you're staying, or what your plans are." I heard my voice in my ears, fading, uncertain.

"I leave tomorrow," he said. "I'd thought you might come with me, but—" Then he touched my cheek, and we hugged, and when he glanced at me as we walked back to Barbara and Frank, I thought of him flying here to win me back, and I realized that he had loved me in his own scattered, spangled way.

Barbara was kissing Frank good night; she hugged him as if she might be considering letting her hands slide lower than the small of his back, and I tried not to let this get to me. I followed him to his car and we drove toward downtown, the streetlamps like little planets against the dark trees and the star-washed sky.

Frank's apartment was on the third floor of a Victorian house at the top of Hill Street. There was a little front room, a kitchen, and a bath off the bedroom, which was a five-walled, oddly shaped room that seemed to have been built by drunk neighbors. We stood in the front room beside the bay window, the treetops of the front yard inches below the sills, and I could see the mossy gloss of the cobblestone street below, the lights of River Street glowing, the buildings amber and shining off the water, and it felt a little like flying, or safer than that, like being in a tree house that you know is sturdy in its cradle of branches.

"I'm going to buy a new plane," Frank said, taking my hands, his plans wrapping around me like the cool, quiet air between us.

"I'm going to buy a car," I said, walking to him, into him, drawing in his smell, which right then was like sun-warmed metal, rain that had barely left the clouds. We kissed for a long time and then we started undressing, his trousers and cotton shirt, my boots and sweater, his hands under my breasts, lifting, fingering the seams of the pull-away panels, not sure what they were, which warmed me in ways I hadn't expected, and I smiled into his neck and slipped the dress straps off my shoulders, held my breath as we fit ourselves together. He was leading me to the bedroom and everything was going fine, I was wet and breathy with anticipation, and then—how could I have helped it?—Terence came to mind, his role-playing and sex toys, the way we were just playing doctor all those years, and I thought of seven years of having been with only one man.

Frank laid me down and we held each other. He felt thicker, muscled where Terence was angled, hairy where Terence was smooth. I didn't know where to begin with all the differences, my mouth missing Frank's as we tried to find each other in the dark, my hands hitting rib where I thought I'd find arm. It made me nervous and I sat up, my mouth dry.

"Are you OK?" Frank asked, sitting up, too.

"Could I have a glass of water?" I asked, buying time.

Frank got up and walked to the kitchen, and I caught the lines of him as he passed, the hinges of his shoulders and hips, the space of his stride, his penis not completely hard, sticking straight out like a guide. He was unconcerned about it, unlike most men—it was all coming back to me now, how they shielded themselves until they had reached what they decided was their fullest glory; this was what I was thinking about as Frank came back with the water, the lines of his back and buttocks outlined now in the bluish light coming in the window, this and Terence and the boys I'd slept with in college, more out of curiosity than anything else, and suddenly the room was very crowded with them all, and I gulped down the water, trying to swallow them again, clear the air.

Frank sat beside me, touched my shoulder. "Are you sure you're OK?"

I reached across him to put my empty glass on the bedstand. I could feel the water sloshing in my belly, the memories gurgling. I belched quietly. "Sorry," I said.

"Would you like me to fart to make you feel better?"

"I've never met a man so willing to accommodate," I said.

We smiled at each other in the dark, our teeth and eyes glimmering, skins blue-shadowed and throwing heat. Frank touched my hair, my cheek, my collarbone. We leaned into each other, and later, when he was inside me, I felt the realness of him, the risky simplicity of it, and then it seemed we were lifting into the quick air, cloud-heavy and constant.

36

I woke up the next morning, my birthday, thinking of my mother and of love. The two feelings mingled and I couldn't tell where one ended and the other began—the oddness of being older than my mother combined with the possibility of starting a life beyond hers, like walking from under porch shadow into the sun. And there was the warm curve of Frank's sleeping self pressed against my back and the nervousness of feeling that new territory.

I sat up carefully so as not to wake him, pulled on my underwear and sweater in the front room, and looked for coffee in the kitchen. The pot was gurgling, almost filled when I heard Frank get up to pee in that loud, authoritative way men do. I was sitting at the table, looking out the front window at the leaves turning in morning breezes when he appeared in the doorway naked, sleep still weighing down his arms and shuffling his step.

"It's my birthday," I said.

"I know," Frank said. He pointed to the newspaper on the couch. "I woke up a couple of hours ago and brought it in, and there you were."

I picked it up. There under the headline, among the photos of Lilly Franklin on the stretcher and her staggering soon-to-be-ex-boyfriend, Charlie, was the photo of my mother and me, my back arched and chubby legs rigid with angry fear, my mother's open mouth a shadow. As always, the article mentioned that it had been my birthday; that my mother was later questioned as a possible organizer. I sat down and thought of thirty years since then.

Frank pulled on his trousers, poured two coffees, and sat down with me at the table. He lifted my feet to his lap, his hands warm against the cool pads of my toes. I looked at my mother's fierce, twenty-two-year-old face, her features narrow and spare. He didn't say anything until I started crying, then he gently placed my feet on the floor and pulled me to him, chair and all. "I watched you sleep this morning," he said. "You sleep beautifully."

I didn't know what to say to this, but something about it calmed me. I sipped my coffee, blew my nose in toilet paper Frank brought me, and thought of Olin's Marilyn in her hopeful, slipping veil. We drank one cup, then another, and then I asked Frank if I could borrow a pair of pants.

"Would you like to help me go plane shopping?" Frank asked.

"I've got to go home," I said.

"It's OK," he said. "It's Sunday and I don't think the plane stores are open on Sundays. It was just my way of asking what you're doing later."

"I'm going to campus," I said. "For the vigil."

Frank walked me downstairs and kissed me on the top of my head before I left.

37

BACK AT MY APARTMENT, I saw that Terence's car was gone, but Olin's was there. I wondered with a surprising, sad tug in my chest if Terence had already left.

Harold's sign for the day: LSD MELTS YOUR MIND, NOT IN YOUR HAND.

I assumed this message had something to do with the evening he'd spent with Terence.

I realized I didn't have my keys, so I knocked softly, then louder. Olin came to the door after the third knock, when I was beginning to think there was no one there and I would have to walk back to Frank's to have a place to hang out, an idea that was not without its appeal. But I wanted to see Olin, and I was happy he was there, even though he gave me a squinty glare in the sunlight. He swung the door open and walked away.

"What's wrong with you?" I asked.

"You left me with Lettie and her racy friends, who do, in fact, play strip poker. They took over the bedroom," Olin said. "I fell asleep on the couch, and they woke me up at four wanting me to follow them home. Not drive them—they insisted on driving—but they wanted me to follow them just in case."

"Were they dressed at that point?"

Olin threw his hands up, and walked into the kitchen. "You know, you leave me and then you make fun of me. It's the same thing over and over."

I shrugged. I sat down on the couch, my purse on my knees. I heard the crackle of Fiona's letter inside and thought about how I would amend it, or if I would just have to start over. Marilyn was still leaning against the upended coffee table. There were little plastic cups and paper napkins everywhere, a pile of CDs on the floor next to the stereo, the multi-colored lights sagging from the ceiling.

"Can I make it up to you?" I called, beginning to pick up the cups and napkins.

"How about joining me in singing 'Happy Birthday'?" Olin said, rounding the corner from the kitchen doorway with a piece of cake one of Lettie's friends had brought for the reception, a lit candle from the table stuffed into the top and tipping precariously. I tried to sing, but it was hard; the words caught in my throat and I kept wanting to breathe. Olin sat the cake down on the couch between us, holding the candle steady. "Make a wish," he said. "Go ahead."

I closed my eyes and thought of my father and Doreen heading south on 77, sunlight in their hair, of Frank looking at my saddest baby picture in the paper, of Olin and how I could always find his childhood face in his smile, right at the corners of the mouth, which turned up exactly like Joanie's, wide with promise.

I blew out the candle, and watched as Olin carefully stood Marilyn up straight and began unwrapping her toilet-paper dress. He folded the long strips of tissue and took it into the bathroom. "No sense in wasting it, right?" he said as he passed me. He came back out with his blue bathrobe and drew it over Marilyn's shoulders, a gentleman on a date, attentive. He tied it in front and stood back to survey his work. "Barbara told me last night she's going to call her people at *Cleveland Tonight,*" he said, without turning around. "About my art happening."

"That's great," I said. I didn't ask him whether he thought he might be the entertainment, or whether it mattered to him.

"She looks good in blue, doesn't she?" Olin said, fingering the hem of one robe sleeve.

"Yes, she does," I said. We both watched her, as if waiting to see if she'd say something, a hello, or thank you.

We decided to eat the cake outside on the stoop. Everything was cartoon-bright with sunlight, the red brick apartments, the yellow-green grass, the snapping blue sky. We were licking icing off our fingers when Terence's rental car pulled into the lot, windows and sunroof open all the way, and then I saw the orange flash of Terence's hair—he was stretched out in the backseat, head against the car door, apparently asleep. Barbara parked and got out, waving at us. "Olin, honey, help me out here, could you?"

I followed Olin to the car. Terence was snoring quietly, arms folded across his chest, frowning slightly in sunlight. "What happened?" Olin asked.

Barbara gave him a steady look. "He didn't get very much sleep," she said. "I thought you might let him rest on your couch. I've got to get back to Vegas."

Olin and I helped a semiconscious Terence out of the car, his legs wobbling at each step, Barbara following. He smelled of cinnamon and hash and cigarettes. His bobbing head and half-closed eyes made me panicky—I wondered if he'd ever leave and then felt guilty for not being more concerned for him. Olin and I staggered inside with him, laid him out on the couch like a heavy coat. He moaned, tried to sit up, fell back against the cushions and started snoring again.

Olin and I looked at Barbara, who was standing in the doorway, watching. "He is one sweet boy," she said.

I couldn't explain the sudden bubble of jealousy stinging my throat. "Are you sure he's OK?"

"Oh, honey, believe me, he's fine," Barbara said smoothly. She started to turn away, then stopped. "My car's still downtown. Could someone give me a ride?" Eyes batting, looking straight at Olin.

"I'll stay here with Terence," I said with a little eye-bat of my own for Olin's benefit.

Olin grabbed his keys, smiling to himself. "This story should be better than the swinging ferry," he said. We followed Barbara outside, and I gave her a hug, wincing as one of her earrings cut into my cheek. "Have a good trip," I said.

I watched them drive off. Inside, I continued to pick up from the party, Terence's snore a rattling bass punctuating my movements. When I came back from taking out the trash, I perched on the arm of the couch and watched him until he woke up, blue eyes focusing on me, squinting, as if he weren't sure where he was.

Neither of us said anything for a while. He seemed to be watching mental replays of the night before, frowning and shaking his head, giggling a little.

"Quite a night, hmm?" I said.

Terence rubbed his face slowly. He groaned. "She kept me up all night."

"No details, please," I said.

Terence broke into a silent laugh that ended in a smoker's cough. "She made me paint her nails!" he said. "Fingers and toes, the whole thing. Soaking, buffing, filing, the works. It took hours." The effort of talking seemed to exhaust him. He tried to sit up, but couldn't; I grabbed his arms and pulled him forward. "My back is killing me from all that kneeling," he said, but he looked at me in a supremely happy way, and I knew he was already putting together his latest X Publishing novel, and that, relieved as I was to have ended my pornographic editing career, I would probably keep an eye out for it, at least online.

Terence shook his head and pushed himself up from the couch. "What time is it? I've got to catch my plane."

Relief and regret at the same time was what I felt, like two currents of water against the skin. I walked with him out to his hulking purple car.

Terence patted his pockets and grinned at me. "Wallet, peekaboo shorts, will travel."

He kissed me on the cheek, and we smiled at each other. What I loved about him right then was his total unawareness of anything relevant to me, like the fact that it was my birthday and that my whole town, anyone who remembered my mother and me at least, knew it. Or that my brother was in love with a doll or my father never cried. But in the end, that wasn't how you moved through time together, unaware. We had cheated ourselves with everything we had decided not to know. I searched for something to say that wouldn't feel purply, dramatic. Good-bye was already thick in the air between us. "Tell Fiona I will get a letter off to her soon, OK?"

"Yes, and send along my congratulations to your father."

We nodded and smiled at each other and said "yes" and "I will" a few more times, until it felt as if we weren't really saying a kind of no to each other, until, watching Terence drive away, I almost believed I'd see him again, maybe at a party where we'd share one glass of wine each, and remember.

38

A FEW HOURS LATER, Olin and I were walking to campus for the Morris P. Alston building bombing vigil. He offered to drive, but I wanted to walk the way my mother had that morning thirty years ago—I could imagine the mixture of excitement and fear swirling in her chest after Lilly's phone call, the squeak of the stroller wheels as she pushed me along, the air crisp and earth-scented, the spring weather and being twenty and having a friend in the movement, whatever that was, quickening her step. We passed Mantle Street, and I could see our father's house, shuttered and quiet, early evening sky warming the windows.

We crossed Trade Street and walked across the green, and I was surprised to see so many people, most of them young, climbing the hill toward the Morris P. Alston building. Neil Young warbled from a sound system beside a podium that had been set up in front of the main doors. Olin and I found a spot on the grass.

"We should have brought some beer," he said, looking around, nodding to the music. It was a party for him in ways it could never be for me, but having him with me helped, as the shadows stretched and deepened on the hill.

It was also a helpful distraction to watch the dozens of college kids passing out white candles to light for the vigil, and I was wondering when college students had started to look so young, their faces open and spare in the fading sunlight. I was thinking about that and about Joanie and where exactly she might have been standing when the photographer snapped us—I had never figured that out because of the agents in the background, you couldn't really see anything else—and then I saw a small-boned woman with graying hair and one arm tucked shyly behind her as she approached the podium, and it took me a few moments of watching her to realize that she was Lilly Franklin, the bomber who'd lived next door to us that hot, sad summer.

"Holy shit," I whispered.

"What?" Olin said.

I pointed, and he looked. "Who is it?"

It surprised me that he didn't recognize her; but I guess he'd been too young to remember her. I wondered what details he did remember; if he, too, needed a photograph to sharpen his memory of Joanie's features again, as I did these days.

Other people were gathering at the podium, men and women in suits with the resigned expressions of academic administration, and then I also recognized Charlie, Lilly's former boyfriend who had caught a piece of shrapnel in the ass and still managed a limp. They stood at opposite ends of the group, apparently ignoring each other. Amelia Flink, the woman who had been blinded in the blast, was being led to the stage by a boy who appeared to be her son. Watson Puckett was taking photographs for the Lotus newsletter, freezing everyone in moments of blue light. I turned and saw Frank coming up the hill. I watched him move through the crowd, his certain stride, his eyes on the sky and then, finding us, on me.

He shook hands with Olin and leaned to kiss me on the cheek, that simple gesture an announcement: We. He sat on the other side of me, smelling of leather seats and fuel.

"Did you fly today?" I asked him. At the podium, the provost was making an introduction.

"No, just did some work on her. Getting her ready for sale."

I didn't like to think of some unsuspecting pilot flying that plane, and Frank seemed to read it. "Don't worry, a better maintenance man than me can take care of her," he said.

The provost finished and a few people clapped. The crowd quieted when Lilly approached the podium. She still looked delicate and vulnerable, her hair tucked behind her ears. I could see where time had changed her—a slight double chin, a thickening at her shoulders and bust—but she still looked like the young woman fresh out of prison that I had half-fallen in love with that summer nearly twenty years ago.

Lilly bent her head as if in a short prayer and cleared her throat. "Many of you are aware of my role in this sad occasion," she said, her voice small and nervous in the gathering evening. "Although I supposedly paid my debt to society, I have never stopped being sorry for what I did."

She paused, and I could hear her breathing, air trembling across the sound system. I closed my eyes and wondered what Joanie might say, what she would have told Olin and me—that she hadn't meant it, the way things had turned out? Or perhaps that everything had happened as it should? I imagined my father and Doreen following the line of the Florida coast in Doreen's Cadillac, golden and quick.

Everyone was silent as Lilly began speaking again. "It doesn't help much to talk about why I did it—I was young, misdirected in my enthusiasm, wanting to be part of something important. I didn't think about the pain I would cause—for the injured, for the college, and for my family. I came here to offer my apologies and my hope that this place is better for it, that we're smarter somehow, and that if our country finds itself at war again, Florence College will be a place where philosophical differences will be settled in peaceful discussion."

She stopped then and for several moments, no one did anything. Then what I was hoping for happened. She glanced in my direction, and I stood up to catch her eye. She saw me, and I think she recognized me, even though it had been nearly twenty years. We looked at each other, and she hugged her damaged arm to her side, as if to protect it.

A few people had started clapping politely, a signal that it was time for the next speaker. Lilly walked away from the podium, back to her place in the semicircle of suits again. I sat down and thought of how much Joanie had wanted to be like her, shaping her pots in exactly the same way, as if to change herself in the clay.

There were a few other speakers, the student government president, the chair of counterculture studies, their voices blending into the soft air. Eventually, someone fired up the Neil Young again. People were on their feet by then, passing out candles, passing flame from candle to candle. Some started to dance, cigarette lighters flickering on and off. Frank and Olin and I stood up to avoid being stepped on. I wanted to find Lilly, to tell her I respected what she'd done, to ask her what she'd been doing with her life since that dry, hot summer when she lived next door to us for a few secret weeks. I thought of her dreams of sailing through her prison bars, starlight caught in her hair, and I thought of my mother and father driving through the night to Ohio after their hasty wedding, the black sky low and hot on the roof of the car.

I thought also of why I had come back, which maybe was because I wanted to know my mother and be different from her at the same time. I wondered what it must have been like for her, that evening when she'd looked down at herself and maybe believed for a moment what Olin had seen, the sequins transformed to fireflies, her life something more than what it was. I could see my thirteen-year-old self batting my glamorous eyelashes, Olin building his flimsy fort, our father pretending he didn't know. I imagined Joanie and Hall drinking until his fingers could barely manage the zipper on her dress that I had helped to fasten before she left. I remembered her face close to mine as she brushed the mascara onto my lashes, her breath on my cheek, minty and warm, her mouth slightly open with concentration, close enough to kiss, and I thought that this was what Hall had seen, too, her mouth opening to his, and I understood it, the need behind it.

Frank took my hand, and the three of us worked our way to the edge of the crowd at the top of the hill. I leaned my head against the slope of Frank's shoulder. He slid his arm around my waist. I touched Olin's arm to make sure he was there. The air was smoky from candles burned out and relit, the smell reminding me of church and Reverend Phil's hopeful sermons and planes leaning into the sky. The candles were a wavering fabric of light, a reversed bowl of stars, a huge birthday cake marking all the years left to me.

"Make a wish," Frank said to me, his lips close to my ear, warm.

I closed my eyes and I did.

ABOUT THE AUTHOR

QUINN DALTON's short stories have appeared in various literary magazines, including *StoryQuarterly, ACM (Another Chicago Magazine), Glimmer Train,* and *The Kenyon Review.* She has been a semifinalist for the Iowa Short Fiction Award and won the *Pearl* 2002 Fiction Prize for her short story "Back on Earth." She lives with her husband and young daughter in Greensboro. This is her first novel.